Praise for Loletta Clouse

Vivid imagery...a decided change of pace.

—Library Journal

Wilder is a delicious tale of intrigue, loyalty and suspense mixed with a good dose of history.

—Knoxville News-Sentinel

An entertaining exploration of inner and outer conflict...deftly handles the characters with attention to historical facts and human emotion.

—Crossville Chronicle

Quickly engages her readers with her smooth style and her comfortable characters.

—Rocky Mountain News

A superb....novel. We look forward to more.

—Kentucky Post

A very good writer. I wonder why more has not been written about this dramatic part of our state's history.

—Knoxville News-Sentinel

MALLIE

MALLIE

Loletta Clouse

Chicory Books
Knoxville, Tennessee
2005

Published by Tennessee Valley Publishing

Order *Mallie* and other exciting novels by **Loletta Clouse**:

Wilder
An epic tale of power, strife, and romance in the East Tennessee Coalfields of the 1930's.

The Homesteads
A bittersweet story of hope and determination to build a new way of life in the rugged mountains of East Tennessee during the 1930's.

Available from:
Chicory Books
PO Box 31131
Knoxville TN 37930
1-865-693-5678
www.chicorybooks.com

Cover photo used by permission of McClung Historical Collection.

Library of Congress Cataloging-in-Publication Data

Clouse, Loletta, 1948–
Mallie / Loletta Clouse.
p. cm.
ISBN 0-9719417-2-6 (alk. paper)
1. Great Smoky Mountains (N.C. and Tenn.)--Fiction 2. Women teachers--Fiction. 3. Mountain life--Fiction. 4. Orphans--Fiction.. I. Title.
PS3553.L648M35 2005
813'.54 -- dc22
2005015878

Printed in the United States of America

Second Printing

MALLIE

Once again, I find myself overtaken by my blessings.
Endless gratitude for my family, friends, and all the
Great people I have met through writing.
And for the Creative Spirit in all of us that makes life
A wonder and a joy.

1

Her pa would not be meeting her at the train in Townsend. Mallie knew this because they had not spoken in the six years since he sent her away. In the fall of 1906, he had sold their farm and gone to work as a logger for the Little River Lumber Company.

Her brother, Cole, also worked as a logger, as did so many of the people in the Smoky Mountains. He had written to her often until the spring of that year when the letters had stopped. She had not heard from him since and she had begun to worry.

Reverend Elijah Thomas and his wife, Abigail, would be meeting the train. They had invited her to teach at Elkmont, a lumber camp on the East Prong of the Little River and she had accepted.

The train from Knoxville had left early that morning stopping at the way station at Walland to switch the coach from the Southern Railway to an engine from the Little River Railroad. It continued its slow eight mile journey along the river until it reached the sawmill community of Townsend.

Years had passed since Mallie's last visit to Tuckaleechee Cove. The place the Cherokees had named the peaceful valley was transformed into a bustling mill town that looked nothing like Mallie remembered.

When W. B. Townsend and a group of investors from Pennsylvania purchased a hundred thousand acres of timberland along the Little River and its tributaries in 1901, they built the sawmill on the first flat place on the drainage of the Little River below the Forks. Now, twelve years later, the screeching whine of the band saw in the mill, just east of where she stood, never stopped. A huge pond held the logs until an elevator could carry them up and through the mill. Daily trains brought more logs while other trains hauled out finished lumber in the other direction. West of the log pond on a spur of the tracks were endless rows of lumber stacked to dry and cure before shipping to market. Bark and bits of broken lumber lay everywhere and the acrid smell of fresh-sawed boards filled the air.

The piercing blast of the mill steam whistle startled Mallie. From the rumbling in her stomach, she guessed the whistle signaled dinner for the workers. The whistle was so loud she imagined folks all the way to Elkmont Camp could hear it. She pictured her brother Cole, as he had described it to her so many times in his letters, coming down off some high and dangerous place to rest a spell and eat his dinner of cold pork and cathead biscuits leftover from the camp breakfast. The thought of seeing him soon made her jump in her skin with excitement.

Fiddling with her hat, she tried to hide her nervousness by tucking the loose ends of her fine black hair back into place. Plain by some standards, her long face held brooding dark eyes that made her appear lost in thought, her thin lips and sharp nose only adding to the earnestness. It was only her easy smile, which came like a light flickering in dark woods, quick and always leaving a person wanting more, which made her beautiful. In her mind, she thought she looked like her mother. The memory of her mother was one of a beautiful woman, eyes always sparkling with curiosity and kindness.

She liked to think of herself as sturdy and practical, not given to foolishness, like many of the well-heeled girls with whom her aunt wanted her to associate, practicing their manners at endless teas and falling for the first man who crossed their path. She, on the other hand, had failed to make a good match disappointing her Aunt Mae who had taken her in after her mother's death.

How tedious it had all become, and she was glad to be home to her beloved mountains where she felt free. Still, she wanted to make a good impression on her new employers for her willful nature had insured she would have to earn her own way. Her white blouse, starched and ironed stiff that morning, now streaked with soot, hung limp on her from the July heat. Adorned only with ebony buttons, the plain black skirt she wore was creased and wrinkled from sitting so long on the train. Never one for patience, Mallie hopped from one foot to the other debating whether to head down the road to meet the

Thomas family when she spotted a surrey in the distance. She recognized the Reverend and his wife and she waved a greeting. The Reverend tipped his hat in his forever-solemn fashion.

Only a few years older than Mallie, the young couple had lived in the valley for four years. "God had directed them to come to the mountains to help the people," Elijah Thomas had told Mallie on their first meeting. Mallie wondered why God so often sent people to faraway places to do good works when it was possible to do those most anywhere, but she had learned through the years that blurting out such comments often made people mad or hurt their feelings. The thought sent a pang of sorrow through her for her mother had tolerated her questioning of things and always patiently answered her endless wonderings without judgment. Eight years had done nothing to soften her loss.

"Miss Hamilton," Elijah Thomas said, jumping from the surrey and proffering his hand.

"Yes, sir," Mallie said, shaking the Reverend's hand firmly.

With a slight wince, the Reverend withdrew his hand. "You remember my wife, Abigail."

Mallie shook her hand more gently and smiled briefly. "Yes, how are you Mrs. Thomas?"

"Please, call me Abigail."

Mallie nodded. "Abigail."

"I'm well, thank you. And how was your trip?"

"A lot of soot and cinders but at least I didn't catch on fire," Mallie said.

Abigail laughed a polite laugh, while the Reverend cleared his throat and made for Mallie's bags.

"Only two bags dear?" Abigail asked.

"I didn't think I would need a lot of the clothes I'd worn in Knoxville."

"Oh, but we do so hope you will be joining us in Townsend for the weekends. You certainly don't intend to spend all of your time in a logging camp."

"That would be very nice," Mallie lied.

"Oh, you simply must come for Christmas especially. Colonel and Mrs. Townsend always throw a lovely party for everyone in town. Margaret, that is Mrs. Townsend, sets up a tree in the schoolhouse decorated with her own personal things brought in from Pennsylvania. She personally buys a gift for everyone. I am sure you would enjoy meeting her. She has such a regard for the mountain folk."

"Yes, I would like that," Mallie said, thinking Christmas seemed much too far away to contemplate.

Abigail patted her arm. "I will talk to your Aunt about having your other things sent up by train."

Mallie simply smiled her thanks and revealed nothing of her plans, not that there was much to reveal. Truthfully, her plans had not gone beyond thoughts of getting back to the wildness and freedom of secluded coves with mountains rising into the mist all around her and streams that tumbled over boulders like liquid jewels.

The Reverend loaded the bags into the back seat of the surrey and helped Mallie in next to them. They had arranged for her to spend the night at their house before heading out for Elkmont the next day. "I appreciate your letting me stay the night at your house," Mallie said by way of conversation. She had never been good at small talk.

"My dear," Abigail said, turning and smiling sweetly. "We love having company. Don't we Elijah?"

The Reverend, who had never asked Mallie to call him Elijah nodded but said nothing.

"Reverend Thomas, I hear they've had a number of teachers at Elkmont," Mallie said.

The Reverend nodded again. "You know that it is not uncommon for teachers to uh…well, find the conditions difficult."

"What conditions?" Mallie asked.

"Well, living conditions can be sparse," Reverend Thomas said, "and of course, the children."

"The children?" Mallie questioned.

"Yes, the children can be a test for the teacher."

"They are very energetic," Abigail interjected.

"We were hoping that because you were from around here, you might have a greater understanding of things," Reverend Thomas said.

It was common for outsiders to think of mountain children as untamed creatures whose natures were unfathomable. "I'm sure I won't have any trouble," Mallie said. It was part of why she wanted to be a teacher. She knew the yearnings of a young mind existed in every child no matter where they were born.

"You have so far impressed me as a person of uncommon reason and practicality not usually found in a woman. I hope you do not disappoint me."

Mallie ruffled at finding herself in judgment by such a pompous man. Reminding herself that she needed this position, she held her tongue.

"Of course dear, I am sure she will do fine," Abigail said, filling in the silence in her cheery way. "We have made arrangements for you to board with the Willis family. Norma cooks for the camp and you can take your meals there if you agree to help. That is until your teacher's salary starts." She added the last part quickly, somewhat embarrassed.

"I'm sure that I shall manage."

"Tomorrow after church, you can ride the excursion train on up to Elkmont. I am afraid it will be packed with people going up to enjoy the mountains. There will, however, be a number of ladies on the train so you will not be alone. I understand your father will not be there to greet you, some kind of unpleasantness between you."

Mallie felt the heat race from her throat to her scalp. She could not find words to answer. Her Aunt Mae had obviously shared confidences with Abigail. She could just hear her saying, "He killed my sister with hard work on that worthless farm and I was not going to allow him to destroy his daughter." How many times had she heard that over the years? Aunt Mae had convinced him to send her away where she could be brought up as a lady, but a broken heart had made him sell her beloved farm to the logging company. She had begged him not to but his heart had turned as hard as a pine knot after her mother died. "My brother will be meeting me in Elkmont," she lied finally. She hoped that he had indeed gotten her letter and would be meeting her there, but she had no way of knowing.

"Elijah could ask one of the women to sit with you on the train, if you like?" Abigail went on undaunted.

"No need for that. I'm sure I'll be perfectly fine."

"We would love to ride up with you but Elijah has the evening service," Abigail said, still apologizing.

"No, I couldn't ask you to do that," Mallie said quickly. "I have put you out enough. I know I'll be just fine." She was eager to be free of the Reverend and his wife despite their kindness to her. In some people, kindness created obligation, and she did not want to be more indebted to them.

Finally, mollified by Mallie's confidence that she would indeed survive the train ride unescorted, Abigail relaxed in her seat. She chatted about who would be at the service in the morning and about the fine sermon the Reverend had prepared while Mallie's eyes scanned the mountains and heard them calling to her above the sound of the band saw. By tomorrow, she would be home.

As the train entered the gorge, the wheels shrilled a high-pitched scream as it took the curves. The stream below laughed in reply as it bounded over huge boulders untamed and undisturbed by the crowds passing by. The track laid the thirteen miles up the Little River gorge to Elkmont was complete by 1908 and soon after visitors discovered the now accessible beauty of the mountains and wanted to ride the train up. The Little River Lumber Company began offering a special passenger excursion train to Elkmont. On this Sunday, the coaches were full of passengers moving from one side of the car to the other not wanting to lose the view as the train crossed over the river.

Even Mallie's heart thrilled at the sight of the foaming water so powerful and determined. Her memories tumbled over each other in a rush just like the river, even as her mind tried to take in all the changes. She would have much preferred to be alone on this trip into the mountains but in the seat next to her sat a tiny woman dwarfed by a large straw hat adorned with organdy flowers. As the train rounded each turn, the woman would suck in her breath and clap her hands in delight. Before the train left Townsend, the woman had introduced herself as Elizabeth Newman of the Virginia Newman's. She was in Maryville visiting her niece and nephew and they were going to spend the day in Elkmont. Mallie had introduced herself but had not offered any information other than her name.

The train groaned and rocked its way up the gorge. Although the grade was a gentle climb, the continuous curves proved a challenge for any engineer. It was necessary to keep the engines fired just right so they would not run out of steam on the long run. The rock walls of the gorge came close enough to touch at times. The rail bed blasted out of rock left craggy overhangs raw from drilling and blasting.

When Mallie was a child, the only way into the farm had been by horse or foot. Now men and women in Sunday finery came all the way from Knoxville by train just for the day to swim and picnic. Rails had replaced the familiar footpaths and wagon roads of Mallie's childhood.

The train slowed to a stop at an open place in the gorge. Passengers got off to stretch and get a closer view of the river. Mallie laughed as the women brushed cinders from their dresses and men slapped their hats against legs to clear them of ashes. When she stepped off the train, a man offered his hand. Mallie hesitated long enough to study his face. He appeared to be older than she was by two decades. He was tall, his tailored suit cut to make the best of his still slender frame. His neatly cut blonde hair set off his eyes, the color of a cloudy day. They looked straight at her with the confidence of a man assured of his place in the world. Thanking him politely, she walked on along the tracks without looking back, but she could feel his eyes on her. When she glanced back, he was with a petite blonde woman young enough to be his daughter who was fanning herself and complaining about the heat. Mallie quickly looked away.

When they boarded the train to continue to Elkmont, the man sat two rows behind her. She could hear his deep baritone voice as he pointed out sights to the woman. The woman called him Pierce, so she was obviously not his daughter; Mallie thought and wondered why she should care.

The train slowed to a stop at a small platform. Steps led up a steep bank to the newly built Wonderland Hotel, a large white frame structure with a porch that spanned the entire front. Several people got off, including Pierce and his companion. Mallie sat watching, while the women fussed with their clothing and the men arranged to have their things carried up to the hotel. As the train chugged slowly away toward Elkmont, she could see Pierce watching her curiously.

When the train pulled into the track yard at Elkmont, it slowed to a stop and Mallie leapt up to get off. Most of the passengers would be riding the train a short distance beyond Elkmont where they would swim and picnic for the day. The engineer who had stored her bags in the locomotive jumped off, placed her things on the porch, and helped her down.

Mallie was shocked to see that the town stretched for as far as she could see on both sides of the rail line. The land cleared of trees was open and there were houses scattered everywhere. They had passed a post office and commissary and stopped at two small wood frame buildings connected by a walkway. Over one, it read Elkmont and over the other read Hotel. She thought it was probably the boarding house for company workers who did not have families.

Mallie, caught up in the changes she saw around her, tumbled backwards and landed with a plop on her suitcase. She straightened herself up as though she had meant to sit down and then she looked around her to see if anyone had seen her.

They had once owned an old dog name Jed and her pa said he was the best snake dog he ever owned. Mallie watched him many times grab up a copperhead and shake it until he was dead. Today she felt like one of old Jed's victims caught off guard and shaken within an inch of her life. Nothing was as she remembered it. Something had stolen her secret world of wild beauty and dark mystery.

2

Mallie, quit dawdling and finish your reading," Rebecca Hamilton said firmly, without turning from the fireplace where she stood stirring the beans. "Your brother finished his work half-an-hour ago."

Mallie made a face then saw her mother's back stiffen. It would mean another chapter to read and missing trout fishing with her pa if she were caught. The outside world called to Mallie like a winter wren announcing spring. It was not her fault that her brother Cole enjoyed his studies. He relished the time he spent with his schoolwork as a relief from the hard work of farming, while Mallie dreamed of running the woods. Her mama insisted they get an education, over Crockett's half-hearted protest. "Times are changing, Crockett," she argued, fighting for the time it took away from chores. "The children are going to need an education."

In truth, he was proud of his educated wife and Mallie knew he collected ginseng all year to have money to buy her mama a book. He loved to tell the story of the way he had stolen Miss Rebecca Grimsley away from her family in Knoxville and whisked her off while her folks just stood with their jaws dropped. "They didn't know what to make of no mountain man stealin' their daughter away," her pa would say, while her mama smiled, color flooding her cheeks.

Mallie would always beg her pa to tell the story repeatedly. To humor her at night by the firelight, he would tell it slowly drawing it out as he patiently sharpened his knife.

He had first seen Rebecca Grimsley on State Street in Knoxville. It was a Sunday morning, April 14, 1889. She was getting out of a carriage at the First Presbyterian Church with her parents and sister. "She had on a blue dress with a high collar that come up 'round her face. Hair twirled around on top of her head like black silk. It was her eyes though that done me in. Like a panther's eyes, big and bold, taking me in and I knowed she had the power to kill me with one word."

At this, her mama always laughed her throaty laugh. "Crockett Hamilton, you are one outrageous man!"

"What did you do then?" Mallie always asked.

"Why I walked right up to her."

"And what did mama say? Did she say the word to have you killed?"

"Why, she walked right past me. Then when I thought all was lost, she turned and give me the biggest smile. That was all I needed. I waited outside until after the service was over. Them Presbyterians can go over long, but finally she come out and I followed her home."

"He waited outside my house for one week," Rebecca said. "Finally, I got a chance to sneak out without my folks knowing and spoke to him."

"Did you think Pa was handsome?" Cole always asked, for he was the spitting image of his father.

"Handsomest man I'd ever seen," her ma would say looking deep into Cole's eyes to answer both his questions. "He had a long beard the color of a hot poker and his hair was like red flames shooting out from his head. I thought Zeus had come to claim me and take me away to Mt Olympus for his queen. That was pretty much the way it was, for your pa said, 'Rebecca, I've come to take you home.' I packed a bag and left that evening. It was the next day before I remembered that I had never told your pa my name."

"I just always knowed it," her pa would say with pride.

Mallie liked that part the best.

Her mama had taught Crockett Hamilton to read and cipher and he had taught her to shoot a rifle. He liked to brag that she never wasted a bullet.

Crockett burst through the door as he did every evening, Mallie and Rebecca looking up their eyes lighting up with pure adoration. He kissed Rebecca full on the mouth, which was his habit and bent down to give Mallie a peck on the forehead. "Get your pole, girl. We're going fishing," he whispered to her. Winking at her, he turned with a grin and said, "How does fresh speckled trout for supper sound, Rebecca?"

"Crockett, the girl has not finished her schoolwork," Rebecca protested, hands on her hips.

"The mountain is the best teacher there is," he said with a nod to Mallie. "It'll learn you everything you need to know to survive."

Before her mama could say another world, Mallie had their poles and was standing beside her pa. She stood rigid, holding her breath waiting for her mama to speak.

"Don't be gone long," her mama relented.

They were out the door of the cabin and headed down the trail before she had time to change her mind. They passed a stand of sourwood where the beehives stood. The bees used the white-tassel blossoms to make honey. Mallie's mouth watered at the thought of golden honey on warm biscuits.

Crockett stopped and called back to Cole, "Chop your mama some firewood, boy."

Cole stood watching them with a look that made Mallie feel a twinge of guilt. She could have gone back at that moment but she loved the time she spent alone in the woods with her pa. With the selfishness of childhood, spurring her on, she turned heading into the cool woods.

The forest floor, blanketed with maidenhair ferns, was quiet except for the call of an occasional red-breasted nuthatch. White trilliums by the hundreds danced in the gentle breeze showing off their pink and black centers. Purple violets and bloodroot competed like small children for attention. The diffused light, through new green leaves of dogwood and redbud, made Mallie light headed. Her pa called to her and she realized he had gone far ahead. She ran as fast as her skinny, eight-year-old legs could carry her, not wanting to disappoint him with her dallying.

When Mallie came upon him breathless, her skin prickly with sweat, he was squatting beside the stump of a fallen tree, his hand caressing the tiny flowers of a plant. "Mallie, this here's a puttyroot orchid. You can make a paste from the bulb that is as fine a glue as you could buy in any store. Can you remember that name?"

"Yes, Pa."

"Say it to me then."

"Puttyroot orchid, Pa."

"That's good Mallie. You remember that now. I fixed one of your mama's blue cups once and it was as good as new.

'Cepting for one small piece, I never could find to save my life."

Mallie knew the cup her pa spoke of, for it sat on a wooden shelf above the stove. Not one to waste a thing, her mama used it for salt. "It's still a real good cup, Pa," she said in his defense.

"Your mama forgive me when she seen how hard I tried to piece it all back together," he said with a wink.

Mallie touched the plant and said the name over in her head. Her pa always taught her the names of plants and how they could be useful. She never forgot the names he taught her and it pleased him when she could repeat them the next time they were out in the woods.

They came upon a thinly wooded area to the right of the trail. A startled white-tailed deer bounded over fallen limbs and small shrubs to stand looking back at them. "It's a doe," Crockett remarked quietly. "I bet there's a fawn around here." He walked to where the deer had been and pulled back a mountain laurel to reveal a spotted fawn curled into a tiny bundle.

"Can I pet him Pa?" Mallie whispered. The land held a bounty of white-tailed deer and her pa often killed one to feed the family, but seeing a fawn was a treat. She was not allowed to have a pet for they could not afford to feed it when there was little enough for the family. Even their old dog Jed was not a pet for he was for hunting and guarding the farm.

"That doe run off to protect its baby. We don't want her to fret," he said, but then he relented immediately. "Just stroke him gentle like."

Mallie eased her way toward the fawn. It looked at her with eyes wide, its body moving in rhythm with its heartbeat. Stroking the soft fur, she cupped the tiny head in her other hand. Holding her breath in wonderment, she felt her pa's hand on her shoulder. They backed away leaving the fawn and neither of them spoke until they were well down the trail. When she finally looked at her pa, she knew he understood how she felt.

When they came upon the branch of the stream where a small waterfall tumbled over mossy rocks, they stopped. The pool at the base of the falls was clear and deep. Mallie could see speckled trout swimming near the bottom and her small body twitched with excitement. She loved to fish and was not at all squeamish about baiting the hook or pulling in a fish that fought and flopped about on the bank.

Baiting her hook, she negotiated the slick rocks with agility. As soon as her line hit the water, she felt the tug and yanked the pole to set her hook. Pulling on the line, she fought to hold on as the trout struggled. Her pa came to help her get it out of the water so she would not lose her hook.

"First fish of the day, Mallie. You caught the first one of the day," her pa said, grinning at her as he held the fish up.

Mallie beamed.

"We'll have us two dozen and be home for supper in no time."

She slipped another worm onto her hook. As eager as she was to catch another trout, Mallie never wanted the day to end. She thought she could sit on the banks of the stream and fish with her pa forever.

A noise from the brush startled them. Three men on horseback emerged from the thicket. Jumping up, Crockett Hamilton nodded his greeting. He had not brought along his rifle, but his hand went to the knife strapped to his side.

They did not see many strangers. Their nearest neighbors were four miles away and Mallie could not go visit her friend Rose unless Cole went with her. Sometimes Rose's pa, Riley, would bring her to visit when he was going hunting with Crockett.

Mallie pulled her pole from the water and stared at the men. She wanted to go to her pa but did not want to appear to be a baby so she sat still and watched.

One man got off his horse and came over to her pa. He took off his hat and held it in front of him. "Crockett Hamilton, don't you know me?" he said.

Crockett squinted in puzzlement. "Ollie Jones?" he said in sudden recognition. Shaking his hand vigorously, he said, "Why Ollie, I do know you now that I seen you up close. I did not know you at first. You're from over in Wears Cove ain't you? I've not seen you in over a year."

"I reckon I've changed a bit. I was sickly over the winter."

Crockett gave a knowing nod. Croup and coughs were constant winter companions and everyone was relieved to emerge alive and well in the spring.

"What are you doing out in these parts?"

"These men hired me to scout for them," he said pointing to the men.

"Walker Stevens," the large man on the sorrel said, introducing himself. "And this is Carl Myers," he said, pointing to his companion.

Mallie watched her pa for he held his shoulders high and tight around his neck as he watched the men warily.

"We're scouting timber for some lumbermen out of Philadelphia."

No one spoke.

"We've seen some fine virgin timber in these parts," Myers volunteered. "Why there's yellow poplar eight feet in diameter at least. And chestnut trees, the likes of which, you have to see to believe," he said excitedly.

"No need to mark trees on my land," Crockett said, referring to the way scouts came through and bought trees on the stump. They would mark the trees they wanted. Then it was up to the farmer to cut the tree down and drag it with a team of oxen to a portable sawmill before he could be paid. "I done sold all the trees I can snake outta here. Men have died trying to get trees out of here," Crockett said. "They ain't a road for miles. And what's left is too big to drag by mule."

The men grinned.

"We don't want just a few trees, Mr. Hamilton," Stevens said. "We represent important investors interested in buying all the trees for as far as you can see."

"They're going to build a railroad," Ollie Jones exclaimed.

Crockett Hamilton's face darkened as he calmly studied each man in turn. "Get your pole, Mallie. We are going home," he said without looking at her.

They had caught only half-a-dozen trout. Mallie started to protest but she saw her pa's face darken and she scurried about to collect their things.

"My land is not for sale," Crockett said.

"Why Crockett, you sold tanbark to the tannery in Walland before," Ollie Jones pointed out. "They's money to be made in timbering."

Crockett put his hand in Mallie's back and pushed her on ahead of him. "My land's not for sale," he repeated.

"We plan on buying upwards of eighty-thousand acres," Walker Stevens called after him. "I'm sure we'll find plenty of folks willing to sell."

"Watch out you don't get caught up in one of them laurel hells," Crockett said, referring to the thick, tangled undergrowth that had trapped many a man in its endless maze. Without turning around, he walked away.

They marched on down the trail toward home without a word between them. The last thing Mallie saw when she turned was the men riding deeper into the woods.

3

Crockett Hamilton concentrated on the warm biscuits and sausage in front of him. The room was quiet except for the sounds of men chewing and slurping their coffee and the clangor of forks on crockery. It took a lot of food to feed men who worked ten to twelve hours a day logging and the men at the table had little time for talk until they finished their breakfast. Food was so important to a logger; every camp had a dining car that served hearty meals. The lumber company had learned long ago that a full stomach made for a loyal worker. Some men chose the camp they worked in by the cook alone.

After his third helping, Crockett drained his coffee cup, pushed back his chair and looked across the table at his old friend, Riley Combs. He was a big man filling the room with broad shoulders and long muscular arms. His face was tanned dark as leather from the sun; despite the wide brimmed hat, he wore every day. Crockett, on the other hand, with his fair skin, which never seemed to darken with the sun, figured he had burned off a few layers of hide over the years.

With a nod, they both rose from the table and headed out. They had been working together for the lumber company since 1906. Unlike Crockett, who now lived from one lumber camp to the next, when Riley sold his farm to the lumber company, he had bought a smaller piece of land in Wears Cove where his son and daughter-in-law still scratched out a meager living. Lumber speculators had driven the price up and he had not been able to buy as much land as he had once owned. He talked about going back there someday to live, but for now, he was dependent on the wages he earned. Almost all the folks around there worked off and on for the lumber company when they needed the money, which was most of the time.

They stood on the porch of the long frame bunkhouse while Riley rolled a one-handed cigarette. The bunkhouse at Fish Camp was so new it smelled of fresh sawdust but already the porch floor held the puncture wounds of the cutter boots the loggers wore. The sharp steel points embedded in the soles and heels made a man more sure-footed when jumping from log to log. Crockett would not hire a man who did not own his own pair of cutter boots.

They had cut most of the hardwoods from the lower regions and they had to move on up the mountain. Since coming to work for the Little River Lumber Company, Crockett had worked Laurel Creek, Hesse Creek Basin, Elkmont and now Fish Camp. The camp built on the Fish Camp Prong of the Little River, had been a favorite fishing camp for locals. Crockett had fished there many times, but now he had work to do.

Before he became foreman of his own crew, he had done every kind of logging job a man could do in his years with the Little River Lumber Company. He had started out as a ballhooter and his job had been to nose the log around on a steep slope until it took off rolling downhill. He had been a chipper, sawyer, choke hooker and skid operator. It was all dangerous work, and he had taken a lot of chances, driving himself and daring the odds doing things he would never let his men do. He had been older when he started and after Rebecca died, he had not cared what happened to him.

Many of the loggers were just boys not yet shaving regular with more courage than sense. He had gained a reputation for being a hard man to work for, but the men trusted him to keep them safe.

The camp was bustling with new workers pouring in daily. The manager, W. B. Townsend encouraged more families than single men in his camps, to cut down on rowdy brawls and drunkenness. A row of portable box houses, brought in by railcar the day before and unloaded by crane, set only a few feet from the tracks. The one-room frame structures were made of rough sawed lumber at the mill in Townsend and brought by railroad as needed to house loggers and their families. They could never be bigger than eight feet wide and twelve to fourteen feet long because they had to fit on a flatcar. Bigger families often used more than one.

Stringtowns, called that because of the placement of the box houses side by side along the tracks, popped up throughout the mountains as the logging played out and the camps moved. Tarpaper insulated the inside from wall to ceiling, but they were often drafty and cold from ill-fitting roofs and large cracks. To save their meager possessions, before moving the families packed their things and sent them ahead by rail.

The only way into Fish Camp was by train because there was no road. The train brought food for the loggers and supplies for the commissary and anything else that was needed. Crockett knew they had brought in more than houses the night before. It had been the talk of all the men as they sat about after supper. The new Clyde Skidder set on a spur line waiting for his crew to be the first to use it.

The Little River Lumber Company had been using skidders in the mountains for years. The steep slopes and rugged mountains had made the use of teams of horses difficult. And as the logs dragged through timber or over stumps, they often became entangled and could be freed only through backbreaking work. The primitive donkey skidder was little more than a steam engine with winches on skids. A horse would pull the steel cable up the mountain where a man attached it to the log. When the signal came, the skid operator would simply engage the winch and drag the log down the mountain, taking with it small trees and soil. Before long, they added a mast to raise the cable, but still dragging the logs created much work for many men with peavey and pry bar to keep the logs moving.

As logging progressed up steeper and steeper slopes, the track for the railcars had more and more switchbacks to reduce the grade, costing the company money. The Sarah Parker, an incline machine, was brought in to try to overcome the problem. Track, which was laid straight up the slope, allowed for pulling the machine up with cable where it could be winched into place. Railcars, winched up by the same method, were loaded and lowered back down the track by the boom on the Sarah Parker.

Still the Little River Lumber Company looked for a better solution. The Clyde Iron Works had designed a new type of skidder they thought would solve the problem of timbering in the rugged terrain. Crockett's team would be the first to test it.

Crockett had sent a fireman on ahead to get the steam up on the skidder. Already smoke filled the air from the skidder and the loader. The steam engines required an abundance of coal to keep the fire hot enough and by the end of the week, a pile of cinders would stack up by the track. There had been talk of switching out to wood to save money. Crockett knew it would make it harder on the men to keep steam up to the one-hundred and sixty pounds needed to work the machines. Wood sent out more sparks and increased the danger of fire. The slash left by the loggers, the limbs and tops of trees, dried out by the sun and wind was a tinderbox and left the men in constant fear of fire.

The previous day the men had cleared a path for the cable that would run high up the slope. As Riley and Crockett headed up the tracks, the other men soon followed. Riley would operate the skidder because he had the most experience and he could be trusted. It took a strong man to work the levers and if the logs hung up, it would take skill to untangle them.

"Curtis, you and Sam come with me up the slope. We'll hook the cable to a stump at the top," Crockett said. "Nat, you get the horse and pull the cable up." Crockett yelled, calling out directions as the men rushed around eager to get to work.

"Riley, you wait for the flagman's signal and then you go to work."

"I won't make a move 'til you send the okay."

Crockett slapped him on the back and headed up the slope. "Let's get to work men."

Attaching the main cable to the stump, a special cable was sent out to the first fallen log. Crockett went down to attach the harness. He took the choker rope, pushed it through a trench dug under the log to accommodate the cable, and hooked the log. When he had done this to four logs, he stood back. He took time to wipe the sweat that ran down his face and surveyed the logs. He had an experienced hook choker on his crew but he had wanted to do the first load himself. Satisfied, he signaled to have the tongs hooked into the logs. With a wave, he gave the sign for the flagman to alert Riley.

The Clyde Skidder had a system of cables. If all went well, the logs would be winched into the air and pulled in across the canyon. Crockett knew that Riley would have to work a complicated set of levers to make the cables work.

The logs lifted into the air, but as the carriage-cable pulled them forward, one of the logs caught on a stump. Crockett gave the signal to the flagman to stop the skidder. They all watched as Riley slowly brought the carriage sheaf back so the log was perpendicular to the stump. He skillfully picked the log up over the stump until it was free. The logs then rose two hundred feet into the air and dangled. They whipped about as they were reeled across the canyon on special cable sheaves. Each log weighed between sixteen and eighteen hundred pounds and if the cable broke, it would lash around killing anyone in its path.

As the logs reached the bottom of the slope, they dropped in piles beside the railroad. A cheer went up from the men. Crockett relaxed his clenched jaw. "All right men, let's get'em outta here." Without wasting a minute, he set the men to task and went back to hooking more logs.

When the whistle blew for dinner, Crockett went down to congratulate Riley. They sat on the side of a railcar and opened their dinner pails. "I couldn't of had a better man on that thing today, Riley."

"'Cepting if it was you," Riley said modestly.

"That's one fine piece of equipment."

"Was you worried?"

"I'll admit to it."

Riley chuckled. "Seeing them logs a swinging around out there changing ends can cause a man to think."

Crockett nodded in agreement his mouth full of cold biscuit and side meat. He searched his pail and found a sweet potato, his favorite. "We'll have this whole dang slope cleared in a day or two."

Riley chewed thoughtfully and then swallowed hard before he spoke. "We'll be able to move higher up into the mountains now. They'll be having us cutting firs before you know it."

"They won't be able to lay track fast enough. We keep this up; we'll soon work ourselves out of a job."

"Not till they's a spur line up every cove in these mountains. At least this skidder don't tear the ground up like a Groundhog does," Riley said, referring to one of the early crude skidders. "I never did like the way them things would take out every little tree, bush and half the hillside just getting the logs out."

"It don't hurt the logs as much neither."

"Still, we have to clear off a lot of trees to hook the cable. Waste a lot of trees."

"The men get paid by the board foot," Crockett said. "They can't do it without this machinery."

"I'm just saying, it don't hurt to leave something. A good rain comes along next thing you know it's done washed half the slopes down into the creek."

"That's no concern of mine," Crockett snapped. " I'm paid to get the lumber out."

"Crockett, when are you going to stop taking your hurt out on these mountains? You think if you tame the wildness out of these mountains, they'll give you back Rebecca."

"You still have your wife, Riley." Crockett said to stop Riley.

"I know, Crockett. I didn't mean nothing by what I said."

Crockett threw up his hand and waved off any more talk on the subject. They sat for a few minutes in silence. "You reckon Maude and Rose will move up from Elkmont?" Crockett asked to show he was not angry. Riley's wife and daughter had been living at the camp at Elkmont. Riley stayed at Fish Camp during the week and took the train down to be with them on Sundays, his only day off.

"I don't reckon. They done got jobs at that new Wonderland Hotel. Maude makes pies for them fine folks and Rose cleans rooms."

"They keep that up and you won't need to log no more."

Riley smiled quickly and then a look came over his face and he was quiet. "Maude told me something when I was home last."

Crockett waited.

"I've been studying whether to tell you."

"Ain't no need to study on it. We've known each other too long for that. Just have out with it."

"It's about Mallie."

Crockett felt his back stiffen and his nostrils flare. It was the last thing he expected to hear. He looked at Riley through hooded eyes. "I'm listening."

"She's come back to Elkmont to teach school."

He was no longer hungry and tossed his biscuit back into the pail. He rubbed his hand across his smooth shaven face. He had given up the beard and long hair when he took up logging.

Mallie would not recognize him. He had changed so much, too much, perhaps. "Six years, Riley. We ain't spoke a word in six years."

"Well then ain't it just about fine time you spoke to that little gal again?"

"I done what I done for her sake."

"I ain't the one that needs to hear that," Riley said. "Don't you need to tell her that?"

Crockett did not answer, for there were things that even Riley did not know.

4

Mallie dipped the dishpan into the stream to get water for the supper dishes. Two speckled trout hurriedly swam away to warn the others. She had been staying with the Willis family for a week, where she helped with chores to pay for her board. Norma Willis and her husband, Dan, cooked for eight loggers who worked for the Little River Lumber Company. They lived in one end of a wood frame building and the boarders lived in the other. They ate in a common area in the middle. Norma cooked two meals a day for the men and packed a dinner pail for them from the breakfast leftovers. Mallie and the Willis' ten-year-old daughter Frannie helped clean up and do the dishes.

The Willis family was lively and fun. They enjoyed what they were doing and they treated her like family from the first day. She loved the raucous loggers with their endless teasing and joking. They would sit up long after dark talking and laughing until someone pointed out that daylight would come early and they had best get some sleep.

"I hate washing supper dishes," Frannie complained as they headed back to the boarding house, arms straining under the weight of the dishpans full of water.

"It won't take long with both of us," Mallie said. "When we're done, maybe your mama will let you walk up to the Wonderland Hotel with me."

Frannie's eyes lighted up and then darkened. "I don't think mama will let me go?"

"And why wouldn't she?"

"She says we don't go where we're not wanted."

There was no resentment in Frannie's voice as there had probably been none in her mama's when she spoke the words. It was just an accepted fact in their lives. Mallie understood the shy, reserved ways bred into them. They would take in a stranger, give them their last bite of food, but they did not go places or mingle with people with whom they did not feel comfortable. Mallie nodded, "I'll ask her myself."

She was meeting her old friend Rose at the hotel where she worked as a maid. She had run into her at the Post Office soon after coming to Elkmont. When she hugged her old friend, the joy of their years together, playing and running the woods flooded back. Without a mischievous thought of her own, Rose was the willing companion to Mallie's endless misadventures. One fall, when they had gone chestnut hunting, Mallie had talked Rose into stomping a sticky chestnut burr with her bare foot. She had once seen Cole do it on a dare from some bigger boys. He had not let on how much it hurt but Rose sure did. Then Mallie did it just to show her how sorry she was even though Rose begged her not to do it. They both walked home hobbling from the pain.

Rose had invited her home Saturday after work to spend the night. She had Sundays off and her mama had promised to make blackberry cobbler.

Frannie rushed ahead splashing water in her hurry.

"It won't do if we don't have enough water left to do the dishes," Mallie called. Frannie was too excited to hear her. In a few weeks, she would be facing a room full of children just as excited and full of energy. She had been up to the schoolhouse to look around. The one-room frame building held a blackboard and a potbellied stove. Long benches with planks attached for desks filled the center of the room. Her teaching supplies consisted of a few pieces of chalk. It was clear to her that she had her work cut out. She could hear her Aunt Mae's voice repeating the words she had said so often in the weeks before she left for the mountains, "What sensible young woman would waste a fine education to teach school for room and board and fifty dollars?" Mallie had never claimed she was her aunt's idea of sensible, just her own.

As they walked the half mile from Elkmont to the hotel, Frannie skipped and ran from one side of the track to the other, her long blonde braids flying behind her. Stumps and limbs from the trees cut down to lay the track littered the landscape. New growth rushed to fill in the spaces.

"Look, Frannie, a persimmon tree," Mallie said. Somehow, the persimmon tree gnarled from age and spotted with lichens, had escaped the axe. They stopped to pick the soft sweet fruit the tree had struggled against all odds to produce. Mallie held the persimmon between her fingers, its golden colors shimmering in the sunlight. She took a bite. The rich, intoxicating smell and powerful earthy flavor took her back to when she was a child. She closed her eyes and held it in her mouth for as long as she could to savor the lush flavor.

"Did you ever eat one before it was ripe?" Frannie asked.

"Only once," Mallie said, pulling herself back from her reverie. "My mouth puckered for a week."

They laughed together, strolling hand in hand until Frannie spied Black-eyed Susan blooming along the sides of the railroad tracks and stopped to pick a handful. She wove one into Mallie's hair before taking off to chase a butterfly.

"Don't get too far ahead," she called. Frannie smiled back at her. How much like Frannie, she had been at that age, one moment a child delighting in everything around her, then the next moment a grownup taking care of her pa and brother as her mama grew ill. For a long time she had been unaware of how sick her mama was because she never complained. Crockett begged her to go to her family who would pay for the best doctors, but she refused.

Mallie took on more and more as her mother seemed to tire more easily until finally she was doing most of the cooking. Cole helped her work the garden, but the planting, hoeing, and harvesting worked them long after dark. Even then, part of the crop was lost because she did not know how to preserve it.

All the while, she believed her mama would get better. Until one day, her pa met them coming in from gathering up the cows and told them that she had died. He took her mama back to Knoxville and returned her at last to the family she had not seen since running off with Crockett. He had her buried in the cemetery of the First Presbyterian Church where they had met. When he returned to the mountains, he was a changed man.

She wanted to go to her pa, but he had closed in on himself and he would not let her in. He blamed himself for her mama's death. He believed that if he had never brought her to the mountains to a life of hardship, she would not have died.

Cole became her only friend. They struggled to keep the farm going even as their pa grew more despondent. When Mallie was fourteen, he sold the farm and sent her away. Furious with him for taking away the only home she had ever known, she had said hateful things. Still her hurtful words had not penetrated the wall of his despair. She had hated him even more for loving his grief more than he loved her.

Her brother wrote to her every few months. He had gone to work with her pa for the logging company soon after Mallie left. Cole's first job was as a flagman for a skidder. He claimed to love logging, but Mallie always wondered, if what the boy who had always loved books, really enjoyed was his father's attention. He often worked side by side with their pa, proving himself day after day in jobs that tested grown men and often found them wanting. The last letter she had gotten from him in April, Cole had written to say he had gotten a job as operator of a log loader. She hoped Rose would know where her brother might be now.

Rose was to meet them at the Wonderland Station, a covered platform near the railroad tracks. A long set of steps led up the slope to the white frame two-story Wonderland Hotel. Men in their shirtsleeves smoking cigars sat in rockers on the long front porch that stretched the length of the hotel.

The July sun was still hot and Mallie sought the shade of the covered station while Frannie played. Rose was still nowhere in sight. Impatient as always, Mallie thought about taking the steps and going around to the back of the hotel to search for Rose, but she knew Frannie would not want to go and she did not want to leave her alone.

As Mallie was deciding what to do, a man came out of the hotel, put on his hat and looked straight at her. He cocked his head as though he recognized her and took the porch steps by two. As he hurried down the long flight of stairs to the platform, Mallie recognized him as the man from the train who had helped her down.

"Good evening," the man called as he neared the platform. "I'm Pierce Gerard. I saw you standing here and I thought you might be in need of some assistance. I am afraid there will not be another train until tomorrow. The last train was through at 5:30."

"I'm not waiting for a train, Mr. Gerard," she snapped. It made her angry that he would think her so ignorant she would not know the train schedule. Then she saw his tightlipped expression.

"I didn't mean to offend you. I mean about the train. It was just my poor attempt at being humorous," he said, with a crooked smile.

Once again, Mallie realized she had let her pride control her tongue. Her pride had been her shield against the arrogance of those who thought mountain people were ignorant and stupid. Sometimes to her embarrassment, it caused her to lash out. Her voice softened, "I am waiting for a friend. She's meeting me here."

"Is she staying at the hotel? I could get her for you. You could wait on the porch. It might be cooler there."

"My friend works at the hotel. She's a maid."

Mallie watched his face for any sign of disappointment. She could read nothing in the stillness of his slate-blue eyes. She could see now that gray streaked his blonde hair and the corners of his eyes crinkled when he spoke. He had an odd reticence about him for a man of the world.

"I might know her, I stay here quite often," he offered.

"I don't think so, she just started working."

Rose appeared from behind the hotel, shielded her eyes from the sun as she searched the platform. Mallie waved to her over Pierce's shoulder.

"There she is now," said Mallie, relief flooding her.

"I didn't get your name," he said.

"I'm Mallie Hamilton," she said holding out her hand.

He took her hand, holding on to it as he talked. "I saw you on the train. When you did not get off with the others, I thought you must live here or are you just visiting friends?"

"This is my home, Mr. Gerard," she said, awkwardly pulling her hand free. She was surprised that he had given her so much thought.

"Have you always lived here?"

"I've been away awhile," Mallie said.

"And now you've come back to marry your childhood sweetheart?"

"That would be no concern of yours now, would it Mr. Gerard?" Mallie blurted out.

"I apologize," he said backing away. "Once again I have offended you." He stood in silence.

Mallie said nothing. She could see the flush rise up over his collar.

"You are a very beautiful young woman, and I assumed you would have a sweetheart."

Mallie almost laughed aloud at his clumsy attempt to flatter her. He obviously preferred women half his age, Mallie thought, remembering the blonde-haired woman on the train. Perhaps, he had thought her young, guileless, and easily taken in. Did he now think that he had cornered some wild native creature and did not know what to do with her, she thought. She enjoyed the fact she made him uncomfortable. Ignoring the compliment she said, "I've come back to teach school. I'm a school teacher, Mr. Gerard."

Rose came up shyly behind Pierce and hesitated. Mallie pushed past him to hug her friend. With her arm around her friend, she said, "Mr. Gerard, this is my dear friend Rose Combs."

"A pleasure to meet you, Miss Combs," he said, with a nod.

Rose looked at him from under her long black lashes and smiled briefly. A scarlet blush spread up her face, darkening her complexion already the color of tanbark. Rose's grandmother on her pa's side had been part Cherokee. The beauty and grace of her had passed like a gift to her granddaughter Rose.

Mallie took her by the hand and called Frannie to join them. "Mr. Gerard, thank you for all your help. We need to be going now."

"I am afraid I didn't do anything after all. And please, call me Pierce."

"You were very kind, Mr. Gerard," Mallie said. Thinking the man to be stodgy and pompous, she did not intend to call him by his given name and thought it unlikely they would ever meet again.

As they walked up the tracks, Rose and Mallie did not speak until they were well out of hearing distance and then they burst out laughing. Frannie laughed too and then asked, "What's so funny?"

"You are so beautiful, you must have a sweetheart," Mallie mocked, her voice deepened.

"You were so kind," Rose said, her hands fluttering around her face.

"I was just being polite. That man is old enough to be my father."

"What are you two talking about?" Frannie said, frowning at them.

"You'll understand soon enough. When you are a little older," Mallie said and pulled on Frannie's braids to tease her. Frannie laughed and then ran off to walk the rails, singing to herself and balancing with her thin arms out stretched.

"I about couldn't catch my breath when I seen you standing down there with Mr. Gerard," Rose said.

"Why would you be so concerned about that? We were in full view of a dozen folks sitting on that porch. What did you think was going to happen?"

"Mallie, you do know who that was, don't you?"

Mallie shrugged. "Just some man who was on the train when I rode in."

She gave Mallie a look she had not seen since they were children playing and Rose had nearly stepped on a copperhead. Mallie had knocked her out of the way and grabbed the snake by the back of the head. She held on to it for an hour afraid to let go until her pa found them and killed it.

"He's an investor in the Little River Lumber Company. He's from Pennsylvania and they say he has more money than Rockefeller."

His money bought my home, Mallie thought. "Having money doesn't give him the right to flirt with young girls." Mallie snapped. She was furious now that she had even spoken to the man.

"I hope you didn't make him mad," Rose said, worry pinching her brow.

"Well, if I did, he deserved it," Mallie said.

"I need this job, Mallie. And you know how you can be."

Mallie laughed. She had not changed so much after all, she thought. "He won't have you fired, Rose. I am sure by now he has forgotten all about us."

"I've seen that look in a man's eyes before and I don't think he'll be forgetting you anytime soon," Rose teased.

Mallie rolled her eyes.

"Well, ain't you the choicey one Miss Mallie," Rose sing-songed. "No wonder you ain't never married."

"Not you too, Rose. I heard enough of that from my Aunt."

"I'm sorry, Mallie. I shouldn't of said that," Rose said, her hands clasped to her face.

"I've just not met the right man," Mallie said, ashamed of explaining herself to her friend. She realized that to Rose not being married was not so much a choice as a sign of not being chosen.

"I understand, Mallie. I loved Ambrose better than anybody on this earth," Rose said. "I'm planning on marrying again as soon as I find somebody to have me, but I won't never love nobody as much again. I'm not sure it's good for you to love one person that much."

Rose had told her that she had been married for less than a year but her husband had died of pneumonia the first winter and she had moved back in with her folks. Mallie watched as tears welled up in her friend's eyes and spilled down her cheeks. "I'm so sorry, Rose," she said. She took her in her arms and they hugged. She thought of her pa and wondered too if it was good to love one person so much. Maybe that was why she was so reluctant to give her heart away to anyone.

Rose pulled away and wiped her tears with the heels of her hands. She smiled at Mallie. "I thought I was done crying."

"Grief catches a person by surprise," Mallie said, gently. "You think you're done with it but it's not done with you." She thought of all the nights alone in her room she cried for her mother wondering if it would ever stop, at times losing her breath, drowning in her grief.

"I'm glad you've come home, Mallie."

"I'm glad too, Rose."

She took Rose by the hand and they walked swinging their arms.

"Now tell me what it is like is to work around rich folks," Mallie said.

"Well, they could use a lesson in picking up after theirselves," Rose said.

They both laughed.

"I expect they are used to being picked up after."

"Ma would still tan my hide if I throwed my clothes around like that and me a grown woman. The worst one is Mr. Gerard's niece. I go in to clean her room and it looks like pigs have rooted around in there."

"His niece?" Mallie said, surprised.

"A little blonde thing always complaining it's too hot or there's a bug in her room."

"She was on the train with him. I thought she was his fiancée. She called him by his given name."

Rose shook her head as if to say there was no accounting for the manners of rich folks. "No, he's a widower. His wife died a year ago."

Mallie regretted being rude to the man but how could she have known. "I am surprised he is here on a holiday so soon after losing his wife."

"I heard he used to bring her down here and they'd ride horses all over these mountains. They say she loved it here. They say she was beautiful and Mr. Gerard was crazy for her. Now, I see him going out early of a morning walking and sometimes he don't come back till dark. Misses his dinner and everything."

"Does his niece like to ride?"

"I've never seen her ride. To tell you the truth I don't think his niece will be back here next time. She don't seem to take to the mountains. I heard Mr. Gerard fussing at her for talking bad to the help. She accused May Simpson of going through her things. It hurt May's feelings something awful. She might of looked at her things but she wouldn't never a took nothing. May's honest as they come."

"I don't doubt she did if they were left lying around," Mallie said. "We were lucky. We never had much to leave lying around. We wore everything we had on our backs." She would never have Rose know of the beautiful clothes she had worn and cared so little for.

"Ain't that the truth," Rose agreed. "Sometimes, I had to stay in the bed while Ma washed and dried my clothes."

"More money than sense, Pa always said." Mallie realized what she had said and looked at Rose to see if she had noticed it.

A look passed over her face and then she looked away.

"We passed a bunch of them women down at the river," Rose said, "with them suits on that looked like a man's long-handled underwear. They was right out there with the men folk. You know Pa, he about had a fit. He said they all ought to be ashamed of theirselves. But it didn't look to me like they was at all."

She gave Mallie a wicked grin. Mallie laughed. She loved having her old friend back and she was grateful Rose had said nothing about her pa. She was not ready for that.

"Rose, you remember that time I was convinced we could fly if we flapped our arms hard enough?"

"You said you had watched a lot of birds and had figured out how they done it. I believed you."

"Well, I was telling the truth about one thing. I had watched a lot of birds."

"We must of jumped off our front porch a hundred times and it four feet off the ground."

"Going a little higher and a little farther each time."

"Then you said we was ready to take off. This time we could get high enough to fly. Just like a bird, you said. So I took off running and I sure enough flew. Then I landed face first and my nose smacked the ground. Blood shot out in all directions. Mama come running and she screamed real big when she seen me."

"She looked at you and then she looked at me," Mallie said. "I don't know who she was maddest at, but I remember she said, 'One of these days, the two of you will break your fool necks and they won't be nobody to blame but yourself. I ought to whoop the both of you, Rose for pulling such a trick, and you, Little Miss Mallie, for putting her up to it.' I was scared I had earned you a busted nose and a whooping."

"You knew when she called you that she was really upset, but she never would of whooped us."

Mallie laughed. "I know that now but I was pretty scared at the time."

"I don't think you was scared of Mama even then," Rose said. "I don't think you was ever sacred of nothing."

Mallie chuckled.

Rose grinned back shyly.

"What are you grinning at?"

"Well, I was thinking you ain't changed a bit."

"I'm glad you find that funny. I know a few folks wouldn't find that so laughable."

"Like Mr. Gerard."

"Maybe," Mallie said grinning.

They walked on giggling and talking like old friends who had never been apart.

The door of the cabin flew open and Mallie found herself in the arms of Maude Combs. The smell of vanilla filled her senses as Maude's plump body, as soft as a feather pillow, folded around her. She wanted to rest her head on Maude's shoulder and let go of all the sadness she had carried so long, but found herself quickly pulled away.

"Lordy honey, let me look at you. You're all growed up and pretty as an April morning."

"Mrs. Combs, it's so good to see you." Mallie said. A tear clinging to her lashes escaped and ran down her cheek.

"Hush, now," Maude said. She took her broad thumb and wiped the tear away. "You're home and there's no need for tears."

"I'm just happy," Mallie whispered.

"Well, now that's all right then," Maude said, patting Mallie's cheek. "Rose and me will just make some coffee and we'll have us some cobbler. You come on in when you're ready."

Mallie smiled. She was pleased that they left her alone for a moment to collect herself. The front room of the cabin was sparsely furnished. The ceiling was low and the fireplace covered most of one wall. A clock sat on the mantle. She remembered the one that had sat above their fireplace. Her pa would wind it once a week. A bed filled one end of the room covered with a quilt. A doorway led to another small room added to the cabin for a bedroom. Next to the doorway was a ladder leading to a loft. It was very much like the cabin where she had grown up. It made her heart ache, tears filled her eyes once more, and she had to shake them off.

Taking a deep breath, she went to the kitchen, a small room tacked onto the back of the cabin with a porch. Maude had a cookstove and did not have to cook over an open fireplace as her mama had done. There were no strings of dried beans hanging from nails or gourds full of seeds for the next year's planting. She supposed folks bought those things now from the company store or had them brought in by train. Pulling out a straight back chair from the table, she sat down.

Rose brought steaming cups of coffee to the table and then helped her mother with the cobbler. Maude set a huge bowl of blackberry cobbler in front of Mallie.

"Oh my, this looks wonderful, Mrs. Combs," Mallie said.

"I reckon you can call me Maude, now. You are a grown woman."

"Thank you, Maude," she said. She took a spoonful of cobbler and held it in her mouth. The tart blackberries swimming in sticky juice made her salivate and memories of hot summer days flashed through her mind. "This cobbler is the best thing I've eaten in years."

Maude and Rose sat down across from her and for a moment, they simply stared. Mallie flushed. She took a sip of her coffee and swallowed hard.

"I just can't get over how much you look like your mama," Maude said.

"Mama was beautiful," Mallie said simply.

"Well, she was that for sure. You've got a lot of that in you with that dark hair and them bold eyes. But it's the way you carry yourself and the way you take it all in. You've got your mama's curious nature, don't you?"

"I reckon I do," Mallie said, feeling both proud and humbled to be compared to her mama.

"She would be so proud of you making a teacher. Don't think she wouldn't."

"I hope so," Mallie said. Her voice cracked and she fought back tears. In her heart, she had always hoped her mama would be proud of her.

"Law, honey of course she would. Think of it, our little girl making a teacher. Of course, I should of knowed it. Your mama was a smart one. She could ask more questions. If I fixed an onion poultice for one of the younguns with the croup, your mama had to know what all was in it and just how I done it so she could make it too. Before long folks was coming to her to have her make a poultice for them. One time I made lye soap and she walked four miles to get me to show her how. It only took one time and she caught right on."

By the time she was born, Mallie realized, her mama had learned so much. It never occurred to her that her mama had to learn to live the life she had chosen. She had been a woman of privilege who had given it up to live in the mountains. How difficult it must have been in those early years, Mallie thought. She loved hearing stories of her mama. It was like having someone give her the words to a song she had been humming for a long time but could not remember.

"I thought Mama knew everything. I thought she was the smartest woman in the whole world."

"Oh, she was that," Maude said nodding. "In the beginning though, she was like a hog on ice when it come to getting by. I don't reckon she ever had to lift a hand to do nothing for herself growing up."

Mallie could imagine her life for it would have been just as hers had been for the last six years. Always someone there to cook the meals and fix her bath, her clothes laid out for her each day. "Do you think she ever regretted moving up here into the mountains?"

"I think living here was the happiest time of her life," Maude said firmly. "She told me that many of a time. Why she said she felt more like herself here."

Mallie smiled. "I feel the same way."

"Besides, she loved your pa," Maude said. "And she was going to be wherever he was and do whatever it took to please him, I know that much."

Mallie winced at the words. Maude reached out and patted her hand. "And she loved you and Cole. There was never any doubt in that. She thought you two was the moon and the stars. Why you younguns was the reason she done every thing she done. She couldn't cook to save herself when she first come up here. I learned her how to cook venison. For a while, that was all she knowed how to cook. Your pa said she cooked it every day for a month until he near about foundered. He never said a word to her though. No, he would of eat deer meat right on before he would of said a harm word to Rebecca."

Her spoon stopped and Mallie held it aloft unable to put it in her mouth. She looked at Rose through hooded eyes.

Rose placed a hand on her mama's arm.

Maude looked at Rose and then at Mallie. "Your pa knows you're here, honey," Maude said. "I made Riley promise to tell him."

Mallie placed her spoon back in her bowl unable to eat another bite. "He won't like it, me being back."

"He shouldn't never have sent you away. It weren't right." Maude said angrily.

"Mama," Rose cautioned.

Maude looked at Rose, her jaw set and then she relented. "I reckon he thought he was doing the best by you."

"Does he ever come to Elkmont?"

"He spends most of his time up at Fish Camp. He don't hardly come down like the other men."

"Truth be told, I don't know if I want to see him again," Mallie said biting her lip, "I didn't come back here to see him."

"You was just a youngun when he sent you away," Maude said. "You was missing your mama. Of course, you'd have some hard feelings, but he is still your pa."

"He never came to see me. He never even wrote to me."

Maude clucked her tongue. "Lordy mercy child, they just ain't no explaining your pa. Your ma and pa was fine folks to neighbor with, but your pa changed after Rebecca died."

"I think he just didn't want us after mama died," Mallie said, ashamed of the pity in her voice.

"Hush that talk, you hear me," Maude said her voice more gentle than her words. "Don't fret on it no more right now. Your pa is not a hard man, but he's got some contrary ways that can set a person to wondering, that's for sure. I just have to believe he means well."

"Thank you, Maude," Mallie said the words catching in her throat. "You are so kind."

"Oh, goodness honey, it ain't hard. There's plenty of love in this house to go around."

Mallie smiled and relaxed in her chair. "Cole wrote to me," she said at last. "He would tell me all about what he was doing timbering and how pa was doing. He wrote me every month, but I haven't heard from him since April."

Rose jumped up to get the coffee pot and lingered at the stove. Maude searched the bottom of her cup. The silence in the room grew louder. Rose came back and refilled their cups and then sat down and looked at Mallie.

"Nobody has seen Cole since early spring," Rose said.

"What do you mean?"

"He just disappeared."

"Without telling anyone where he was going?"

"There was an accident," Rose said.

"Oh my lord, was he hurt?" Mallie screamed.

"No, Mallie. He was operating a log loader."

"That was the last thing he told me. He was so excited that he had gotten a new job. He was going to be making more money and he was proud."

Rose hesitated.

"What happened, Rose? You have to tell me," Mallie insisted.

"He had only been working on the log loader for little over a week. He was working over at Hesse Creek. Local folks call it The Hurricane but the timber folks called it Hesse Creek. They couldn't build the railroad direct up Millers Cove there 'cause some folks wouldn't sell their land so they had to go up through Davis Branch just west of Kinzel Springs. It was a roundabout way to get to there but the lumber company was determined to do it."

"Rose," Mallie said gently.

"I'm sorry, Mallie." Rose shifted in her seat, sat on her hands and looked down at her lap.

Maude took over the story. "Everybody said he was doing a fine job, Mallie. It takes a heap of skill to guide a sixteen-foot log hooked onto a thin cable onto one of them flatcars. Them logs have to be balanced just right. Three logs on the bottom, two on the second row and one heavy one on top so the load will ride just right."

Mallie rubbed her forehead.

"I'm getting to it," Maude said. "You see it was when he was loading that top log that the cable broke. It weren't his fault. It just snapped under the load."

"But you said he wasn't hurt."

"It wasn't him, Mallie," Rose said. "When that cable breaks it whips around something awful."

"Someone else was hurt?"

"Dave Morgan was killed."

"Killed?"

"It was nobody's fault," Maude said.

"But Cole took it real hard," Rose said.

"He always took things hard," Mallie said. She felt sick for Cole. He had always been the sensitive one. The one who loved education and should have been the one sent away to go to school. Instead, he had stayed behind and tried so hard to please his father. "How did Pa take it?"

"He asked him a lot of questions," Maude said. 'Did he check the cable before he started? Had the tongs been set right to balance the log?' Cole took it as your pa accusing him of not doing his job right."

"So he left," Mallie said. She could feel her anger at her pa swell up in her chest.

They both nodded.

"And no one has heard from him since?"

"Not a word," Rose said, "except..."

"Except what?"

"Somebody said they thought they spotted him up near Clingmans Dome one day dressed like a mountain man with a long red beard."

"I wouldn't put no stock in that, Mallie," Maude said. "I think most likely he went to Knoxville to live."

"Then why didn't he come to see me?"

"Maybe he needs some time. Time and the Good Lord heals all."

Mallie thought time had healed nothing. If anything, with time, things had grown worse. Now she had lost her beloved brother. Sadness spread heavily through her limbs and her head dropped.

"You need some rest," Maude said. "You can share the bed with Rose tonight and tomorrow we will bring your things over."

Mallie looked up. "Bring my things over?"

"We can't have you living with strangers, when you have family here," Maude said.

Rose got up and put her arms around Mallie. "We all talked it over," Rose said. "You are going to stay with us."

"It was Riley brought it up. Soon as he heard you was in town," Maude said proudly. "We got plenty of room. We don't have to take in boarders like some folks. We do have one young feller comes through here now and again. Riley met him and took a liking to him so he lets him stay here when he's passing through, but he mostly camps out."

"Come on Mallie, it'll be fun," Rose said excitedly, cutting Maude short. "Like when we was girls."

She hugged Rose and whispered, "Thank you." She knew in her heart those days were lost to her and she wondered if anything would ever be so simple again.

5

Sweat beaded out on Crockett's forehead as he climbed toward the ridgeline of Dripping Springs Mountain. After a succcssion of hot July days, even the early morning sun shone like a lighted match. Above him, the spruces and balsam trees lined up like soldiers on guard. The thick tang of balsam gum filled the air. When he crested the top of a long climb, he threw off the tow sack he carried across his shoulder and leaned his rifle against a boulder. The path was a familiar one since he had made this climb so many times. Every Sunday, when he had the day off, he would take his hunting rifle walking as far as he could make it in a day and get back by dark. Sometimes he misjudged what he could do, driven to go further each time. Night would fall like a cool damp curtain. He would build a fire if he had to, knowing many a man had been lost in these mountains, and come in just before daylight to start work.

The clear blue sky was a stark contrast to the deep green of the spruce trees. Only a few wispy clouds floated aimlessly. They had not logged in this area or on Meigs Mountain to the north. The terrain was too steep and inaccessible. Crockett knew that would change in the coming years. The new Clyde Skidder was just the beginning. The Lumbermen would find a way to get the trees out. It was just a matter of time.

Crockett cupped his hands and collected water from one of the many springs that had given the mountains its name. He drank deeply, tasting thc cool, sweet water and then rubbed his hands over his face.

A rustling in the laurel thicket caused Crockett to ease his rifle into his lap. A ruffled grouse, startled by his presence, flew from the thicket less than six yards from him. He did not raise his gun to shoot it but merely watched its frantic flight.

Rubbing his hand along the barrel of his gun, he thought of the winter he had spent making it. Making a rifle was a long slow process. The barrel, shaped on an anvil from soft iron, had to be carefully rifled by cutting a twist into the bore with a special wooden guide made with a knife. A good stock had to be shaped from maple or walnut and a bullet mold forged. It took time, patience, and skill that not many men had. He thought he might be one of the few men left in these parts who could do it and he had lost the heart for it. He had made another rifle for Cole for his twelfth birthday.

Deciding that time was wasting, Crockett loaded up his gear and headed up the narrow trail overgrown in places by high bush huckleberries. Before long, the trail opened up to a heath bald, grassy and nearly flat where he had sometimes grazed his cattle. Scattered about were pines and scrub oaks with rhododendron and laurel threatening to take over.

Game, he observed, was not as plentiful as it had once been. Only a few years ago, by this time, he would have seen a dozen deer and a flock of wild turkey. He had seen a few signs of bear and only traces of wild hogs having rooted along the trail.

He hiked down a long trail bordered on both sides by galax. Crossing a footlog and walking up a small bank, he stepped out of the woods and saw his farm. It changed a little each time he saw it as nature took back the land he had worked so hard to claim.

Crockett had been on his own since he was fourteen and had run off from the Pennsylvania coalfields. He did not intend to spend his life underground as his pa had, giving his life up to darkness and drink and an early death. When his ma married another coal miner, after a mining accident killed his pa, he figured it was time to move on.

Working at whatever odd jobs he could find, he found himself one day in the Smoky Mountains. By that time, he figured he had enough abuse at the hands of other men to relish the thought of spending the rest of his life alone in the mountains. He lived with a family over at Whiteoak Flats while he dreamed of owning his own land. He did plowing and harvesting and whatever needed doing while he scraped to save a little money. He trapped furs for five winters and collected ginseng and chestnuts to sell at the store to buy a piece of land high up on the mountain.

All the while, he was learning the skills he would need to make it on his own. Wanting to know more than just how to build a cabin and a springhouse, he learned how to fashion his own axes and yokes, and repair a broken harness. With a froe and mallet, he learned to split shingles.

In the beginning, when he was building his cabin and clearing the land, he thought he could live there forever alone. It had taken a lot of hard work and ingenuity to survive the first year. He had hunted and fished for food and picked wild berries and gathered chestnuts to feed himself. With very few tools and no one to help him, he had girdled the biggest trees and then burned them off.

The work never ended so he was unaware of the growing loneliness in him until sometime after the third winter when it drove him out and down the mountain. He spent two weeks on the Bowery in Knoxville, mostly drunk and in the company of women who made him feel even lonelier.

When he wandered aimlessly up the street that morning, he had no idea it would change his life. He had not even known how close he was to losing it until he looked into Rebecca's eyes, even though she always made him feel it was the other way around. If she had married him to spite her family, as some folks said, he could not tell it in her voice or the way she looked at him even after her family disowned her.

Grass and vines hid the rock fences built around the garden to keep out the livestock. He had cleared enough land for a garden before Rebecca came to live there, but they never seemed to be able to rid the land of rocks. Each time he plowed, more rocks would pop up out of the ground like harvesting potatoes. Rebecca liked to joke that rocks were their biggest crop.

Near the orchard, the bee stands were empty and silent even though the sourwood trees still beckoned. The peach trees Rebecca had so loved had dropped their fruit. It lay on the ground rotting. He remembered how Rebecca had learned to make a tea from peach tree leaves that she swore could cure any ailment. She had believed it so strongly, but in the end, it had not saved her.

The front porch of the cabin sagged and lent a sad frown to its face. The chimney leaned away from the cabin and a large stone had fallen from the top. A snakeskin hung from one of the rocks about half way up. Birds nested in the eaves, their droppings spotting the logs. The land around the cabin, once cleared had sprung up all around with tulip poplars.

Walking to the front porch, he sat down hard, leaning his rifle against the railing and putting his sack on the rotting boards of the top step. He felt wilted and alone in the place that had given him such joy. Still he came to be with her, the only place he felt her presence.

"Rebecca, I've made a mess of things," he said simply. "I thought I was doing right by our younguns, but without your sweet hand to guide me I've lost my way." He put one foot on the porch, his hand on his knee and leaned against the railing. Eyes closed, he let the warm sun lull away the pain. Sometimes he wished he had buried Rebecca here on the farm so he could be nearer to her, but he knew if he had he would not have been able to sell the place, it would have been like selling her soul. He knew that some of the families continued to live on their farms after they had sold off the land but at the time, he had wanted nothing to do with the place. Rebecca's death had made all his dreams turn bitter in his mouth.

He thought of Rebecca's beautiful face and the way she would look up through her dark lashes at him when she sat quilting by the firelight, the glow on her face. He could still conjure up her trilling laugh and the way her smile spread across her face when she was especially pleased with herself. Once she had made Mallie a doll from cornhusk, her nimble fingers fashioning the tiny arms and head and the long skirt. It had delighted Rebecca as much as it had their daughter.

Crockett opened his eyes expecting Rebecca to be there, but he was alone. Still he spoke to her. "I guess you know Mallie has come back." He waited. "I thought I was doing the right thing when I sold this place and sent her to live in Knoxville. Your sister promised to give her a good life. I did not want her to have to work like we done. I thought in time she would see it that way."

He shook his head and chuckled. "She's made a teacher. Ain't that something? I know what you are thinking. Our

Mallie sitting still long enough to make a teacher. I thought the same thing, but I know you're proud."

A wasp droned loudly above Crockett's head. He looked up to see it hover around the nest and then dart away purposefully. An Eastern Phoebe had built its nest on a porch rafter, the mud and moss nest stuck securely to the wood. The fledglings peeked over the nest and stretched their necks, mouths open. The mother was no doubt nearby waiting for him to leave before coming to feed her babies. He felt no urge to move on just yet. The babies would have to wait.

"Now she's come back, to trade a good life for a hard way to go, I'm afraid. She's that much like me," he continued. "Mule headed as the day is long." He shook his head as memories flooded back like high water rising. "I've seen that girl go ginseng hunting all day without a drop of water or nothing to eat and not complain for fear I wouldn't let her come back with me."

He grew suddenly serious. "It was Cole I thought was most like you, always dwelling on something. But it was me he was taking after. I think the dark times comes to Cole like they always come to me. I never told nobody about them times but you, Rebecca. In your loving way, you done what you could to help me, but sometimes I had to go off by myself until it was done with me. When the dark times come, covering me like a heavy coat, I done all I could to fight it off but it would get the better of me. It would just hold me tight in its grip like a panther playing with its prey until it was ready to let go of me. Sometimes it would bring me to the point of dying, like after you was gone. I hoped it would take me then, but that ain't the way it works."

Crockett shifted his weight and rubbed the nape of his neck. He closed his eyes for a moment before he spoke as though speaking the words would make the truth too real. "Cole has got that in him too. I just never seen it then even though it was right out there for me to see. We would be out hoeing corn. You know how awful a job that was," Crockett said shaking his head, "and he would cut me a look. I thought it was just him being youngun like not wanting to work. He would never say a word to me; just give me this strange look. What good would it have done anyhow? The work had to be done. Still, he always acted like he had something bearing on his mind."

Stretching his limbs, Crockett reached for his sack and rifle. Then he set them back down. "I thought the younguns would be better off without me with you gone. I just wanted to go back living alone like I had before. I can see now where that was selfish of me. Now I'm afraid that both our younguns have come to hate me. Mallie's turned against me and Cole has gone off to be by hisself and I don't know what to do to help him." He dropped his head into his hands. "I'm lost, Rebecca," he cried. "Every way I turn, I seem to head down the wrong path. I dream every night that I am lost in a laurel hell and can't find my way out. I slide on my belly through mud and over rocks and down slicks, but I never find the end. I wake up beat down before I ever set my feet on the floor come morning."

He dried his eyes with the backs of his hands and squared his shoulders. "The Devil is working hard to break me down and use my faults against me. I'm afraid that without you to guide me, he's got the upper hand. I know you've gone to a better place and it ain't right for me to worry you but I need you. I need you to help me, Rebecca."

He waited, searching the sky for a sign. The sun bore down on him like a threat from a cloudless sky. He stood up, suddenly ashamed of his emotions and the need he felt for his wife gone eight years now. "Forgive me Rebecca for being a weak man and burdening you with my thoughts. I just wish I could have had you with me a little longer."

He bent to pick up his sack. The sun struck something in the dirt by his foot and flashed off it like a tiny beacon. Crockett scratched around in the dirt with his finger. It was a piece of blue pottery. He held the shard in his hand and smiled. It was the chip from Rebecca's cup. The missing piece from the one he broke and mended so long ago. He had searched the house over for it even taking up the floorboards in the kitchen to see if it had fallen through a crack. Now here it was in the palm of his hand. Smiling, with a calm spreading through him, he closed his fingers over it and whispered, "I'll be going on now, Rebecca. I got something I have to do before I head back. I know you'll understand."

He headed up the mountain to a cave above the farm. Laurel still bloomed in places, as the way grew steeper. A blowdown slowed his pace as he worked his way over fallen tree trunks and pushed through the brush toward a cliff face and a narrow ridgeline. Bellying over a tree trunk he noticed a copperhead only inches from where he planned to set his foot down. Just as he was figuring out how to get his rifle around to get a shot, it crawled languorously away. Letting out his breath, he eased off the log. He thought he was strong enough to stand a copperhead bite, but he did not want to test that out today.

Breaking through the thick tangled brush, he stood on a craggy outcropping to catch his breath. Steep ravines fell off on either side as the ridgeline snaked ahead of him.

He cut down through a stand of high-bush huckleberries and stopped to pick a handful remembering he had forgotten to eat the biscuit he had packed that morning. He knew bears liked huckleberries too. He had seen signs of bear scat on the walk up and trees scarred from their big claws. Panthers roamed these ridges too, their screams echoing through the valley. Only the strongest survive up here, he thought.

A jagged rock shot out from the cliff to his left and he headed toward it. Below the rock, the ground dropped off sharply. He worked his way along a narrow ledge to a crevice where time and nature had split the rock. Turning sideways, he inched his way through the slit to an opening big enough to move around in. Over time, a boulder had broken off and wedged itself over the top of the opening forming a cave.

There was no sign that anyone had been there. There were no cold blackened ashes from a fire or marks of a boot print. He stooped down and studied the ground. Close to one of the boulders in the dry soil, he thought he could see the serpentine marks of a tree branch as though someone might have used it to erase his tracks. Smiling to himself, he remembered teaching this trick, he had learned from an old Cherokee man, to Cole on their first hunting trip to hide his favorite spots for game.

This cave had been the first place he had come looking for Cole when he disappeared the morning after the accident. It had been his favorite place when he was a boy. He had taken his rifle and his gear but said not a word to anyone when he left. Crockett hoped he had headed out to Knoxville or over the mountain to North Carolina. He would have a better chance of surviving. When word came that someone had seen a redheaded man up near Clingmans Dome dressed like a mountain man, he had started walking the mountains looking for his son.

The sack he had left the last time was gone. It had not been ripped open and left on the ground as though an animal had found it. He had wedged a rope into a crack and hung the bag five feet in the air and now it was gone. He tied the rope around the top of the sack he had packed that morning with coffee, salt, a flint rock, a hunting knife and gunpowder. He had thrown in a pair of wool socks at the last minute. He had no way of knowing if it was Cole taking the sack but he felt some comfort in leaving it.

It was summer now, but fall would set in soon. The temperature at that elevation could drop without warning. A cold rain could chill a man until he could not think straight. First, he would start to shiver uncontrollably, his body shaking until his teeth rattled. Then his mind would play tricks on him leading him away from a safe place to wander the woods aimlessly. Crockett knew a man over near Blanket Mountain found by his wife as rigid as a post. He had come halfway down the mountain and had wandered around his own land unable to find his cabin a few hundred yards away. If the boy were up here, he would need to come down before winter.

From his shirt pocket, he pulled a small book, *Walden's Pond* by Henry David Thoreau. It had been Rebecca's favorite. She had read it aloud to the children at night before bed. She would forgive him for leaving it here if there was a chance it would bring his son the peace he was seeking. Placing the book on a rock ledge, he took one last look around before working his way back out of the crevice. He would need to make good time if he was to get back to Fish Camp before dark.

He had not done right by either of his children and now all he could ask was to know they were safe. Next Sunday he would be back walking the ridgeline.

6

At last, Mallie had the children separated by grades with the boys on one side of the classroom and the girls on the other. She looked around the classroom and counted twenty-five students on this the first day of school. Many of the students she had met already from her time in the camp, but some of the children had walked for two miles that morning to attend.

This, she reminded herself, was what she wanted to do, to come back home and teach the children who lived in her beloved mountains. That morning she had put on her white blouse starched and ironed until it hung stiff on the hanger, and pulled back her hair into a severe bun to appear older.

The rough paper tablets and pencils bought by the students at the commissary for the price of two eggs lay on their wide plank desks. Some of the children, scrubbed clean for their first day of school, looked at her eagerly while others appeared to have slept in the clothing they were wearing. Some of them had shoes but most were barefoot since it was still warm.

She wrote her name on the blackboard. "My name is Miss Hamilton," she said. "I am to be your teacher. I know some of your names already, but I want to learn every student's name so let us go around the room and please tell me your name. Let's start here," Mallie said, pointing to a tiny girl on the first row.

At first the girl hid her head in her thin arm. Her brown hair, brushed smooth and plaited into two braids fell around her face. Then she looked up at Mallie through dark lashes. Mallie smiled at her and then turned to look at the other students so as not to embarrass her. The girl's mother had brought her to school and they had stood outside for a long time before she talked her daughter into coming in. Mallie suspected she had never been away from home. Her mother had told Mallie the little girl's name was Willow.

"Her name is Willer, Willer Mathes," the little girl next to Willow said boldly. "And my name is Penelope Joy Smith." The girl, big for her age and dish faced, had taken on responsibility for Willow like the natural mother she would grow up to be.

"Thank you, Penelope," Mallie said. She did not press Willow to speak, for shyness was something she understood. As she continued around the room and each child spoke, she studied their faces and memorized each name. Only two bigger boys in the back of the room showed any signs of surliness and she wondered how long they would be content before they caused her any problems. She was nervous at the thought but dared not showed it.

"Now, how many of you know your letters?" she asked. Her instructions when she was hired had been to teach writing, arithmetic and reading. With the older students, she was to add geography and history. Since many of her students attended school only a few months of the year and often moved from camp to camp, she would first have to determine how much they had learned.

She sent some of the older students to the blackboard with the younger students to start them on the alphabet. The only way to teach so many grades was to put some of the students to task while she worked with the other students.

Frannie was the oldest girl in her class. Mallie knew that she had been up since dawn and had washed the boarders' breakfast dishes before coming to school. She was glad her mother thought it important enough to have her at school. Gathering some of the students into a reading group, she asked Frannie to read first. She was surprised to discover that her reading was very good. "Thank you, Frannie," she said.

Frannie sat down smiling, pleased with herself.

Mallie surveyed the group. "John, would you read for us," she asked. The other children giggled and Mallie shot them a look that quieted them down.

"John can't read," Jimmy Neil said. "He can't hardly talk."

"John," she said, ignoring Jimmy.

The boy, thin and pale, took the book in his hands and gave her a pained look. Slowly, the words came out. "The...boy...ran...to...."

Mallie knew she had made a mistake by making the boy read. It was painful to hear his halting attempts but she let him continue rather than stop him in the middle. Struck by his bravery, she said simply, "Thank you, John."

"Yes…ma'am," he said.

She watched as he sat down limp as a sack.

"Now, you read Jimmy," she said, turning to the boy who had spoken up.

The rest of the morning went quickly and Mallie was pleased to see the students working diligently. She looked at her watch and realized that it was time for the noon break. "Children," she said standing up, "put away your things. It's time for dinner break. If you brought something to eat, you may go outside under the shade tree to eat. If you are walking home, please be back in one hour."

The children quickly filed outside. Mallie collected the dinner pail Maude had packed for her. She stopped to stretch her shoulders and realized how tired she felt. Still, she was happy that her first day appeared to be going so well. Walking outside, she called to John to go to the spring and bring back a bucket of water.

He nodded at her. "Yes…ma'am," he said politely.

She wondered if that was the most he ever said, but she could tell he was pleased that she had singled him out.

It was too far for her to walk home to the Combs' cabin for dinner each day, so she joined some of the girls under the oak tree. She unpacked her dinner of two biscuits slathered with huckleberry jam and an apple. She ate the apple first.

The children, happy to be free, wasted no time but began immediately to play. The girls quickly drew out hopscotch games in the dirt. The boys chased each other around in a frantic game of tag.

Willow, who had sat down by Penelope to eat, got up and came to Mallie. She stood looking at her feet until Mallie patted the ground next to her. Willow sat down and fingered the fabric of Mallie's skirt. Cautioned repeatedly by her professors about the need for discipline in dealing with children, what she felt now was a tenderness rush over her. Reaching out, she brushed the little girl's bangs from her face and cupped her chin in her hand. Willow bit her lip and smiled a crooked smile. Mallie took a stick and wrote her name in the dirt. "That is your name. See, I spelled it out for you W-i-l-l-o-w. Can you say it for me?"

"Willow," the girl whispered softly.

"You are a very smart young lady. Someday you are going to be able to write many words. Right now, we will start with your name, how's that?"

Willow nodded, lost in her thoughts as she traced the letters with her finger.

Mallie relaxed against the tree trunk feeling happier than she had in years. Maude and Rose had made her feel a part of the family. They seemed to expect nothing of her but to have her there with them, unlike her Aunt Mae who constantly reminded her of the privilege it was to live in their home. At every turn, she brought up how much money it took to send her to school and to feed and clothe her in a style suitable for a young lady. Mallie made a point of never asking for anything.

Sharing the room with Rose was like having the sister she always wanted. They laughed together like young girls. Rose, the youngest of a houseful of brothers and sisters had always shared a room with two or three other sisters. Maude too seemed happy to, once again, have girls giggling and sitting up until all hours talking.

It made Mallie think of the times she and Cole had acted the fool, laughing over nothing at all.

Her only regret was that Maude and Rose were gone a lot of the time working. Much of her free time, she spent reading and preparing lessons for the children. She tried to help out by cleaning house. Her few attempts at cooking were such failures that she soon gave up unless Maude was there to show her what to do. She remembered having cooked for her family when her mama was ill. They never said anything about how bad it was but she laughed to herself now at what they must have thought about her pitiful efforts.

She stood up and dusted off her skirt. Walking to the steps of the schoolhouse, she called to the children to gather for the afternoon classes. They lined up in front of her and took turns drinking from the bucket of water John had brought from the creek. They shared the one dipper passing it on after they drank. The boys' faces were red and streaked with dirt where the sweat had run down. The girls' hair, combed neatly that morning, stuck out from their plaits and curled around their pink faces.

John walked up and presented her with a small branch from a sourwood tree. She remembered how her pa had prized his sourwood trees. He always said the best honey came from the sourwood tree and he would harvest it as soon as the flowers stopped blooming so it would not mix with the nectar of other flowers. He never cut one down to use for firewood.

She wondered how many of the children understood how the bees made honey from the sourwood flowers. They had watched bees flying from flower to flower she was sure. Did they know the bees were collecting nectar and storing it in their stomachs? Did they know that tiny grains of pollen clung to their legs and brushed off on the stigma of other flowers? She remembered how excited she had been to learn such things. "Oh John, how nice," she said, taking the branch and examining it closely. "I'll use this for our science lesson this afternoon."

He beamed. "Yes...ma'am."

As she directed the children back into the schoolhouse, she turned to look up at the mountains. Storm clouds were gathering, brought in by a gentle breeze. They swirled about like the thoughts in the back of her mind. She wondered if her brother was really living up in the mountains. What kind of shelter had he built for himself? Was he sitting alone in a cave or a lean-to he had built from fallen trees, the mist thick around him? She tried to picture her sensitive, tenderhearted brother living a life of such solitude and it made her throat close up.

If the rains came, she knew her pa would go on working. She knew from Cole's letters that many of the men moved around from camp to camp and left when the snows came, but her pa worked on through snow, mud and miserable cold rains. Bad weather always made a difficult job even more dangerous. Cole had written to her about a train wreck on Jakes Creek that killed two men in 1909. The engineer, Gordon A. Bryson and the brakeman Charles M. Jenkins had died when the train overturned on a sharp curve coming down the mountain fully loaded on rain slick tracks. The wreck, still not cleared days later when the first excursion train brought its load of holiday visitors up the mountain, presented an alarming sight. Even though the accident had made both the Knoxville newspapers and Mallie read every word, her Aunt Mae refused to discuss it.

Someday soon, she would have to go up the mountain. If Cole did not come down to her, she would go up the mountain in search of him. A clap of thunder brought Mallie back from her rumination. Her plans would have to wait until she had a day alone for there were folks who would not approve of her roaming the mountains alone and for now she had children to teach.

As she turned to go back into the school, she saw a man riding up on horseback. Sitting tall on the buckskin, he wore high boots and dark rough serge pants, his hat pulled low over his eyes. He took off his hat as he approached and she recognized Pierce Gerard.

Sweat gleamed on the buckskin's flanks from hard riding. Pierce dismounted like an experienced rider and rubbed the horse along its neck for a moment before turning to stand awkwardly at the bottom of the steps, hat in hand. He looked up at her. "Oxydendrum arboreum," he said finally.

"I beg your pardon," Mallie said.

"The leaves you hold in your hand. The scientific name for sourwood is Oxydendrum arboreum."

Mallie had forgotten she was still holding the leaves that John had given her. She glanced down at them and then looked at Pierce. His boots cost more than she would make in a year of teaching, she thought, and yet they were scuffed and muddy from use. His damp hair stuck to his forehead and dark stains had formed on his shirt. "You know a lot about trees." It was more a statement than a question.

"I have studied them quite extensively."

"I suppose you have to protect your investments," she said.

"It's both a business and personal interest."

If he caught anything in the tone of her voice, he ignored it. He was either a man without emotions or one who had learned not to reveal himself. "One of the children brought the leaves to me and I thought I might use them to teach a science lesson this afternoon. In fact, I need to be going. Was there something I could help you with?"

"Oh, I am so sorry to keep you. I was just riding by when I saw you standing on the porch."

She watched as he gripped his hat tighter and shifted his weight. He was as uneasy as a young man come to court her and the thought almost made her laugh. "It's just that the children are waiting." She could feel them behind her gathering in the doorway to listen. Throwing a glance behind her, she could hear them scramble to their desks.

"Yes, of course. I apologize for the way I look. I was out riding."

"I can see that. Do you ride often?"

"Yes. Every day if I have an opportunity. I ride as far up into the mountains as I can. It's beautiful and I find peace up there."

She thought the sadness in his eyes belied his words. "I haven't seen you riding through here before."

"I remembered you said you came back to teach."

"So, you didn't just ride by and see me." Pierce Gerard had been nothing but nice to her and still her guard went up when he came around.

"Let me say I rode by in hopes of seeing you. I was wondering if you might like to join me for dinner at the hotel on Sunday. They serve a very nice meal on Sunday."

Mallie was so stunned she could not speak. It was the last thing she expected and she simply looked at him unable to form a response.

"It would give you an opportunity to meet some very nice people," he continued. "I mean if you are concerned about being alone with me. Or you could bring along a friend."

"My friends all work there, Mr. Gerard."

"Well, of course, I understand if you would be uncomfortable."

"It wouldn't make me at all uncomfortable Mr. Gerard," she said defensively. "I meant they would most likely be working." That was not the whole truth since she knew Rose had the day off. "If I might ask, Mr. Gerard, what is your interest in me?"

"Miss Hamilton, please forgive me if I've offended you. I am afraid I am not very good at this. My wife was quite outgoing. She was the one who directed our social life and I left that all to her. She had a wonderful way with people and I perhaps relied on that too much."

"I heard about your wife's death, Mr. Gerard. I am truly sorry."

"Thank you," he said simply. "I promise you, my interest in you is simply as a dinner companion. I will let you go now. I hope I haven't kept you too long."

"I am surprised you are still here," she said.

His eyes widened but he made no reply.

Mallie blushed. "Oh, now I am the one to apologize. I am too plain spoken I am afraid." He had the grace to smile kindly and she returned a closed mouthed smile.

"I like that about you," he said. "I find that too often the people I meet now … well, I find I don't have the patience I once had."

"You are very kind," she said. "I didn't mean here in front of me, I meant here in Elkmont. I thought you would have returned to Pennsylvania by now. Are you spending the summer here?"

"Actually, I am planning on building a summer cottage."

"Here at Elkmont?"

"Why, yes, here at Elkmont. I've come to enjoy the place quite a lot."

"What about your niece?"

"She has returned home," he said. "She never warmed to the place as I have."

Mallie could see a frown appear on his brow and then disappear. From what Rose had told her, his niece had been completely miserable at Elkmont and had managed to make everyone else so. She had wondered earlier if his interest in her was as a companion for his niece, but now she knew that was not true. "I'm sorry to hear that," she said.

"Yes, well, I won't bother you further," he said, politely.

As he turned to go, Mallie called out to him. "I would be happy to have dinner with you Mr. Gerard." She could not imagine what had made her do it. It was not pity for his loss, for she had known many people who had suffered greater tragedies. He sparked an odd curiosity in her that she wondered if she would come to regret and she had decided he had something to offer her after all.

He turned back to face her and smiled. "That would be very nice Miss Hamilton."

"There is one condition however."

"Of course, whatever you need," he said without hesitation.

"I would like for you to take me horseback riding."

Pierce stood studying the ground as if pondering her request, and then he looked up. "Noon," he said with a nod. "They serve promptly at noon and I understand they are quite serious about it."

She laughed. "I'll be there, on time."

"I'll be happy to escort you."

"The walk will do me good," Mallie said. She wondered what people would think if they saw her stroll along on the arm of Pierce Gerard.

"At noon then, Miss Hamilton," he said politely.

"At noon, Mr. Gerard."

She watched him mount his horse and ride away slowly. His interest in her was a puzzle. People had told her before that she was difficult to get to know. Perhaps that was what intrigued him. What would he do when he realized she guarded her independence far more than he could ever imagine? Almost immediately, she regretted agreeing to have dinner with him. Too much in her life needed working out to add a further complication. Then she realized there was no one in her life now to tell her what she could or could not do. The thought was both exhilarating and saddening.

Rose would have a fit when she found out she was dining with Pierce Gerard. There would be no end of teasing and speculating on the day as they went over what Mallie was to wear and how she would do her hair. Rose would know everyone staying at the hotel and his or her social status and discuss it endlessly. It would serve no purpose to keep it to herself for Rose would find out soon enough. She would never forgive Mallie for holding out even though there was no explaining to her why she was doing it. Rose would never believe she was having dinner with him in exchange for a horse.

As she turned to walk back into the schoolroom, she could hear the children running back to their desks. The word would be all over the camp by dark. Shaking off the thought, she walked to the blackboard to start the afternoon lessons.

7

It was time for Cole to break up camp and move. He had bivouacked near Buckeye Gap for longer than he felt comfortable and it was time to move on. It was impossible to camp in one place for long without leaving some footprints.

Whenever possible, he camped near old trails so as not to call attention to a new footpath created by his comings and goings. Generally, he picked a place that was invisible from the trail and opposite ridgelines, preferring a place near tall evergreens to hide his camp smoke. Sometimes he made another camp some distance away and more visible to throw off anyone passing through. He knew where cattle were grazed and favorite fishing holes and he avoided those places. On occasion, he had camped near streams in laurel thickets where he had to crawl in and out, but there it was dark and damp. His favorite places were high up in the mountains where he could look out over the ridgelines and see the clouds drift overhead.

His first night in the mountains he had spent sleeping up against a fallen log. His mind had not been clear when he left Elkmont and night had fallen before he realized it. Surviving the night by covering himself with leaves, by morning, they sparkled with the frost that had formed on them. He knew he had been lucky and that he would have to be more careful if he were to make it over the mountain alive.

The next night, high up on Clingmans Dome, he built a bed of balsam branches and at dawn headed on over to Newfound Gap and down the mountain to North Carolina.

The Smokemont Logging camp hired him on as a cook. He refused to work as a logger. The work suited him fine and he lived with a good family. Still, after a month, a local man working on the railroad was cut in half between two railcars and Cole packed up and left. He drifted for a while and then got a job in the cotton mills. The work was dirty and confining. The living conditions were worse than any he had seen in the logging camps. Before long, he bought a knapsack and some supplies and did the last thing he would have believed possible, he headed back home to the Smoky Mountains. That had been over two months ago and he had come to be at home high up in the mountains.

He packed the canvas knapsack with a hatchet, a canteen, his tin of dry matches and a pouch with a piece of eyeglass and candle. His simple cooking utensils included a small cook pot, a cup and a fork and spoon. He added his ammunition and flint and a small bag of jerked venison. In the next day or two, he would have to hunt for meat. He wore a sheath knife and carried a jackknife in his pocket. Rolling up his blanket, he tied it to the bottom of his knapsack. Brushing away the signs of his campsite with a balsam branch, he stood back to check his work. He had learned a lot during his time on the mountain. The knowledge had come to him from deep buried memories awakened through need and whispered to him by mountaineers long dead. It made him feel stronger and more alive than he had ever felt to know that he could never tame the mountains but he could survive on his own wits.

Satisfied with the job he had done of covering his camp, he put on his pack, grabbed his rifle and headed down the mountain. The morning fog was still thick as he slipped onto the old trail. Moving quietly, he listened for sounds of other men and searched the trail for signs of recent footprints.

Today, he would walk over the ridgeline and down to the farm. He thought it might be Thursday or maybe Friday but he was not sure. It had been twenty days since any rain had fallen although clouds had gathered a time or two. The air was taking on a tang in the evenings and fall would soon be turning the leaves to ruby and gold. No wind stirred the trees and the sky was clear blue.

Going along the ridgeline, he planned on dropping down to cross Miry Ridge and on to Dripping Springs Mountain. He would rest at the slit in the rock above the farm before heading down. The bee stand at the farm had been gone for a long time, but the last time he visited a swarm had taken up in a tree nearby. The thought of honey and butter on a warm biscuit made his mouth water. There would be no warm biscuits but he would settle for a comb of sourwood honey. He wiped his mouth with the back of his hand and pressed on.

It did not serve him well to ponder things. It was best to keep moving. His long red beard fell on his chest, his hair, tied back with a string, stuck out in places. It had been a month since he had last viewed his face in a stream. When he rubbed his hands over his face, it felt gaunt and his arms were sinewy. He thought he might be unrecognizable to anyone who had known him. In the two months he had been back in the mountains, he had not spoken to another soul.

The warm sun had burned off the last of the fog and heated up the day by the time Cole dropped down off the last ledge to the cave. He eased his pack off and hid it along with his rifle in a stand of laurel before he worked his way along the crevice to where the rock opened up into a small room. The tow sack was hanging there just as it had been many times before. The first time he came to the rock, he had been homesick, lost and in need of something familiar. The sack had been hanging there and he knew who had left it. He almost broke down as the months of pain washed over him and he almost went down the mountain then, but he did not. Living on his own in the mountains was his act of contrition and he did not know how long it would last. He was not even sure what his sin was but he knew somehow that the mountains would give him a way to redeem himself.

Still, he had taken the sack because as much as he had learned to live on his own in the mountains, only a fool would turn down such a gift. Even the most seasoned mountaineer knew that living in the wilds was a tenuous thing measured in hours and days.

Cole took the sack and sat down on a rock. With a silent prayer of thanks, he opened it. He took out the supplies one by one and chuckled to himself with pure joy when he saw the coffee and dry socks. He knew from watching nature that all animals sought comfort and felt pleasure in it and that he was no different from them.

As he stood up, intending to take the sack out and load the things into his pack, he saw something on a rock ledge just above his head. He sat the sack back down and reached up his hand brushing it over a flat object. When he lifted it off the ledge and looked at it, a knot tightened in his stomach and tears spilled over his cheeks for the first time since his mama had died. Holding the book to his face, he smelled the leather binding. Opening it, he looked at pages now crisp and brown with age.

A noise brought him back and he shut the book quickly. Reaching for his rifle, he remembered he had hidden it along with his pack and cursed himself silently for his carelessness. Slinking back against the rock wall, his hand went to the knife at his waist.

A tall dark haired man not much older than him emerged from the slit. Blinking as his eyes adjusted, the man looked around, taking in the sight of the open sack with its contents lined up on the rock.

"Hello," the man said, "anybody here?"

Cole wondered what kind of fool called out like that. Then the man walked right toward him. He stepped out, knife pulled. The man looked at the knife and then at Cole.

"You're Cole Hamilton," he said with a smile.

Cole stared at him but did not reply. The man ignored the knife and stuck out his hand. The smile never left his face.

"I'm Will Stenson. I'd heard mention of you but I never thought we'd meet."

Cole put away the knife and shook the man's hand. "How did you know it was me?" His voice sounded strange in his ears. He had found himself talking to an animal or two at times but he was never sure he had spoken aloud.

"Well, there can't be that many red haired men roaming the mountains now can there?"

"So there's talk of me?"

"Some. To tell you the truth, I thought it was mostly made up, all that talk of a wild man living high up in the mountains. Now, that I get a good look at you, you do look pretty wild," Will said, a grin splitting his face.

Cole stepped back relaxing his posture. "What are you doing up here?"

"I'm studying the plants. I am a botanist. These mountains have more diverse species than anywhere in America. I am looking for rare species. "

"You're a botanist."

"Yes, you know about botany?" Will asked.

"I know plants."

"Then maybe you could help me."

Cole said nothing. Will watched as he stuck the book inside his shirt and returned to loading the sack.

"That is if you have time," Will said breaking the silence.

Cole turned to see Will, arms crossed, leaning back on the rock wall, his head cocked to one side and his eyes full of sport. "I could have killed you Will Stenson, as soon as you were inside the cave. You could see I had a knife."

"I knew you wouldn't," Will said simply.

"And just how could you know a thing like that."

"Let's say I'm a pretty good judge of character. You wouldn't be up here if you were the murdering kind."

Cole knew he was right. A man who would run off like he did wouldn't be likely to kill a man. "Let's get out of here. You first."

They eased their way through the slit and came out into the bright sunlight. Will's pack lay on the ground. "You left your pack out where it could be seen," Cole said shaking his head. "You're a bigger dang fool than I thought."

"I'm not hiding from anybody," Will joked.

Cole ignored the remark.

"You are right. It was careless of me, Cole, but I've been up here for two weeks this time and all I've seen are deer, squirrels and grouse and they are not likely to run off with my pack."

"From the looks of the thing a bear couldn't carry it off. What have you got in that thing? It's dang near as big as you are."

"I need a lot of things for my work, my journals and my books, a compass, a few maps and, of course, my food and cooking utensils," Will recited.

Cole shook his head. He dug his pack and rifle out from hiding. He added the new supplies and then folded the sack and put it to into his pack. "You got everything you need right here," he said with a sweep of his hand.

"I don't see you turning down help," he said pointing to the now bulging pack.

"I can find my way around without a map, tell you the habits of every creature up here, dress out wild game and catch fish without a hook, but I can't grow coffee or weave a pair of dry socks. Even a seasoned mountain man knows better than to turn down help," Cole said. He realized he had spoken more words than he thought he still had in him and it annoyed him that it felt good.

"Then you won't mind if I tell you I took a few things the last time I was here, just some coffee and a little salt. I left most of it for you."

Cole laughed despite himself. "Well, I guess I was wrong about you. At least you ain't a complete fool."

"Who leaves you these supplies?" Will asked.

Cole looked at him through veiled eyes.

"Crockett Hamilton, your father. He leaves it."

Cole said nothing but went on gathering his gear.

"You said I was not a complete fool," Will said, finally.

"Well, I was being generous," said Cole.

Will laughed, his teeth shining through two weeks growth of beard. "I admit I have a lot to learn. I have studied a number of books on camping in the wild."

Cole snorted. "No book can teach you that. You have to use your wits and have some common sense. Things I am beginning to suspect you are in short supply of."

"You could teach me."

"I travel light."

"One day. Give me one day."

Cole studied the man. His eyes were dark and earnest. "Get your pack," Cole ordered wondering how much a man could learn in a day about surviving the mountains when some men spent a lifetime and never learned it all. Despite himself, he found he liked Will and trusted him. "But you are not to tell a soul you seen me. And remember, I didn't come up here for company."

Will grabbed his hand and shook it hard. "You won't regret this. I am a very good student."

"I already regret it. Now, let's get on down the trail. We got to make camp before dark."

"I learned that one on my first trip out."

Cole thought about his first night out but said nothing. If Will wanted to believe he was the expert then so be it. "And don't make so much noise."

Will put on his heavy pack and Cole took the lead. Fifty yards down the trail, Cole could no longer feel Will behind him and turned to find him gone. He shook his head and started on down the trail when he thought better of it. Heading back up the trail, he found Will holding something in his hand. When he looked up to see Cole standing there, his face lighted up. "Look, it's a nut or some fruit from this tree. I remember how it had small flowers in the spring."

"That's an oil nut tree. If you open that up, it is oily inside. You don't want to do that though because its rank smelling and poisonous."

"I noted the flowers of many of the plants in spring and now I like to see the seeds they produced," Will said. "Take this calycanthus floridus," he said, touching a nearby shrub, "in the spring it had white, bell-shaped flowers and the seeds have wings."

"That's a silverbell. I thought you were looking for something rare."

"Yes, I am."

"Then your first lesson is to learn what's common and ignore it. This plant grows all over these mountains. If you spend time looking at it, you will never see what is rare. That goes for surviving too. Train your eyes to see what is different, like the ground tore up from some animal rooting, the way the trail looks from up ahead and behind you, look for rocks and mossy patches and things to remind yourself of if you get lost."

"Have you ever been lost up here?"

"It's harder to get lost if you're not headed no place particular. But I have wandered around a bit."

Will smiled. "What did you do?"

"Built me a camp and waited till daylight. Things are always clearer in daylight. Now, let's get on down the trail while we still have some."

Cole watched as Will put the nut in a small pouch attached to his belt. He could only shake his head in wonder, surprised the man had made it this far.

Entering the clearing where the cabin stood always brought back a flood of memories. Cole waited to let Will catch up. Will had asked a hundred questions along the trail. His curiosity about the plants and animals of the Smoky Mountains seemed endless. After the months of isolation, being with another person, especially one so inquisitive, had left Cole exhausted. He decided to break his own rule and stay at the farm for the night. Being with Will had sparked something in him that he thought he had put aside, a longing for life, as he had once known it.

"We'll camp here tonight," he said, when Will caught up with him.

"It's an old farm," Will remarked. "Does anyone live here?"

"Not anymore. It belongs to the lumber company."

"Will they mind us staying here?"

"Don't much care," Cole said, with a shrug.

"Still, you wouldn't like anyone to know we are here?"

Cole nodded. "I know how often the timber scouts came through checking things out to see if anyone is living on the land or camping out in a claims cabin."

"Claims cabin?"

"The lumber company builds a cabin on a piece of land, sends somebody up here now and again to live in it. After a while, they claim the land. They are not likely to be back through this way for months."

"I've stayed in a few of those cabins. I wondered why it seemed like there hadn't been anybody around for a while."

"There's a fire pit out back of the cabin. What say we set some snares and have us some rabbit for supper?"

"This is your farm, isn't it?"

"For a man who don't know nothing, you are sure full of lucky guesses. It belonged to my family once. I grew up here."

"Why did you sell it?"

Cole looked at him.

"I'm sorry. That's none of my business."

"Pa sold the place after my mama died."

"I am sorry to hear about your mother," Will said. "My father died before I was born. How old were you when she died?"

"Fourteen."

"And then you went to work for the lumber company?"

"We held on to the farm for a while. My pa didn't have much use for it with Mama gone."

"Do you miss it?"

"It was hard work," Cole said flatly. "And we hardly had a thing we didn't make or grow. All this land had to be cleared of trees, some of them thirteen feet across. You see them rock fences, they was all made from rocks carried out of these fields. Most times it was just me and Pa to do the work."

Will grew quiet and a cloud passed over his face for a moment and then it was gone and his smile was back. "You must have had some good times working with your pa and all."

Cole hated to admit that he had good times, but that he had not known it until they were gone. "Hang your pack up here," he said, pointing to a rusty hook on the back porch, "and let's get those snares set."

Will hung up his pack.

Cole took a length of braided fishing line from his pack and then hung it up. "Have you made a snare before?"

"I've tried but I've never caught a rabbit."

"Then you are doing something wrong. A rabbit is the easiest thing in the whole dang world to catch. A rabbit is something you can catch any time of the year. They don't hibernate like bears. And they can be found most anywhere in these mountains," Cole said.

"When did you learn to set a snare?"

"When I was five," Cole said. "Caught two rabbits that day. After that it was my job to set the snares from then on."

"Did your pa teach you?"

Cole nodded.

"I envy you that."

"Don't never envy nobody," Cole said simply.

"Wise words from a man of your advanced years," Will teased. "I'll take that into consideration."

"It's still not too late for me to go back on our deal," Cole said dryly.

"What do you want me to do?" Will asked, suppressing a grin.

"Look for a young sapling growing near some bushes or tall grass. Bend the sapling over to form a trigger for the snare."

Will quickly found the spot and cleaned the sapling of its branches while Cole formed a noose with some of the fishing line.

"You don't need bait for a rabbit. They'll just run through coming and going and get caught in this line. That'll trigger the sapling."

Will made the next snare. He looked at Cole when he finished.

Cole examined the snare. "I have to admit, you learn quick."

Will smiled.

They set two more snares along the perimeter of the farm before they headed back.

"Do you think we'll catch a rabbit?" Will asked.

"I sure hope we do."

"Do you like rabbit?"

"I like it a heap more than jerky and that's what'll we'll be having if we don't. Have you never eat a rabbit?"

"No," Will admitted.

"What have you being living on up here?"

"Rice, dried beans, hardtack and some dried fruit."

"Got that out of a book did you?"

Will chuckled. "Yes, it was the same book that told me to bring along extra socks."

"Come on let's get that fire built. You do know how to build a fire?"

"Of course, you just rub two sticks together."

Cole stared at him. "One more remark out of you and you can watch me eat rabbit tonight." He grabbed Will by the neck and pushed him on ahead.

He could hear Will laughing to himself all the way back to the farm.

The men sat by the fire and watched as the two rabbits they had dressed earlier roasted on sharpened sticks. The smell made Cole's mouth water. He busied himself sharpening his jackknife on a flint rock. He studied Will, who sat contentedly leaning against his pack, studying the braided fishing line they had used for the snare. He had to admit that Will had an interest in everything to do with the mountains and took no offense at anything. It was hard not to like a man like that even for someone as hardened as Cole thought he had become. "What made you come to the Smoky Mountains to study plants?" he asked.

Will looked up. He looked at Cole for a moment as though forming his thoughts. "My father was a botanist, William

Dawson Stenson. I am his namesake. Perhaps, you have heard of him. He came to this area many times."

Cole shook his head.

"He froze to death near Clingmans Dome, caught in a sudden snowstorm. My mother always believed that he would die someday out in the woods. He would get caught up in following a species and forget the time, she said. All I have left of him are his journals."

"I'm sorry about your pa. So you followed in his footsteps," Cole said. Struck by the power that even a dead father wielded over a son, he could only think of his struggles with his own father.

"Yes, exactly. I became a botanist with the hope of continuing his work."

"What does your mother think of that?"

"She doesn't like the idea of course," Will said, matter-of-factly. "She wanted me to become a banker. I think she worries that I will meet the same fate as my father."

"She's afraid you will die in the mountains like your father did?"

"Yes."

"You can't hold that against her."

"I don't. It is just… I'm sort of hoping she's wrong," Will said, a wry grin splitting his face.

"Then you don't want to stay up here too long. The odds will turn on you."

"I'm willing to take that chance," Will said. "What about you, aren't you afraid the odds will turn on you?"

"I am not afraid of dying," Cole said simply. He did not say that living tested him more. "Now, when did we start talking about me? You got brothers and sisters?"

"I've talked more about myself than I ever have," Will said with disgust. "Stenson's are not people to talk about themselves, about growing up or anything in the past."

"Why not?"

"It's impossible to change. You just got what you got."

"Don't you have any good memories of growing up?"

"This will be a good one," Will said with a smile. "Every day now is a good memory. And to answer your question, I have an older sister who married a banker and lives nearby my mother. My mother remarried and had two other daughters but not another son."

"Are you close to your sisters?"

"My oldest sister, yes. Mary Anne took care of me when I was young."

"I have a sister, Mallie. She lives in Knoxville. I used to write to her but not since…the accident."

"Mallie," Will said, "that's a pretty name. Is she older or younger than you?"

"Younger, by two years."

"What's she like?"

Cole laughed, but he felt pierced by a sense of loss. "Mallie was always the independent type. She had a mind of her own even when she was a little bitty girl. Mama used to say you could see the mischief working alive in her."

"So she hasn't heard from you since the accident?"

"I couldn't write to her after that."

"Don't you think she must be worried?"

"It bears on my mind."

"I could get word to her that you are all right."

"No, it's best the way it is for now. She might try to find me."

"Why don't you want her to know you are here? No one holds the accident against you. Logging is a dangerous business. Men are hurt or killed all the time. You know your father doesn't blame you or he wouldn't bring you supplies."

"I hold it against me," Cole said, with more anger than he intended. Then more softly, he said, "There are just times in a man's life when he needs to be alone. It's better for him and better for other folks."

They sat for a long time in silence.

"You had a book in your hand," Will said, "when you were holding the knife on me. Did your father bring that too?"

"*Walden Pond*," Cole said. "It was my mama's favorite book. She used to read it to us at night."

"'I went to the woods because I wished to live deliberately, to front only the essential facts of life, and see if I could not learn what it had to teach,'" Will quoted.

"You know the book?" Cole asked.

"Yes, it was always a favorite of mine."

"Then you know it goes on, "'When I came to die, discover that I had not lived.'"

They both sat lost in their own thoughts until Will spoke. "I'm getting pretty hungry," he said sheepishly. "I stayed up here longer than I meant to. I was down to eating rice mostly."

"Why didn't you head on down? No sense in starving yourself to death looking for some plants."

"This may be my only chance to see some of the plants my father wrote about. With the heavy logging going on they are likely to disappear. Many of them need the shade of trees. They can't survive in heavy sunlight."

"And men can't survive without jobs," Cole said defensively.

"I didn't mean to offend you. I was just saying what I know to be true."

Cole nodded.

"With the trees gone, other plants like blackberries and fire cherries move in and crowd out everything else. Soon all the animals that lived on the seeds and nuts from the trees move on for lack of food. Things like white tailed deer and wild turkey are the first to go. Then the birds will go because they too need the trees."

Cole had seen that with his own eyes. The herds of deer that used to roam the woods and fields had dropped off. "When I was a boy, deer were nuisances to anybody trying to farm around here," Cole said, conceding nothing.

"They survived farmers and hunters but they won't survive timbermen. Already there is some talk the government will put closed-seasons on hunting to try to protect the animals that are left."

"You mean the government can tell me when I can hunt and when I can't?"

"The state has already formed a game and wildlife commission to look into it."

To Cole, the animals, birds, and fish had seemed plentiful. There had always been more than a man could use or so he had believed. Just like the trees, they seemed to exist in an endless supply stretching on forever.

A sound like a woman's scream came from the ridgeline above them. Will sat up straight and looked at Cole.

"Panther," Cole said.

"I've never heard anything like that before."

"Not many panthers left around here," Cole said. The words made him uncomfortable after their earlier conversation. "You hear one now and again. Once you've heard a panther scream, you're not likely to forget it."

"They are dangerous, aren't they?"

"You don't want to run up on one. You can sleep in the cabin tonight if you want. I'll keep the fire going."

"I'm not afraid," Will said.

Cole believed him for the look on his face was one of fascination. "It wouldn't hurt when it comes to panthers to be just a little afraid."

Will nodded.

"Now, let's eat these rabbits before something else does."

Cole watched as Will sat on his haunches and tore off pieces of flesh with his teeth. He grinned at Cole with his mouth full. "I do like rabbit," he said.

Cole had a feeling there was very little that Will did not like about the woods and life in general. "Eat up then, we got us an early morning ahead of us."

He added more logs to the fire. He would keep it going all night for he knew what Will was yet to learn. The scream of the panther was just one of many things to be feared and the rest could never be fully learned.

He shook Will awake before dawn. He sat up and took the piece of wood Cole handed him as though he had been expecting it, but then he looked at it.

"What's this?"

"It's called a punk. It's made from a piece of rotted out wood. When you don't have coal oil to make a torch, you have to make do. This here wood will smoke but it won't burn."

"And why do we need it to smoke?"

"We are going to rob a bee tree. Come on, let's get going, it's nearly daylight."

Will was up instantly.

"I scouted a tree out last time I was through here. We need to get there before the sun comes up and warms the bees and they set to swarming the hive."

"But we don't have any gear. What's to keep the bees from stinging us?"

"Well, if we do it right, this smoke will confuse 'em and we can get the honey comb out before they figure out what's going on."

"How did you learn to rob a bee tree?"

"My pa used to have bee stands. He'd take the honey every year and never get a sting."

"What about you, did you ever get stung taking honey?"

"I ain't actually ever done it myself, but I've watched my pa."

"But you've never actually done it?" Will asked, astonished.

"Ain't that what I said? Now, do you want some honey or not?"

They could hear the bees when they got within sixty feet of the tree. A black cloud came out of a hole.

"They're swarming. They'll be flying off soon," Cole said.

"Why don't we just let them go?" Will reasoned.

"Because they'll come back and they won't like us being in their honey. If we smoke them out, it'll take them a while to get over it."

Cole lighted the torch and let it start smoking. "I'm going to take this torch and stick it right in the middle of them bees and they should fly off. I'm going to need you to hold me up there."

They walked to the tree, Cole holding the torch low to the ground. They stood watching the swarm, the sound like the grind of a band saw in their ears. Cole looked at Will and grinned. "You ain't afraid of getting stung are you?" he asked.

"I don't know. I've never been stung before."

Cole looked at him and shook his head. "Where the hell did you grow up?"

"Philadelphia."

"Dang Will." Cole said, shaking his head.

"Hoist me up. I'll do it," Will said.

Cole hesitated a moment and then let Will climb on his shoulders. He handed him the torch and watched as Will shoved it into the cloud of bees. The swarm scattered into the woods but not before a dozen dazed bees flew around Cole stinging him on his back and legs. He danced around in pain, hurling Will from his shoulders. Will landed face first in the field. He rolled over laughing as Cole tore off his shirt and slapped himself with it to dislodge the bees.

"We need to get the honeycomb out before the bees get their senses back," Cole said through gritted teeth.

"Tell me what to do."

"Roll that old stump over to stand on and then put your hand in and get a comb," Cole directed.

Will walked to the tree, shimmied up it and without hesitating, stuck his hand into the hive. Jumping to the ground, he proudly held up the comb. Walking to where Cole had thrown the tin cup he had in his shirt, he put the honeycomb in it.

"You are one brave son of a gun," Cole said. "Where did you learn to climb like that?"

"I do have a few skills."

Cole carefully put his shirt back on. "Well, I wish you had told me about this one before you let me get stung all over."

Will dipped his finger into the honey and stuck it into his mouth. He closed his eyes and savored the rich flavor. "This is most delicious thing I have ever tasted."

Cole could see that Will's hands were swelling with bee stings but he made no complaint. "You took a lot of stings."

Will looked at his hands as though just realizing he had been stung. "It does hurt a bit."

"Well, if it makes you feel any better, it was worse on the bee. Rub a little honey on your hands. It will help with the pain."

"They die after they sting, don't they?" Will pulled out a stinger still lodged in his hand and rubbed honey on the spot and then licked his finger.

Cole could tell that Will enjoyed the experience as much as he did the honey. "This honey would be a sight better with some hot biscuits."

"I don't see how it could be better than this."

"That's 'cause you risked your life to get it."

"I appreciate you letting me."

Cole laughed. "Let's get back to camp and fix us some breakfast. I've got a little bit of cornmeal. I reckon hoe cakes will taste just as good with this honey."

As they walked back to camp, Cole took the time to point out to Will plants that mountain folks had used for food and to cure a variety of ailments. "This is Joe-Pye weed. My mama used to make a tea out of it to cure a fever," Cole said, pointing to a tall lavender flower. Will listened intently, his brow furrowed. Cole surprised himself with his knowledge "This is chickweed. It grows in meadows and woods and you can eat it. Mix it with some chicory. You can eat it young just as it is or cook it down in a pot. It tastes right good." He broke off a piece and gave to Will who chewed on it as they walked on.

"A man can survive up here if he knows how to live off the land," Will said. "It's a bare living. I reckon though if a man don't want too much," Cole agreed.

"What more could a man want?" Will asked.

Cole looked at Will. His eyes were like those of a man who had come home from years of wandering. It was a wonder what he saw through them.

Will sat on his haunches finishing the last of his hoecake smeared with honey. He popped the last of the honeycomb in his mouth and chewed it.

"We need to break up camp. I never meant to stay here this long," Cole said.

Will held his palm up.

Cole waited patiently.

"Now that was good eating," Will said at last.

"Well, it appears you like rabbit and you like honey. Is there anything you don't like?" Cole had longed for fresh honey, but his enjoyment of it had been nothing compared to Will's.

"I can't think of a thing," Will said sincerely.

Cole believed him.

After they finished breakfast, Cole set about covering any signs of their camp.

"Why do you always do that? Cover your tracks."

"For exactly that reason. I don't want anybody tracking me. Where I am and what I'm doing is my business until I decide otherwise." He could not explain that it gave him a sense of control over his life that he had never had before.

Will took a cup of water and pulled out a small mirror and razor from his pack. Cole watched as Will shaved his face and trimmed his hair. Will caught him watching in the mirror.

"It wouldn't hurt for you to do the same," Will said. "You're a scary sight to come up on in the woods."

Cole felt his long beard with his hand. "I reckon this beard serves me well enough."

"You're right. One look at you, a panther would run for the hills."

"Well, then that's reason enough not to shave it off," Cole said. "You headed back down the mountain?"

Will nodded. "I wouldn't go but I promised to meet up with a man in Elkmont. He's due there any day. I could take a letter to your sister. Mail it to her when I get back to Elkmont. Just to pay you back. You say she lives in Knoxville?"

"You don't give up easy do you?"

"Wouldn't be any trouble."

"She's going to school there to make a teacher. She's probably out by now and teaching."

"I could find out for you? Maybe go see her. Does she look like you?"

Cole smoothed back his hair with his hand. "No, she's not nearly as scary looking. Here, she sent me a picture," he said searching through his pack. He pulled out a picture of Mallie posed stiffly in a white suit, holding a rose in her hand. A wide brimmed hat covered her hair swept up on her head. She had sent it to him as a joke because it was not at all like her, but every time he looked at the photograph, he saw the beautiful woman his sister had become.

Will took the picture. He looked at it for a long time before he handed it back to Cole. "She's beautiful, Cole."

"Yes," he said, nodding.

"Then let me carry word that you are well."

"Just that then," Cole agreed, "no more." He doubted that Will would ever see Mallie. He doubted that he would see Will again.

"I'll be back in two weeks," Will said, as they dusted out the last of their tracks. "How will I find you?"

"I'll find you, if I want to. Won't be too hard the way you stomp around up here talking to yourself."

"You know these same Appalachian Mountains run through Pennsylvania. I've hiked through most every mile of them. They're very similar in a way; we also have white-tailed deer, ruffled grouse and brook trout. There are places just as wild as this. I suspect we have a lot more in common than you might think Cole Hamilton."

"And I suspect you know more about surviving in the wild than you let on Will Stenson."

Will grinned and shook Cole's hand. "You're a good man, Cole. Like you said, even a seasoned mountain man never turns down help."

"Go on now, get on down the mountain," Cole said.

He watched until Will was out of sight before he headed back up the mountain.

8

The beatings started a month after his mother remarried. At six years old, Will knew they were wrong even if his mother tried to convince him otherwise. "Mr. Warner is a good man, Will," she would always say. She never referred to her new husband as anything but Mr. Warner. "He only does this because he wants you to grow up to be a fine, upstanding gentleman."

He never blamed his mother for marrying Mr. Warner. There had never been much money, for his father had not been a man overly concerned with practical matters. Their plight, after his father's death, had been one of even greater hardship, moving from place to place, existing on handouts from stern faced family who never approved of the marriage in the beginning.

As he walked through the woods on his way back down the mountain, he collected seeds from the trees and plants along the way. In the spring, these same plants had born flowers. With each season, the complex cycle of life was carried forward by nature in an endless struggle to assure the survival and continuation of itself. Sometimes he felt like one of the many seeds he collected. To ensure his survival, he had built a hard shell around himself to protect that part of him that would one day burst free. Vowing early on to survive his stepfather's intense hatred, he decided not to take it personally. He did not waste time wondering why his stepfather hated him or why he alone had been singled out for the most brutal of punishments. He was glad that such treatment did not fall on his sister.

It became clear to him early in his life that he had a brilliant mind. It was a gift, he felt, from the father he never knew. It would serve him well in his struggle to outwit the cruelty and injustice inflicted upon him almost daily.

Mr. Warner was not one to tolerate noise or laughter in the house. The dinner table was a place for solemn recitation of the day's school lessons. Will made it into a game. He soon discovered that his stepfather, a conductor on the Philadelphia Railroad, was not very bright. As long as Will recited something without hesitation and with confidence, Mr. Warner was none the wiser. He would fold his arms in front of him and nod his head as though he understood Will's recitation which was often little more than gibberish. His sister, Mary Anne, begged him not to do it. She feared discovery of such a trick would bring on a beating that Will would not survive. It was the game, he told her, that kept him alive.

He and Mary Anne were only truly free when their stepfather was away and they were allowed to play in the woods behind their rambling Victorian house. In the summer, they would lie down and watch the sun sparkle through the canopy of leaves and talk for hours. If Will was being punished and could not go out, he never argued. He was always respectful, never looked Mr. Warner directly in the eyes and never talked back. Then late at night, he would climb out his window and head to the woods. Sometimes he would stay there until just before the sun came up. Even as a boy, he was never afraid in the woods even though he had been small and thin for his age.

One day, locked in the attic as punishment, he had found his father's journals, buried under a pile of blankets in an old trunk. That was when he knew at last that he would make it. Somehow, he felt his father had left the journals for him and had found a way to lead him there. He knew also that his stepfather would destroy the journals if he found Will reading them, so he always put them back as he had found them.

At fourteen, Will grew to over six feet tall and filled out. There developed about him an air of resolute determination. His stepfather never touched him again and there grew between them an uneasy truce. They were both relieved when Will left for school on a scholarship.

As Will continued along the trail, the autumn sun was warm, and a gentle breeze stirred, rustling the leaves sending them twirling to the ground. He sat down near a clump of goldenrod. Taking out his journal, he wrote down what he had collected that morning putting the date and location. He imagined his father watching over him cautioning him to be thorough in his descriptions. In his imagination, during those long hours spent in the attic, he had closed his eyes and walked every step his father had taken in these mountains. Now, when he walked through the mountains over the steep ridgelines and looked out over the rugged valleys, he felt he had been there before. He never stopped wondering what his life might have been like had his father lived. Perhaps they would have taken this journey together, his father imparting his knowledge of plants to his young son. Of one thing, he was sure, his father would have been proud of him.

His father had been inspired by the early 'plant hunters' who first discovered the Appalachian Mountains in the eighteenth century. Men like William Bartram, who had come to the mountains in the late seventeen hundreds and published a record of his travels. Will had found a copy of the book among his father's papers. Andre` Michaux from France and John Fraser, a Scotsman, had all studied the flora of the Southern Appalachians during those early exciting years when botanists first entered the area to discover and collect hundreds of new species. It was Asa Gray, considered by many as America's first great botanist, however, whom his father most admired. He knew this because his father had corresponded with Asa Gray until his death and kept all of the letters. When Will read the letters Asa Gray wrote, he too was swept away by the description of such an exhilarating country where the only marks made on the land were by bear or Indian.

A monarch butterfly probed the goldenrod for nectar. It reminded him that it was time for the autumn migration. In the spring, monarchs migrated to Canada and returned to Mexico in the autumn. He looked around for a cluster but could see no others. Reaching out his hand, the butterfly fluttered and then perched on his finger. The monarch raised his rust colored wings and then lowered them slowly. The next time he raised them, he flew away into the woods. Smiling to himself, Will closed his journal and put it back into his pack.

A lone cloud covered the sun and then drifted away. There would be no rain today. Will looked at the lush plant life all around him. It had not rained in some weeks. It took a lot of rain to maintain such an abundance of plants. Just like the plants, he longed to feel it on his face, to collect it dripping off a boulder, to hear it percolating through the soil.

He wondered as he had many times before about the first man to set foot on these mountains. The Cherokees had lived here for hundreds of years before Hernando De Soto and his men explored the area, before naturalist William Bartram came in 1699 to collect plants, and long before a farmer's axe felled the first tree to clear a field. Untouched by man, he could only imagine how magnificent the primal forest must have been.

He needed to work his way down to Elkmont. It had already taken him longer than he intended to get this far after leaving Cole on the mountain. Meeting Cole had been like finding the brother he never had. He had liked the man immediately, and hoped that he found the peace he was looking for. It was difficult to understand why he tortured himself over what had happened. Will had no time for that. From the moment he had escaped his stepfather's house, he had discovered he had an infinite capacity for joy. His natural sunny disposition expanded each day until he laughed easily and saw humor in most things.

It seemed at every turn he found something new to explore and he would find himself wandering off the trail. He was in constant danger of getting lost because he forgot to watch for signs or let too much time pass before he stopped to set up camp. He imagined his father had done much the same and it had led to his death. Cole had cautioned him against just such foolishness and he was trying to do better but there was a feeling with him always now that he could never be lost again. How could he be lost, he thought, when he had at last reached his destination? It was a miracle to him that he had traveled this far. Now, here in the Smoky Mountains he was at last truly free.

9

In the end, she had worn the plain shirtwaist dress. It was a soft blue trimmed in black and belted at the waist. Mallie liked the unassuming cut of the skirt, which ended just above her ankle.

"You need to stop hiding your light under a bushel, Mallie Hamilton," Rose told her.

"I am not out to impress anybody," she stated flatly.

"Mallie, when it comes to men you are just like a stinging nettle. Any man tries to get close to you soon learns better."

Rose had said it jokingly but the truth of it hurt. She had brushed up against stinging nettles as a child and the burning sensation on her skin had lasted for hours. It bothered her to think the sting of her words caused men to shy away, but she could not help it. "Maybe so Rose, but I am just who I am. I don't know how to be anybody else and truth be told, I don't want to be."

"I like you fine just the way you are Mallie," Rose said, giving Mallie a hug. "I always have. But I'm not looking to marry you."

"Rose, I don't want to marry anybody, most assuredly not Mr. Gerard. If I do marry someday, they'll have to take me just the way I am."

"You just forget what I said," Rose said. "Go have yourself a good time."

Mallie smiled at Rose. She gave her hair one last look in the mirror before she went out the door.

Pierce insisted upon picking her up in a surrey for the short ride to the Wonderland Hotel. The sun was warm, but with each gentle breeze, leaf after leaf fell spiraling down in front of them whispering of autumn.

Pierce was polite and reserved, complimenting her on her outfit as he helped her into the surrey. “I think we are going to have nice weather today,” he said.

“I always love the weather here in the mountains, Mr. Gerard. I love it when the clouds gather over the mountains and the mist hangs all around, or when the sky is clear and the sun burns hot but the woods are cool and protecting. I love it when the snow drapes the hemlocks and sparkles on the rhododendrons.”

He stared at her, his hands going slack on the reins. Mallie waited for him to speak, wondering if she had gone on too long about the weather. Time stretched out between them as she amused herself by watching the haunches of the horse as it plodded along flicking flies with its tail. She wondered what the horse looked at for amusement and the thought made her smile.

“You seem to be a woman of enviable contentment, Miss Hamilton,” Pierce said.

“It is not mine by nature but a state of mind I choose most often, Mr. Pierce. Please, would you call me Mallie?”

“I would be delighted Mallie, but you must call me Pierce.”

“I’ll try, but you know I was taught…”

“Not to call your elders by their given name?”

Mallie blushed for he had read her mind.

Pierce smiled and his face lighted up.

She smiled back at him and watched as some of the sadness slipped off his shoulders and he relaxed. “Pierce,” she said trying out the name, “what is it that you do?”

“I’m an investor,” he said simply.

“So you give people money and they make you more money,” Mallie said.

He laughed as though she had just pointed out the absurd. “It works something like that.”

“You invested in the Little River Lumber Company?”

“Yes.”

“And has it made money for you?”

“Yes, a great deal,” he said honestly.

She liked the way he seemed not to be shocked by her bold questions but answered them simply. “But sometimes you lose?”

"I am afraid so, Mallie. There is always an element of risk. I don't invest unless I think the odds of winning are in my favor."

"Would you ever take a risk even if you didn't think you could win just because you wanted something so badly?"

He did not look at her, but she could see the truth written on his face and it surprised her. He had taken a risk asking her out to dinner.

"It would be a rare experience," he said, starring ahead.

They rode on chatting about nothing in particular. When they reached the hotel, he helped her down. "I'm forty two," he said, as he took her hand.

"I'm young enough to be your niece," she said. She waited to see the shock on his face before she laughed. "Now let's go meet your friends."

The dining room was a large open room paneled in chestnut. Sturdy chestnut beams supported the ceiling. Ladder-back chairs surrounded the plain wooden tables covered with oilcloth. The tables were being set with steaming platters of fried chicken, country ham, corn bread and pitchers of lemonade.

The room was filling up with people all who seemed to know each other. As Pierce led her about the room speaking to everyone in turn and introducing her, he was confident and gregarious, a man in his element. With her, he was always shy and hoarded his emotions.

He led her to a couple standing near a table at the center of the room. "Dr. Carrington and Mrs. Carrington, I am so glad you could join us," he said shaking hands. "May I present Miss Mallie Hamilton."

Mallie shook hands.

"Miss Hamilton is the school teacher at Elkmont," Pierce informed them.

"How delightful," Mrs. Carrington said without any real interest. "My husband is a noted physician in Knoxville."

"And someone else I would like you to meet," Pierce said rescuing her. "Mr. Henry Vickers. Good to see you again." They shook hands and he introduced Mallie. "Mr. Vickers is with the government."

Before Mallie could speak, the dinner bell rang. It was so loud it made her wince and she had to resist putting her hands to her ears. More people rushed in from outside packing the room with eager diners who took their places at the tables. When they sat down, Mallie noticed one empty seat at the table.

At the last moment, a waiter brought in more platters and bowls until the table was too full to hold more. Everyone started to eat, the clanging of silverware and glasses filling the room.

"Oh, venison," Mrs. Carrington exclaimed. "I was so hoping for venison,"

"Sometimes some of the local men supply the hotel with deer, rabbit or grouse," Pierce explained.

"Do you like venison, Miss Hamilton?" Dr. Carrington asked politely.

"I've eaten my share. We used to live on it. I shot my first deer when I was ten. Pa let me dress it out because I shot it. Of course, he had to tie it up by its hind leg while I skinned it from the hock to the neck."

While Mrs. Carrington stared at her with shock, Pierce looked at her with a gleam akin to adoration in his eyes. "Mallie was born here. She grew up on a farm nearby," he said.

Mallie wondered how Pierce knew that about her. She had never told him that. He must have been asking about her.

"Miss Hamilton, Pierce told me that you had been away for a number of years and that you have come back to teach. I imagine things have changed quite a bit since you were a girl?" Mr. Vickers asked

"When I was growing up, weeks, sometimes months would go by and we wouldn't see another soul but family. Now there are so many people."

"The Little River Lumber Company has brought jobs and prosperity to the area," Dr. Carrington said proudly.

"That's true," she admitted.

"You don't seem particularly pleased by that."

"When I was little, Pa would gather ginseng and sell chestnuts to get a little cash money. Sometimes, he would skin chestnut bark and haul it out to sell, but mostly we made do with what we had. It could be a hard life but I never wanted to trade it. I could be wrong but a little cash money seems a sad trade for the way they've skinned off the mountains around here."

"Why, young lady, there's enough trees in these mountains to last your lifetime. I would think you would be grateful for the progress that's being made around here," Dr. Carrington said his face growing blotchy as he spoke.

He looked to Pierce, who drank his lemonade and calmly buttered his cornbread. If her words had offended him, he did not show it. Still she wondered if she should apologize for his sake for the boldness of her words.

"Actually, Mr. Carrington," Mr. Vickers spoke up.

"Dr. Carrington," Mrs. Carrington corrected.

"What?"

"Dr. Carrington," she repeated.

Her husband waved her off.

"Dr. Carrington," Mr. Vickers said. "You make a good point. The trees will last, I estimate somewhat less than Miss Hamilton's lifetime at the rate they are currently being logged."

"Mr. Vickers is with the United States Forest Service," Pierce said. "He is looking into acquiring land for national forests."

"Yes, I am surveying lands in the east to make recommendations to the government to consider and approve land purchases under the new Weeks Law."

"Surely, Pierce, this is not something you are advocating," Dr. Carrington said.

"There have been a number of gains made in the scientific research of forest management. You as a scientist can appreciate that I am very interested in learning all I can about these new methods," Pierce said. "To protect my investments," he added.

"Well, yes, of course," Dr. Carrington said, nodding vigorously. "That is all well and good, but what this area needs, if we are ever to have real prosperity, is a road over these mountains into the trade centers in North Carolina. When I talk to my business associates in Knoxville, it is their fondest wish that these mountains would disappear."

Mallie choked on the bite of food she had in her mouth. Sputtering and trying not to cough, she held her hand to her mouth. Pierce handed her a glass of lemonade and she drank, tears rolling down the sides of her face.

Mrs. Carrington launched into a discussion of the many methods she used on her children when they were choking. The men looked on helplessly. Embarrassed, Mallie apologized and waved off their concerns. She blotted her face with her napkin and looked up to see a man standing at the table. He was handsome beyond reason with dark hair curling around his face and the nape of his neck. His face, tanned brown from the sun, had a cut on the cheek from shaving. His clothes, creased as though he just unfolded them before putting them on, fit his broad shoulders and slim waist perfectly.

He smiled as Pierce rose to shake his hand. "Will Stenson," Pierce said, "late as always."

Will smiled, his face open and friendly. He seemed not at all embarrassed by his lateness.

Pierce introduced Will all around saving Mallie for last to give her time to recover from choking. When Will reached to take her hand, she looked into his eyes and saw herself reflected there.

"Mallie Hamilton," he said beaming.

As he took her hand, she noticed his was rough and scratched from briars. When she finally pulled away, she looked around to see everyone looking at them. Will seemed not to notice.

"Sit down and eat Will," Pierce commanded, "before they take the food away."

He sat down across from Mallie. Piling his plate high with food, he ate with singular relish.

"I take it has been some time since you have had a good meal?" Pierce asked with a wry grin.

"As a matter of fact, I had quite a fine rabbit only two nights ago," Will said. "You haven't eaten rabbit until you catch it and cook it over an open fire." He looked at Mallie when he said it and his eyes sparkled.

She blushed and turned to see Pierce staring at her. The crease between his brows deepened for a second before he relaxed.

"How long were you up there this time?" Pierce asked.

"Two weeks," Will answered, between bites.

"Will is a botanist. He is studying the plants in the Smoky Mountains."

"Tell us, Will," Mr. Vickers asked, "have you made any great discoveries?"

"Just recently, I made a quite remarkable discovery," Will said looking at Mallie.

Everyone waited, but Will said nothing more. Finally, he turned his warm gaze on the group and continued to eat his meal.

"You have been in the mountains for the last two weeks?" Mallie asked tentatively.

Will nodded. "I've been here since early spring. I go up for two weeks at a time. Then I come down for supplies. Mr. Gerard is financing my study."

Pierce looked uncomfortable. "Botany is a hobby of mine."

Mallie remembered that Pierce had known the Latin name for sourwood when he had talked to her in the schoolyard. He was a more complicated man than she had thought. She had always believed that rich men amused themselves with poker and smoking cigars.

"I am keeping detailed journals of what I find," Will said enthusiastically. "But there is so much to study. I make crude sketches but I admit to being a very poor artist."

"Don't be modest," Pierce said. "I've seen your sketches and they are excellent."

"I am afraid they can never capture the true complexity of many of these plants. Or the mystery."

"And what do you find so intriguing about the plants of these mountains, Mr. Stenson?" asked Dr. Carpenter.

"Nature left to her own has provided the perfect home for such an abundance of plants I could never name them all. There are five species of trillium alone including a rare painted one. There are ferns, mosses and fungi in endless variety. The Rhododendron catawbinese grows higher than a man's head with rose-purple flowers the size of plates. And if you have ever brushed the snow away to see a bed of bluets blooming along a mountain stream you will never forget it."

Mallie looked at Will. His hands were lifted palm up and his shoulders pulled up around his neck straining with the intensity of his fervor. The people around the table sat wide-eyed. Mrs. Carrington blinked her eyes rapidly and patted her lips with her napkin.

Then Will laughed. "I'm afraid I get carried away. Being in the mountains lifts ones spirits and leads to the use of superlatives in an attempt to describe such beauty. I am sure you agree or you wouldn't spend your holidays here?"

His enthusiastic tone left no room for argument. The group laughed and nodded in agreement.

"Mrs. Carrington," Will said, his voice intimate, "did you know there is a shrub blooming in the mountains right now that has a very unusually shaped red pod. When it opens up there is coral fruit inside. The mountaineers call it hearts-bustin'-with-love." Will looked at her with an intensity that caused her to suck in her breath and fan herself with her napkin.

"How very quaint," she said breathlessly.

When Mrs. Carrington seemed close to fainting, Will pulled away and took a long drink of his lemonade. He looked at Mallie over his glass. His eyes sparkled with a secret mischief and she had to catch herself to keep from laughing.

He turned to Pierce. "I know you will find this interesting, Mr. Gerard. Most trees I have noted are right-handed. That is they will spiral to the right, whereas, an elm, if it is going to twist at all, will twist to the left. Now, botanists have long thought that this was due to adverse conditions. You know, if the trees are exposed to a great deal of high wind and severe weather, they will twist. But recent studies have shown that if you transplant a seedling from a twisted tree it too will be twisted no matter the conditions."

Mr. Vickers sat, chin in hand, studying what Will had said.

Pierce nodded his head excitedly. "Yes, yes, very interesting," he agreed. "Mr. Vickers, I am sure you agree, given your knowledge of forestry."

"A mystery indeed," Vickers said.

"Mr. Vickers is to be in town all week. I hope we will be able to meet and discuss this further."

"I'd be delighted of course, Mr. Gerard," Will said.

"Are you sure you won't stay at the hotel? I am sure we can provide you with some fine accommodations," Pierce said.

"Thank you, sir. That is kind of you but I have a place to stay that suits me just fine."

"As you wish," Pierce nodded.

"I am afraid I have bored our companions with all this talk of trees," Will said, turning to Mallie. "Why don't you tell us something about yourself, Miss Hamilton? You are a teacher, I believe."

Mallie searched her mind to remember if anyone had mentioned to Will that she was a teacher. "This is my first year to teach, Mr. Stenson," she said. She felt unsure of her voice.

"Call me, Will," he said as he leaned closer.

She felt herself grow warm and her cheeks burned. "Will," she said.

"And where do you teach?"

"Why, here at Elkmont."

"Here at Elkmont," he said, surprise in his voice.

"Why, yes. Does that surprise you?"

"It pleases me greatly. It means I will have a chance to see you again."

Mallie thought how much she wanted that and it made her cheeks grow warm.

"And are you enjoying it?"

"What do you mean?" she asked. She worried that Will had read her mind.

"Teaching," he said.

"Oh…yes," she stammered. "I find there are days I love it. That I was able to reach the children is my greatest joy, but there are days I fear I despair at my own shortcomings." What she had said was true but it had not been her intention to confess her feelings so openly to a man she hardly knew.

"I think the children must be very fortunate to have you," he said.

"Thank you, Will," she said.

Mrs. Carrington was still fanning herself from Will's attention. Mallie did not want to fall so easily for his charms, but it was impossible to resist his cheerful good nature. She was well aware that he had not singled her out as special for he had gone around the table engaging each person in conversation entertaining them in turn with his stories.

Will caught sight of the dessert tray and waved the waiter over. Will took two pieces of pie and ate them both while Mallie ate her slice. She recognized the apple pie as one Maude often made. It was still warm with lots of cinnamon. She had to remind herself to chew slowly for she did not want to embarrass herself again by choking. Sipping her coffee, Mallie watched the way Will kept his eyes on her.

Will chewed, and with his cheeks still full he popped in another bite. Finally, he closed his eyes and leaned back in the chair. It was hard to imagine that anyone in that dining room could have enjoyed his or her meal more than Will.

Pierce stood up and announced that the men would adjourn to the front porch for a cigar while the women had time to freshen up. Mallie had no desire to be alone with the insipid Mrs. Carrington but she had no choice.

Leaning into her, Pierce whispered, "There's a riding habit laid out for you in the room at the end of the hall. I hope it is the right size. I have arranged to have the horses brought around. Meet me at the back of the hotel. I should be finished with business within the hour."

"Surely not your room," she said.

"I own a number of rooms at the hotel."

"Oh, of course," she said, feeling foolish.

"And Mallie," Pierce said as he turned to go.

"Yes?"

He leaned toward her once again and spoke. "I would prefer it if you did not mention this to anyone."

She looked at him surprise widening her eyes.

"We don't need any boring company tagging along," he said with a glance toward Mrs. Carrington.

Mallie nodded.

Turning to shake Will's hand, Pierce said, "Young man, come outside and tell me more about your discoveries."

"Yes, sir," Will said, shaking his hand vigorously.

He turned to Mallie. "It was nice meeting you, Miss Hamilton," he said politely.

"It was nice meeting you, Mr. Stenson," she said.

He hesitated, and then he started to say something, seemed to think better of it, and withdrew behind a closed mouth smile.

Mrs. Carrington took her by the elbow and led her away.

"Will," he called after her.

Confused she stared at him until she realized he was telling her to call him Will. "Will," she mouthed.

She could feel his eyes on her as she turned. When she turned around again, he was standing on the porch talking to Pierce. They were engaged in lively conversation, Will gesturing excitedly while Pierce stood with his back to her nodding his head, one hand on his hip, smoking his cigar. Will's bold laughter rang through the open window. It followed her down the hall and she thought she could still hear it long after she had closed the door.

10

Carefully laid out on the bed was the riding habit. Mallie wondered if Pierce had placed it there himself. The thought that he might have been the one to lay out the habit, perhaps thinking of her as he did it, made her blush. Then she realized that men like Pierce did not do such things. He had most likely instructed the maid to do it.

When she put it on, she marveled that it fit perfectly. She fingered the rich fabric. The brown tweed riding skirt split to allow riding astride. The tailored jacket flared at the hips flattering her figure. She wondered if it belonged to his dead wife.

Walking outside, she found Pierce standing next to two chestnut quarter horses. His eyes grew large when he saw her. "Thank you, Pierce. And thank you for the loan of the riding habit. It is so beautiful."

"I had it brought in by train especially for you. I am so glad you like it. But it isn't a loan. I meant for you to have it."

"Oh, no, I couldn't keep it."

"It would please me if you would."

"All right then, thank you," she said. She would leave the riding habit in the room when she changed, she thought, as though she had simply forgotten it. She wondered if she should be upset that he had assumed she would not have the proper riding clothes but she was too relieved not to be wearing the clothes of a dead woman. "This is a beautiful horse," she said, running her fingers through the dark mane and stroking the horse's neck. The deep rich chestnut of its coat glistened in the sun.

"Her name is Lady," Pierce said.

"Hello, Lady," Mallie said, stroking the horse's nose.

Pierce helped her mount her horse in what seemed like a familiar gesture for him. He adjusted the stirrups to fit her and the thought lingered that he must have done this so many times for his wife.

"Are you a good rider?" he asked.

Mallie knew this moment would come and she was not sure how Pierce would react. "I haven't been on a horse since I was a child," Mallie confessed. "My brother and I used to ride our mare bareback through the woods to visit the neighbors."

His face showed no signs of disappointment. "Then I will ride lead," he said. "Don't worry; Lady is very docile and quite sure-footed."

They rode up past Elkmont and along Jakes Creek past the Appalachian Club. The club, built in 1910, was a hunting and fishing lodge for wealthy men from Knoxville and Maryville. Now their wives and family often joined them on weekends to enjoy the scenery.

Now, the lumber company had sold some of the logged off property to the wealthy for summer cottages. "Is this where you plan to build your summer cottage?" she asked.

"I haven't decided. Perhaps you could help me pick out a spot."

They rode along the stream until they came to a place where the water bubbled over the rocks into a clear pool. "Here," she said. "Put it right here with the back facing the stream. Will you have lots of windows?"

"If you like," he said, smiling at her playfully.

She laughed. It surprised her that he could be lighthearted. "Yes, big windows in the back and a porch that runs the length of the house so you can sit at night and hear the stream."

"I'll instruct my architect to draw up the plans just as you have described."

"That's just the way I would have it if it were my house. You, of course, might prefer something different."

"No, I would prefer it just as you say and I'll build it right here on this spot. I'll buy it tomorrow."

"It is beautiful here," Mallie said. Would he indeed buy the property so easily on her word or was he merely showing her how little it meant, she wondered.

"I would imagine you know many beautiful places here."

"I always thought the farm I lived on when I was a girl was the most beautiful place on earth, but it was higher up in the mountains. I don't think you would want to live that far away from folks like yourself. You see the poorer you were, the higher up you had to go because the folks who could afford it took the bottom land."

"And you were very poor?"

"I didn't know it then. Everybody we knew was just like us. We always had food because we worked hard. We made a garden every year so we had beans, corn, cabbage and Irish potatoes and turnips. We would put by what we could for winter in a root cellar under the cabin or in a hole, we lined with straw. Mama had an apple and peach orchard. She made jams and jellies from some of the fruit and dried the rest. In the winter, she would make stack cake that filled the cabin with the smell of those apples and the cinnamon and cloves. I could hardly eat my supper for the want of that cake."

Pierce was watching her intently. "That sounds delightful."

She blushed at the intensity of his gaze. "It sounds like I am a woman with a considerable appetite."

They pressed on toward Meigs Mountain skirting the Dan Cannon place crossing near enough to the house to cause the chickens to scatter. Beyond that, a half mile was the Combs place. They passed behind it and headed up the ridgeline, riding through cleared fields and crossing several small branches before winding upward through a hemlock grove where the trail leveled out. The trail was an old Indian footpath, narrow and worn in places, now used by settlers.

"You ride rather well, actually," Pierce said suddenly.

"It's easier with a saddle," Mallie said honestly.

"Yes, I would think so," he said, with an amused smile. "Christina loved beautiful saddles. Wherever we traveled she sought them out and bought only the finest."

"Christina was your wife?"

"Yes," he said simply.

"She was a good rider?"

"Christina did everything well. She came from a prominent family in Philadelphia. She was given riding lessons from an early age."

"How did you meet her?"

"We had known each other since we were children."

Mallie took that to mean that Pierce had also grown up wealthy. She imagined them attending the parties, sharing all the same friends. Writing to each other from wherever their families vacationed for the summer until they could see each other again.

"Christina was a perfect compliment to my more reserved nature," Pierce said. "I am not unaware that I sometimes come off a bit stodgy."

Pierce caught the smile that was tugging at Mallie's lips. "So, I see you have seen that trait in me," he said teasingly.

"I thought it was just around me that you acted…well, reserved. Today, at the hotel, you seemed quite at ease."

"An act I have perfected in a number, but not all situations. Christina was comfortable with everyone. At parties, she was always flitting about laughing and making everyone feel special. She had endless patience with people she thought influential in some way. She could listen to them prattle on endlessly only to laugh about it later. We were the perfect compliment to each other. Without her I find it all so tedious." He said it as if he was holding a bitter pill in his mouth. "What did you think of our little group today? I am sorry to have inflicted Mrs. Carrington on you today. I am afraid Christina tolerated her company far better than I can."

If he meant to test her, she knew she could not compare to his wife for she did not suffer fools well. "Mrs. Carrington went against my grain a bit."

Pierce chuckled. "I couldn't have said it better. I think you and I are more alike than you might think. That is what I like about you Mallie. You speak your mind."

"I've had that said about me before. Well, that last part anyway," she said with a grin.

"There have been people who have tried to make you be what you are not. I can see that in your eyes. You are a woman of spirited temperament, Mallie. Never knuckle under," he said.

She did not know what to say. It was easier to be a person of spirited temperament, if one were a man, especially a rich one, she thought.

"What did you think of our young botanist, Mr. Will Stenson?" he said.

She could not tell him that since dinner she had gone over every word Will had spoken, recalled in her mind his strong jaw line, the tilt of his head when he laughed and the way his eyes sought her out. She could not tell him that even as they rode together thoughts of him had slipped in and out of her mind unbidden. "He is an interesting man," she answered.

"I knew his father when we were boys. He died before Will was born. That's why I've taken an interest in the boy."

"You are very kind to support him in his studies," she said, without looking at him.

"He is a very determined young man. He would get here without my help I am sure. You know he doesn't quite approve of me."

"What do you mean?"

"The logging, the railroad through the mountains," he said, with a sweep of his arm. "He thinks it will destroy the plants."

"What do you think?"

"I think the boy is a dreamer and idealist. People need jobs."

"But you have an interest in the plants and trees here. I heard you discuss it with Mr. Vickers."

"I am interested in the scientific management of forest. We have learned a great deal in the last few years that if these methods are applied they could be of benefit."

"To the company and your investments?"

"To everyone involved. I believe that these forests are to be used for the greater good of the people. Will is not interested in providing a better life for the people here. He wants the forests left alone. He doesn't approve of me but he takes my money anyway."

Mallie did not like the tone of condescension in his voice. She wanted to ask him about it but he rode on ahead. She realized that she had been holding herself rigid in the saddle the entire time they had talked about Will. Suddenly, she relaxed and let out the breath she had been holding.

When they reached Curry Mountain, they headed down a steep slope to the left stopping to admire the huge outcroppings and rocky overhangs of Buckhorn Gap.

"Nature can make a man feel powerless," Pierce remarked. "These rocks have been here since time began. At every turn, man has had to battle nature to survive. Just look what it took to build a railway up the Little River, the engineering problems of cutting through rock and up steep grades, the winding curves of the river. Still repairs are a constant. It seems nature is always trying to take back the land."

She looked at him and his face was tight, as though he was struggling to hold back a tide of forces that threatened to take him over. Perhaps he had been a man who felt in control of his life until his wife died and now he wondered what power he truly had, she thought. "I've never felt that way," she said gently. "When I am here in the mountains, I feel more alive. When I am away from here, I feel like part of me is missing. You see the streams, the cliffs, the trees, and the wind all work together perfectly. When I am here I feel a part of that perfection, like my life is just as it should be."

"Then you are truly blessed," he said, with a sad smile.

They crossed the creek several times. It was shallower in the dry September weather, but fallen tree trunks washed downstream, formed natural dams that gave mute testament to the power of the spring rains.

The virgin forest around Mallie reached to the sky for sunlight, leaving her in the cool dark below. Golden leaves from the maple trees rained down around her covering the ground and mossy rocks like radiant jewels. The creek seemed to be racing them downstream and sometimes it was so loud it drowned out all thought but the beauty around her. Pierce looked back and caught her smiling. "Enjoying the ride?" he asked.

"Yes, very much, it is so peaceful here."

Passing through the deep shade of rhododendrons growing tall around them, Mallie wondered how anyone could ever find their way through such entangled growth. Before there had been this path over the mountain, what brave souls had trod these hills, she wondered.

The trail grew rockier as they emerged from the tunnel of rhododendrons. The sound of water splashing on rock grew louder. Mallie thought she recognized the place. Pierce stopped his horse ahead of her and as she joined him, she could see a waterfall. "I used to come here as a child," Mallie marveled, taking in her breath. "My brother and I would swim here."

"Would you like to stop for a moment?"

"Could we?" she asked, already dismounting.

Hopping about on the rocks, Mallie soaked up the beauty as she watched the late afternoon sun sparkle on the foaming water. She dipped her hand in the water and pressed it to her face. It was cool to touch and smelled of moss and damp leaves. Closing her eyes, she savored the flood of memories that rushed through her mind like the cascading waterfalls.

"I know about your brother," Pierce said.

Mallie opened her eyes, snapped back from her dream. "What do you know?"

"I know about the accident and I know you think he is up in the mountains somewhere. I know you intend to try and find him."

"How do you know that?"

"Isn't that why you asked me to take you horseback riding? You really want the horse. You were hoping that if you went riding with me, I would offer you the use of a horse. So you can go riding up in the mountains looking for your brother."

"Yes," she said honestly. It surprised her that he knew so much about her. He had known all along that she had wanted this from him. Walking up to her, he stood looking at her so close she could see the specks of dark blue in his eyes. Her heart raced when he took her hands.

"I understand how important this is to you, Mallie. That is why I have arranged to have both horses stabled at Dan Cannon's house. He is to get them ready for you anytime you ask."

"Thank you, Pierce."

He let go of her hands and backed away. "I know you will do as you please, but I would prefer you not ride alone. It is not safe. That is why I am leaving both horses."

Mallie nodded. "That's so generous of you." Her mind was already racing ahead to her next chance when she would be alone and could ride up the mountain.

"I wanted to do it for you, Mallie."

"Thank you again. And I really have enjoyed our ride."

She could tell that he was searching her face for more, but she could not say anything. Finally, he turned and walked back to the horses.

"I had better get you back before dark," he said.

They rode back into the woods, crossing several small streams and into the cool canopy of the trees. Just as they emerged from the shelter of the rhododendrons, a ruffled grouse flew from the bushes in front of Mallie, startling her horse. The horse reared up catching her by surprise and throwing her backwards onto the trail. Landing hard on her backside, she jumped up quickly, grabbing Lady's reins and speaking to her in a soothing voice.

"Mallie, are you all right?" Pierce asked as he rode up. He jumped from his horse and came to her.

"I'm fine," she lied, "just knocked the wind out of me."

He took her by her shoulders and studied her face. "You look pale. Won't you sit down?"

Mallie thought Pierce was the one who looked pale. His face had gone ashen gray and drawn. "I've never known Lady to do that," he said.

"It was my fault. I was daydreaming. I should have been watching closer," she said. She was afraid that he would take back his offer of the horses if he thought she had been hurt. Her hip ached and she would have an ugly bruise in the morning. Gently taking his hands from her shoulders, she turned to hide the pain and pretended to brush leaves from her skirt. When she turned back, he was standing so close to her she nearly cried out. She put her palm against his chest.

"Mallie," he whispered, his brow furrowed with concern. "I wouldn't want anything to happen to you."

"Help me back up, please," she said.

Reluctantly, he helped her back on the horse. They rode on in silence, Pierce taking the lead, glancing back at her occasionally.

Mallie reassured him with a smile. As much as she wanted the gift of the horses, she feared that by accepting it, Pierce might expect more of her than she could give. She had held herself so tightly bound for so long; she wondered what she had to give any man.

Even though she had reassured him she was not hurt, Pierce insisted upon her coming back to the hotel where she could clean up and get a light supper before he took her home. The meal consisted of warmed over food from lunch. Mallie had no appetite for anything, but picked at her plate. The time stretched on endlessly while she chatted and smiled at everyone at the table.

Finally, she asked him to take her home because she had to be at school early the next morning. He seemed surprised at the reminder that she had to work for a living.

"I apologize for keeping you so long," he said. "Of course, you must have time to prepare for your students tomorrow."

She waited in the surrey while Pierce went back to speak to a man. She could tell by the way his voice grew louder that they were discussing something of importance. It reminded her that Pierce was also an important businessman who did not tolerate well any affront to his authority. This was a different side of him than she had seen on the mountain where he had been solicitous and caring. With a palm up to cut off the conversation, Pierce walked off.

"I'm sorry to keep you," he said, climbing into the surrey. "That was an important matter that had to be attended to."

She merely smiled not wanting to pry. The evening air was cool and Mallie closed her eyes and breathed it in. "It's a lovely evening."

"Soon the nights will be turning cold. The leaves are already changing colors."

He had already turned back into the gentle Pierce she had seen on the mountain, Mallie noted. He sat back in the seat and his shoulders relaxed. "I enjoyed today, Pierce. Thank you for everything."

"Thank you, Mallie. It has been a long time since I have had such a pleasant day. Now, it may be a while before I have such a day again. I have to return home on business."

"Was that what the conversation at the hotel was all about?" Mallie asked.

"Yes, but it's nothing really. These things happen. I had hoped, however, now that I might stay here longer. I had hoped to see you again very soon. Would you like that, Mallie?"

She wondered what her face showed for inside she was a pool of swirling emotions. Pierce was a man old enough to be her father, with a life she knew nothing about filled with wealthy and influential people. He was a complicated man still reeling from the loss of a wife he loved. Still, he was kind, for even after knowing her motives, he had taken her horseback riding. Against her better judgment, she answered, "Yes, Pierce I would like that."

They rode in silence each lost in thought. When the surrey finally pulled up at the Combs house, Mallie ached in every part of her body. The fall from the horse had caught up with her and she wondered if she could manage the short walk to the cabin. When Pierce helped her down, she had to fight the tears that welled up in her eyes.

"Thank you again, Pierce, for a lovely day. And thank you for the use of the horses."

He held her hand as though to shake it but instead he bent and kissed her briefly on the forehead, an odd gesture that left Mallie feeling puzzled. Turning quickly, he walked back to the surrey. She stood on the porch watching as he drove away. The night mist was forming in the valley, its tendril reaching out to her. She leaned forward on the porch rail and let it caress her cheek, soothing away her confusion.

Then she turned and opened the door, prepared to greet Rose and Maude whose endless questions she would have to answer. The only light came from the kitchen. She called out but no one answered. Surprised but relieved to be alone at last, she gave in to the pain and hobbled toward the kitchen, groaning with each step. She thought she might be able to fix a compress for her bruised hip before the Combs' family discovered she had been hurt, but when she reached the open doorway, her breath caught in her throat. "Will!" she cried out.

Will Stenson sat at the kitchen table drinking coffee. He smiled up at her. "Did I scare you?"

"What are you doing here?" she asked, noticing his dark eyes were more brooding in the dim light.

"I live here," he said with amusement. "Or at least sometimes I do."

"You are the boarder?"

"I'm the one," he said with a grin.

"Where are the Combs?"

"They expected you back hours ago. They walked up to Billy Elders' place. I suspect they'll be back soon since it's almost dark."

"I didn't know I would be gone this long."

"Horseback riding with Mr. Pierce Gerard."

"How did you know?"

"I saw you two riding off. I am very surprised he would take you riding."

"I asked him to take me riding and he was kind enough to do so," Mallie said defensively.

Will chuckled.

"What are you laughing about?"

Will did not answer; instead, he studied her, his face growing more serious. "I heard you groaning in there, are you hurt?"

"My horse was startled by a grouse and threw me. I'm a little bruised."

"Want me to take a look? I have some experience treating accidents in the woods. Of course, mostly gun shot wounds and snake bites. You don't have either of those do you?"

"I'm just sore from landing on my…" Mallie said.

"Ah, so you broke the fall with your backside. Then I recommend a cool compress." He jumped up and went outside. When he came back, he was carrying a bucket of water from the stream. Dipping a cloth into the bucket, he wrung it out and handed it to her.

When she took the compress from him, their fingers touched and she could see a look flicker in his eyes before he smiled and looked away. "Thank you," she whispered.

"You should have put that on right away to stop the swelling, but maybe it will help now," he said. "Is anything broken?"

She shook her head. "Why did you say you were surprised Pierce… Mr. Gerard, took me riding?"

"Well, for one thing, he just recently started riding again. I heard he hadn't been on a horse since the accident."

"What accident?"

"You don't know, do you?"

"Know what?"

"That's how his wife died. She was thrown from her horse and hit her head."

Mallie suddenly felt weak and ignoring her pain sat down. "I would never have asked him, if I had known."

Will reached across the table and placed his hand on hers. She watched his hand cover hers as though it were someone else's. When she looked up, she saw a deep well of suffering in his eyes that belied the gentle smile on his face.

"Maybe he needed you to ask," he said.

Tears spilled over her cheeks and ran down her face. "He talked about his wife but he never mentioned the accident. I feel terrible."

Will came around the table and knelt in front of her. He gently wiped the tears away with his thumb. "He must think you are pretty special."

"How could he think that, he hardly knows me?"

Will stood up and went to the stove. He poured a cup of coffee and put it in front of Mallie. "Because I know how he feels."

Cupping her coffee in both hands, she drank slowly staring into the black liquid. She cast a quick glance at him as he walked around the table and sat down again.

"I wouldn't waste too many tears on Pierce Gerard," Will said at last.

"Mr. Gerard has been nothing but kind to me," Mallie said. "He has been nothing but a gentleman."

"Yes, Mr. Gerard is nothing if not a gentleman."

"You don't like him?"

"Let me tell you something about him I know for sure. He never does anything without a reason."

"What reason does he have for supporting you?"

"He was in love with my mother."

Mallie could not hide her surprise. "He told me he had been friends with your father."

"Yes, but he knew my mother first. Her father was the gardener on the Gerard estate. She grew up there. He told her he loved her, but his family would never have approved the marriage. It was planned all along that he would marry Christina. Then my mother met my father and they were married within a year."

"And you think he always loved your mother? That he gives you money because he feels guilty that he never had the courage to marry your mother?"

"Whoa, that's a lot to think about. I don't dwell on any of that. I just have always known what I wanted to do with my life and when Gerard offered, I took him up on it."

"Do you worry about what he might expect from you?"

"I could ask you the same question."

"Yes, I worry," she said. It surprised her that she could so easily tell him something so personal. She felt at ease sitting in the kitchen alone with him as though they had known each other forever. "You know he has offered me the use of his horses any time I want."

"And are you going to take him up on the offer?"

"I have to go find my brother. He could be living up in the mountains. I just need to know that he is well."

"Cole Hamilton."

"Yes, do you know him?"

"I saw him less than a week ago."

"You saw him! Where did you see him?"

"I ran into him up near your old farm, in a cave."

"I know the one," she said. Then she hesitated to ask the question she wanted most to know. "How was he?"

"He wanted me to tell you that he was doing fine and that he loves you very much."

Mallie jumped up, sending searing pain through her hip. She hobbled toward Will and he came around the table to take her by the arms. "You have to take me to him," she pleaded.

"He told me he was not ready to face anybody yet. He's working out a few things. I think in good time, he'll come down on his own. In the meantime, he doesn't want you to worry about him."

"If you don't take me, I'll go on my own," Mallie said defiantly, hands planted on her hips.

"I believe you," Will said, with a wry grin. "The thing is if he doesn't want to be found, Mallie, you won't find him. Besides, I promised him, I would just get word to you that he was all right. He thinks you are still in Knoxville."

"When you saw me in the hotel, you knew I was Cole's sister."

"He showed me your picture."

"He carries it with him?"

"Yes, Mallie," Will said gently.

Will looked into her eyes.

She held his gaze.

"He talked about you a lot. He admires your courage and your independence."

Mallie closed her eyes and savored her brother's words.

"But I fell in love with you," Will said, "the moment I heard your name. It was like I knew it before he said it."

"Will," Mallie said, drawing in her breath. It was just as her pa had described meeting her mama. "Don't talk like that."

"Then when I saw you in the hotel, I was sure," Will said, ignoring her plea.

"Will, how can you say that?" Mallie said weakly.

"Because you know it too, Mallie," he said simply. "I could see it in your eyes."

She looked into Will's dark eyes and the knowing spread over her. Finally, she put her forehead on his shoulder and let out a sigh. "Oh, Will, you don't understand. I don't want to fall in love with anybody," she said into his shirt.

Will laughed and wrapped his arms around her. Feelings of peace came over her, as she buried herself in his arms. She knew he felt it too.

11

Crockett groaned as he turned over in his bed. His muscles ached from the long days and he wondered if he might be getting too old for such hard work. The men worked ten to twelve hours a day with only Sundays off. He knew that more hours than that and a man could get careless. Without some rest, a man could become a danger to other men as he grew weary and his mind became clouded.

He was always the first up, rising by five to light the coal oil lamp in the boxcar he shared with Riley. Breakfast was served at six, and he liked to have some time to think on what the men were to do that day before he joined them to eat. The work, always dangerous, became more so as they moved up the steeper slopes where machinery was prone to tip over onto workers and logs could slide out of control.

Slipping on his overalls, he tried not to wake Riley sleeping in the bed across from him, as he went out into the chill October air. It did not help matters that the temperatures were dropping at night leaving a frosty coating on everything until well after sunrise. They worked in all kinds of weather; heat so bad it dried a man out like a tobacco leaf, and bitter cold that froze a man's clothes on him so that they stood up when he took them off at night.

He could see a light on in many of the boxcar houses. As he passed by on the way to the outhouse, he could hear the voices of men and women talking and babies crying through the thin walls. Unlike most lumber camps that hired seasonal workers who moved on, the men who worked for the Little River Lumber Company worked year around. Most of the men were from around there so they had brought their families with them, which made for steady workers with close ties. Crockett knew them all and their families. Many of the families, related through marriage, had lived near the Little River for generations.

The camps usually moved once a year but sometimes they stayed only six months, according to the amount of timber. It was hard on the families and Crockett suspected that Fish Camp was one of the harder places to live. It offered little in the way of comfort for the wives who followed the men here.

The boxcar houses sat right off the main track, leaving little room for the children to play. Every day the trains rumbled by, empty or other times loaded with logs, whistles always screaming. Smoke filled the air from loaders, skidders and supply cars all passing by within a few feet of the houses.

When Crockett opened the door to the boxcar, he was surprised to see Riley still in bed. He was usually up and dressed by the time Crockett made it back from his morning trek.

Bending down in front of the potbellied stove, Crockett blew on the few coals left. He added kindling and the fire blazed. They seldom bothered with a fire in the mornings but he thought Riley might be suffering more from the cold than he had let on. Although Riley had said nothing, Crockett had noticed the man grimacing with pain and had seen the red swollen joints of his hands.

"Riley," Crockett said, shaking the man gently. "You awake?"

Riley groaned.

Crockett could see that his eyes were open. "Riley, what is it?"

"Help me up, Crockett."

"Are you sick?"

"It's my rheumatism."

Crockett pulled back the quilt that covered Riley and reached to help him sit up in bed.

Riley moaned.

Crockett hesitated.

"Go on now, help me get my legs on the floor," Riley said through gritted teeth.

"I don't know Riley, appears to me, you are in some pain."

"If I can get moving, I reckon I'll be all right. The pain is always worse at night. I can't hardly sleep."

Crockett reached for his legs, but as soon as he touched them, Riley cried out. "You can't stand for me to touch you. And you've got a fever," Crockett said, testing the man's forehead with the back of his hand. "Why didn't you tell me you was this bad off?"

"'Cause you wouldn't of worked me."

"I'm sending for the doctor."

"Just boil me up some of that willow bark in my pack over there. That will ease the pain till I can get up and around."

Crockett put more wood in the stove. He dipped some water from a pail by the door into a small pot on the stove. Searching through Riley's pack, he found the willow bark and dropped some into the pot. He knew Riley drank willow bark tea every night to ease the pain, but he had thought little of it. "I'll make your tea and then I'm sending for the doctor."

"Crockett, I ain't never seen no doctor."

"I ain't neither but I reckon now is the time. The company hires a doctor to look after us and the way I see it we might as well use him."

Riley did not protest, which worried Crockett more than the fever and the swollen joints. He blamed himself for not noticing that the man was suffering. The night before he had not finished supper nor eaten his two helpings of cobbler as he always did. The men had teased him about it, but Riley had put it off as a bellyache. He had left the dining car early and had not joined the men in the social car for cards. Crockett had dismissed it as a passing thing. Now, he wished that he had paid more mind to his friend.

He handed the cup to Riley, but the man could not hold it. Crockett held him up and fed the tea to him slowly. "You lay back down here. I've got to go get the men started working, but I'll send for the doctor and be back here by noon to see about you. I'll have Emma Ward check in on you 'til I can get back. You know her, she's Dell's wife."

"Don't worry about me. I know you was trying to get done what you could before the snows set in. Last night when I was laying here, I heard a hoot owl hollering late into the night."

"I heard it, too," admitted Crockett. "That means it will be turning off cold here soon."

"I sure do hate to let you down."

"You're not getting out of work that easy," Crockett joked. "Them trees will still be there, snow or not. I'll save'em for you."

The big man tried to smile but it came off as a grimace. He closed his eyes and Crockett slipped out the door. It was nearly daylight and the men would be at breakfast. He could feel his stomach rumble, but he would have no time to eat.

Walking over to the newly built commissary, Crockett thought about what he was to do. Without Riley, he would be short one of his best equipment operators. He had a man out with a broken leg from a rollover and just last week Joe Smith fell trying to rig a tree and broke his back. He could not put a green man to doing that, so he had taken one of his best workers and put him to rigging. If Riley could not work again, and he suspected as much, he would be short three good men.

"Howdy, Alfred," Crockett called out, as he entered the commissary. "Do me a favor and call for Doc Wilson." Just the week before, a telephone line had been strung from Elkmont to Fish Camp allowing for communication between camps.

"You ailing?" Alfred asked.

"It's for Riley."

"Should I tell him to hurry?"

"He ain't hurt. It's his rheumatism. I reckon he'd appreciate it though if the doc could come on soon enough."

Alfred left to make the call. Crockett wondered if he should send a message to Maude. He decided it would be best not to worry her until the doctor had seen Riley.

"I got a hold of the doctor," Alfred said, coming from behind the counter. "I think I woke him up. I checked the schedule of trains coming and going and Dr. Wilson can catch a ride up or take the speeder car and be up in an hour's time."

"Thanks Alfred," Crockett said, shaking the man's hand.

"Riley must be bad off to lay out of work," Alfred said. "I never knowed that man to miss a lick."

"He's a good man," Crockett said, turning to go.

"Be hard to replace a man like that."

Crockett nodded.

"I reckon the doctor will fix him up though."

"I reckon so." Alfred stood waiting for him to say more, but he turned and walked outside. It would be all over camp soon enough that Riley was sick. He would not be the one to carry tales. The sun had still not burned off the morning fog and it felt like a heavy blanket on his shoulders. He knew that if he lost Riley, he would be losing more than a good worker. He would be losing the best friend he ever had.

"The man will be lucky if he ever walks again," Doctor Wilson said as he stood talking to Crockett outside the house. "He has as bad a case of rheumatoid arthritis as I have ever seen."

"Ain't there nothing you can do?" Crockett had taken off from work at dinner, eaten his pork biscuit while walking to make it back before the doctor left.

"I've given him aspirin. He will have to stay in bed. That's about all that can be done. There is no cure for what he has."

"Have you told him?"

"I told him he would need some weeks of bed rest. I didn't tell him that I was not hopeful he would ever walk again."

"Thanks for not telling him he might not walk again."

"It's never good to take a man's hope away. I understand his wife lives in Elkmont."

"She has a cabin past Jakes Creek."

"I've arranged to take him back with me by speeder. He will need a lot of care."

"Let me have a word with him before you go."

"Do you have some men who can help me get him on the speeder?"

"I can do it."

"He's a big man."

"He wouldn't want nobody else to do it."

"All right, bundle him up. It could be a rough ride. The slightest movement hurts him right now."

Crockett steeled himself to face his friend. He opened the door, walked inside to where Riley lay, and looked down at the man's tortured face. "Hey old man, I hear you done it up right this time. How are you feeling?"

"It's pretty tough. I hurt near all over."

"Doc's going to fix you up, I hear."

"He wants to send me back down to Elkmont."

"Well, that won't be for long. You can rest better down there. Too much noise up here for a man to rest anyhow.

Maude will take good care of you and you'll be back working in no time."

"I don't know, Crockett. I ain't never knowed a man to get over the rheumatism."

Crockett could read the worry in his friend's eyes. "You'll just have to see to it that you are the first."

Riley smiled weakly.

"Now, I'm going to have to bundle you up, Riley, for the ride down. This is going to hurt. If you want, I'll get some men to help."

"I'd just as soon you did it. I don't want more folks than has to see me like this."

"The men are at their dinner. It will just be me." Riley did not make a sound as he wrapped him in a quilt and picked him up in his arms, but his face grew ever more ashen. Crockett carried Riley outside to where Doc Wilson waited. The speeder was a four-wheeled rail buggy powered by gasoline. It was only big enough for two men and was used for quick repairs on the railway and for emergencies. Riley would have to sit up in the seat all the way back to Elkmont. As he eased him into the seat, he could see Riley grit his teeth.

"I'll be back," Riley whispered.

"I won't give your job away," Crockett said. He stood, his eyes following the line of the tracks, long after the speeder had disappeared down the mountain. Then he turned and went back to work.

12

Crockett sat down on a stump and rested. It was not yet noon, but he was weary to the bone from work and worry so the long walk to Gatlinburg had tired him out more than it should have.

It had taken him two weeks of asking around to find Sam Melton's widow. She was in her seventies now and living with her grown daughter. When he had first met Sam and Lizzie, they lived in a cabin up near Goshen Ridge. Lizzie married Sam when she was fourteen and they had eked out a bare existence high in the mountains. She was a quiet woman, not given to socializing, but Lizzie had loved Rebecca and they had spent long hours together talking.

Crockett hoped when he went looking for Lizzie that she had a secret she would share with him. As he stood up to walk the last mile to the house, he hoped that Lizzie's folks had passed on a long held knowledge of healing.

Lizzie had been a baby in 1837 when the Cherokees were moved out. Crockett had heard it rumored that her folks hid out in the mountains for months, almost starving to death, living off the pity of settlers. Finally, they had passed themselves off as Black Dutch to escape going to Oklahoma.

The house sat back from the main road a few hundred yards. The small yard was tidy and the place well kept, but the house was dark and quiet. Crockett knocked on the door and waited. When no one answered, he knocked again. Then he called out Lizzie's name. He was about to knock again when he heard a noise behind him.

"My ma's home but she won't come to the door," a woman's voice spoke.

Crockett turned to find a tall, dark haired woman about his age standing at the bottom of the steps.

"I've come looking for Lizzie Melton," he said.

"I'm her daughter, Martha," she said, sticking out her hand.

Crockett shook her hand and she graced him with a sweet smile. For some reason he could not discern, her smile made all the loneliness he felt rise up and lodge in his throat. "I heard she lived here with her son," he said, his voice coming out raspy.

"No, Bob lives next door with his wife, Violet. I live here with Ma. She lost her sight last year, but she is still as feisty as ever." Martha closed her eyes and shook her head gently, chuckling to herself.

Crockett noticed how her long eyelashes made shadows on her brown face and that her cheeks were smooth and rosy. He looked away, ashamed of his attraction to her. "I'm Crockett Hamilton," he said at last. "I knowed your folks when they lived over on Blanket Mountain."

"Rebecca's husband," she said, "I've heard Ma speak of you."

"Then you think she'll see me? I have something important I was hoping she would help me with."

"Come in," she said, "I'm sure she would like to see you. I just walked home to feed her a little dinner. I made a nice venison stew. Won't you come in and eat with us?"

"I don't want to be no trouble."

"It won't be no trouble," she said simply. "Violet looks in on Ma, but she's gone to stay with her folks in Cades Cove for a few days. I don't like leaving her alone, but I teach weaving at the Pi Beta Phi Settlement School most days."

Crockett followed Martha into the small house. An old woman sat by the fire. The long plaits of hair piled high on the back of her head had turned gray and her face was grooved with deep wrinkles. Thrown over her lap was a beautiful woven blanket. He wondered if Martha had made it.

"Ma, I've got somebody come to see you. It's Crockett Hamilton."

"Rebecca's husband," she said, turning toward Crockett. Her sightless eyes sparkled in the firelight.

"Yes, ma'am," Crockett said, taking her hand.

"Rebecca told me you'd be coming," she said matter-of-factly.

Crockett felt the floor falling out from under him. He looked at Martha, who showed no surprise at her ma's words.

He looked back to Lizzie. "Then you know why I'm here," he stammered.

"I suspicion you want me to help you with your friend."

Before Crockett could answer, Martha spoke up. "Pull up a seat," she said pointing to a straight back chair. "I'll heat up the stew." She left Crockett alone with Lizzie.

"I told Rebecca things I never told nobody except one of my younguns. That was because I looked on her as a daughter. I knowed she would use what I told her the way it was meant to be used."

"She never told me what you shared with her. I just knowed that the two of you talked."

"She come to you in a dream, didn't she?" she said chuckling.

"I reckon she did," Crockett admitted.

"It's nothing to be ashamed of," Lizzie said. "She'll come to you as long as you need her to."

Crockett let out a sigh. He could never imagine not needing Rebecca.

"Tell me about your friend that's sick," Lizzie said.

Crockett described Riley's painful swollen joints and loss of appetite. "The doctor said he never heard of nobody being cured of rheumatism."

Lizzie's face showed nothing. She sat quietly, the fire casting shadows on her face. Crockett thought she might have fallen asleep and he was wondering if he should shake her gently when Martha came to say dinner was ready. He reached for Lizzie's arm to help her into the kitchen, but she shook him off and with the help of her cane walked to the table and sat down.

"Set yourself down, Crockett," Martha said, nodding toward a chair. She grinned at him as though to say 'that's just Ma, don't pay her no mind.' Spooning out the stew, she broke off a piece of cornbread and placed it by her ma's bowl. Her movements were easy and graceful like someone comfortable with herself. She poured fresh buttermilk in Crockett's glass and then bowed her head to pray. He had not prayed before Rebecca came into his life and he not prayed since the day she died. Once again, a forlorn feeling swept over him and he lowered his head.

"Now, Crockett," Martha said looking up, "eat your stew while it is still hot."

He realized how easily Martha said his name, as though he were an old friend stopped by to visit. He spooned the stew into his mouth and realized how hungry he was with the first bite. He had eaten very little that morning, stopping only to eat a cold biscuit and drink water from a spring. The buttermilk was thick and sweet and he drank it in big gulps. When he sat the glass down, Martha was looking at him. "Sorry, I reckon I've eat with lumbermen so long, I forgot my manners."

"It's good to see you enjoy your food," she said. "Would you like more?"

"No, thank you. That sure was good though."

"If you've had enough then, Ma has agreed that I am to fix you a potion to help your friend."

Crockett had not heard a word from the old woman. If there had been a sign between the mother and daughter, he had not seen it. Martha got up to clear the table. Lizzie stood up. "Martha knows what to do," she said. "Your friend should be better in two weeks."

Crockett could not hide his surprise. "I.. . .I.... thank you," he said, taking her hand to shake.

Lizzie squeezed his hand hard. "I'll just tell you this once, Crockett Hamilton. Give up your pining. It ain't good for the living or the dead." She let go of his hand and walked into the other room.

It was an odd thing to say and Crockett stood puzzling over it. He jumped when he felt a hand on his arm. He looked up to see Martha, motioning for him to follow her. They went out the back door to a porch boarded up to form a room. Dried plants tied together with string hung from every rafter. A long plank nailed to the wall formed a table. The plank held jars filled with herbs. Martha took a small bowl and began to mix herbs from different jars. Her movements were practiced and efficient. "Rheumatism is not an easy thing to cure. You will need to brew a tea three times a day for your friend."

"Riley. His name is Riley."

"Let the tea steep for ten minutes before you give it to Riley."

"Your ma give you the secrets?" he asked.

"Since I was a little girl," Martha said without looking up. "It has to be passed on. I was the one chosen." She put the herbs in a pouch, put the pouch into a bag and added more dried herbs she pulled from the bundles handing from the rafters. She handed the bag to Crockett. "I am sorry I can't tell you what's in this. I can only tell you that it will help Riley. That much I know."

"You've been more than kind. I have cash money. I can pay you for your trouble." He started to reach into his pocket but her look stopped him.

She put her hand on his arm and looked into his eyes. "If your friend gets well, it will be payment enough," she said sincerely. "You will come back, Crockett Hamilton and tell me, won't you?"

Even now he wondered if he could come back. Just looking into the dark warmth of her eyes felt like a betrayal and frightened him more than the most dangerous logging job. "That's little enough to expect, I reckon," he said, clutching the sack more tightly in his hand before he set off toward Elkmont.

Now, within a few hundred yards of the Combs' cabin, he found he needed to collect his senses. He knew that Mallie was staying with the Combs. She would not be expecting him and he was not sure how she would feel about him. He had not been to Elkmont since spring. Secretly, he had hoped that Mallie would come to him. Sometimes when he heard the train whistle, he pictured her getting off, her hand to her forehead as she searched for him. As the weeks went by and she never came, he decided that she still blamed him for sending her away and was not intending to forgive him. With each passing day, the thought of facing her became more difficult. His reluctance angered Riley.

It was just past four on Sunday and the camp was quiet. It was a time for many families to be together for the first time all week. The whole Combs family would be home, he thought as he eased himself off the stump and he wondered if that would make things easier. No matter, for the sack he gripped in his right hand was more important than his pride.

Stepping up onto the porch, he knocked softly. The cabin was strangely dark and quiet. When no one came, he opened the door slowly and called out. "Riley, are you here?" No one answered. A roaring fire burned in the fireplace and the room was stifling. Crockett walked to a bed and looked down at Riley's face. His heart sank into his shoes. Covered in a half dozen quilts, Crockett thought he looked buried alive. Shaking off the thought, he put his hand on the man's chest. His eyes opened, dull and unfocused they slowly widened. "Riley, it's me, Crockett."

"Crockett," Riley said hoarsely.

"I come to see how you was doing."

"I reckon I'm fairing all right. Help me up so I can see you."

Crockett set the sack he was carrying on the bed, reached his arms around the man, and pulled him up on his pillows. As he leaned Riley back on his pillows, a moan escaped his friend's lips. He was shocked to feel the big man's ribs and his backbone sharp against his skin.

"I've fell off a might, I reckon. I don't have much appetite."

"You'll put it back on when you get back to work," Crockett said confidently. In truth, his friend's loss of appetite worried him most of all. He had never known Riley when he was not hungry. His ability to put away a dozen biscuits and a pound of sausage with gravy for breakfast was legendary around the lumber camps.

"Pull up a chair. It's good to see you."

Crockett moved a straight back chair closer to the bed and sat down. "You're looking some better than the last time I seen you."

"You never was much of a liar," Riley said, cutting his eyes at Crockett.

"I reckon I never got the hang of it."

"No need to start practicing on me. How is it going up at the camp? Have you moved on up?"

"They've done laid track up past the fork this week."

"I wish I could be back to working. Laying here is a tiresome job."

"What does the doctor say?"

"I reckon he done give up on me. He come by twice a week for a while and then he said there weren't nothing more he could do."

"Where's Maude and Rose…and the rest of the family?" Crockett asked. He had been unable ask where Mallie might be.

"Maude and Rose has gone over to the farm in Wears Cove to see our son, Joe. She's got it in her head that we need to move on back over there where there's family can look after me."

The thought that Maude did not believe Riley would be getting well worried Crockett more than the doctor's words. "Riley we've known each other a long time."

"That's the truth, Crockett."

"If I asked you to do something for me, would you do it?" Crockett reached and got the sack he had set on the bed. He put it in his lap and laid both his hands on top of it.

"Have I ever turned you down for a thing?"

"No, I can't say as you have."

"I'll do anything I can for you, but you got to see looking at me I ain't got much to offer," he said.

"You remember old Sam Melton lived up Goshen Prong?"

"Let me think back. Can't say as I remember too much about him. Him and his wife kept to their selves mostly. Didn't he die not too long back?"

"Died two year ago this winter."

"That long. Time does go by don't it, Crockett? Reckon they'll be asking about me like that before long."

Crockett nodded but was too intent on his story to dwell on what Riley had said. "His wife, Lizzie, is a healer."

"You don't say. Can't say as I knowed that."

"Lizzie was never one to have much to do with strangers. She took a liking to Rebecca though."

"I can see that. Rebecca had a way of treating folks that just naturally made them feel at ease."

"I always thought so, but I appreciate you saying it."

"What's all that got to do with me doing you a favor?"

"Now, don't get so all fired impatient. You ain't got no where to go just yet, have you?"

Riley chuckled for the first time. "What you want wouldn't have anything to do with that poke you are holding on to so tight would it. You've been sitting there looking like you was praying over it this whole time."

"I've been studying on this since you got sick, Riley. And it come to me one night as clear as if they was in front of me, Lizzie and Rebecca walking in the woods. Lizzie was pointing to plants and Rebecca was nodding like she understood just what she meant."

"What do you think they was saying?"

"Secrets. Lizzie was sharing secrets she had learned from her family. Things she had never told nobody outside the family."

"What kind of secrets?" Riley said puzzled.

"She had all sorts of remedies for ailments passed down through her family. I think that was what they talked about all them times."

"Come to think of it, Rebecca used to fix me a tonic when I had trouble sleeping. Made from passionflowers, I think she said. It would put me out like a baby."

"You are going to think this is strange, but I got to thinking that Rebecca was trying to tell me something. In my dreams," he said hesitantly.

Riley's face showed nothing. "Go on."

"She would be listening to Lizzie and then she would turn and motion for me to come over to her but as hard as I tried, I couldn't walk. I couldn't get to her."

"Crockett, you know what I think?" Riley said, his head tilted, mouth screwed to one side.

"I see the look on your face and I don't want to know," Crockett said. "Just hear me out."

"I'm listening."

"It come to me that Rebecca was trying to tell me that Lizzie had the answer."

"The answer to what?"

"The answer to what ails you. The morning after my dream, I went looking for Lizzie. It took me two weeks to find her. She'd moved over to Gatlinburg to live with her younguns after Sam died. Then I had to talk her into trusting me enough to help me. She only done it 'cause she thought so much of Rebecca." Crockett reached into the sack he held in his lap and pulled out the leather pouch Martha had given him. "She give me this," Crockett said, not mentioning Martha.

"What's in it?" Riley asked.

"She wouldn't tell me what's in the pouch, but she did give me some dried bloodroot and skunk cabbage to mix with it. She said to brew up a batch of this and you was to drink it three times a day and you'd be up walking within two weeks."

"You don't reckon that stuff will kill me do you?"

"Hell Riley, I don't know," Crockett said exasperated, "looks to me like you're half dead already."

"And I thought I had you fooled," Riley joked.

"Sorry Riley, I didn't mean that," Crockett said, too intent on his mission to joke back.

"No, you got a point there," Riley said agreeably. "I don't have much in the way of choices. I reckon it's worth a try."

Crockett took a deep breath and relaxed in his chair for the first time since he had first sat down. He realized how much stock he had placed in a bag of herbs. Certain of himself these past weeks, he worried now that he was only creating false hope in his friend. He closed his eyes and hoped that he had been right about the dream.

A noise at the back door caused him to look up. Rebecca stood in the doorway of the kitchen, looking more beautiful than he had ever seen her. Loose tendrils of her long dark hair curled around her face and her eyes were bright and questioning. Jumping up quickly, he caused the chair to fall backwards with a loud bang. He started toward her when she spoke.

"Pa," she said.

The sound of her voice startled him. It was a women's voice but it was deeper, fuller than his wife's was. He could see now that she was taller, her shoulders held upright and her gestures bolder as she brushed the hair from her eyes.

"Well, Crockett," Riley said finally. "Ain't you going to speak to your daughter?"

13

Mallie?" he asked, the name sticking in his throat. The last time he had seen his daughter he had stood behind her, his hands on her shoulders. Rebecca's sister had not invited him in when he had taken Mallie there to live. He had left her on the steps and walked away, not turning around until he was out of sight. He wanted to go to her and take her in his arms as if she were still a little girl, but the woman who stood before him now stopped him with her eyes. She looked directly at him and met his gaze without blinking. The silence grew with all that was between them.

"Crockett Hamilton, you might as well get your glad pants on," Riley said, breaking the silence. "Your daughter has come home and there ain't a thing you can do about it but be glad for it. And Mallie, I've knowed your pa a long time and they ain't no sense in trying to out stubborn him."

"Riley, don't take it upon yourself to stir this pot," Crockett said angrily.

"I reckon somebody has to or the two of you will stand here all day," Riley said with a chuckle, ignoring Crockett's anger.

"You've shaved off your beard," Mallie said at last.

Crockett felt of his face as though he had just realized that he no longer had the long red beard he had worn when Mallie was a girl. "Six years now," he said. "You're all growed up."

"Six years now," she said a hard edge in her voice.

Crockett nodded. "You look like your mama."

"So folks tell me. I can't see it. Mama was so beautiful."

"When I saw you standing in the doorway, I thought you was Rebecca."

"Mama's been gone eight years."

"Some memories just grow harder with time like stones."

Walking to the fireplace, Mallie started to put down the firewood she was holding. Crockett rushed toward her just realizing she was carrying a heavy load. He took the wood from her arms and added it to the fire.

"Riley gets cold. The chill hurts his joints. I have to keep the fire going," she said matter-of-factly.

"You've been taking care of him?"

"When Maude and Rose are working," she said.

"How are you making it?" he asked. Crockett thought they talked like strangers waiting at the station for the train to take them to their separate lives.

"The neighbors have been real good to help out. Some of the men come over and chop firewood and the womenfolk bring food. These are good people. They'll help you if you let them."

Crockett caught her accusing tone. He knew that when Rebecca died so many of his friends had tried to help and he had spurned them, turning them away at the door preferring to be alone in his misery. "Riley tells me you made a teacher," he said, trying to change the subject. "You always was a smart one."

Mallie looked at him, her shoulders thrown back. "Cole was the smart one. He was the one who wanted to go to school."

"Your Aunt Mae would only take you," he said.

"You meant to send us both away?" Mallie asked accusingly.

Crockett stood up and backed away at the sound in her voice. He had not meant his words to come out that way. Unable to find the words to explain he said, "I shouldn't have come like this."

"Why did you come?"

"I come to bring Riley some medicine."

"You never meant to see me?"

"Mallie. . .I...."

"I guess I shouldn't be surprised," Mallie said, her voice cracking. "You never wanted anything to do with me after Mama died."

Crockett held out his hands, palms up and willed the words to come to him, but his thoughts swirled like a flooded stream and he could not catch hold of anything. Mallie turned her back to him. He paced the floor and then lighted by Riley's bed. "I reckon I'd best be going. I just come to bring you them herbs."

"You ain't going no place," Riley said, fury in his voice. "Now settle yourself down. You are a prideful man and you don't like to have the truth spoke to you, but I'm going to say me some things here today."

"You are a good friend Riley, but I don't need to hear…."

Riley held up his hand to silence Crockett. "You can tell me after I've said my piece that it ain't worth a tinker's dam, but I intend to say it."

He motioned for Crockett to sit down. Crockett picked up the chair where it had fallen and eased himself back into it. "Come here, Mallie," Riley demanded. He patted the covers, a grimace popping up on his face. Mallie came and sat at the foot of the bed. "I've worked mules with more sense than the two of you."

Crockett, chin in hand, looked away. The fire was crackling, wet knots exploding out onto the hearth like falling stars. He could see Mallie out of the corner of his eye, her arms folded around each other, back ramrod straight, head held high.

"Mallie, you come by it honest, but that ain't no excuse," Riley said sternly. "You may think that it wasn't fair losing your mama and being sent away like that, but what is done is done."

"Riley, I was just a little girl who had lost her mama. I didn't need to lose my pa, too."

"Mallie," Crockett spoke up, "I done what I thought was best for you. I couldn't stand to see you work yourself to death on that worthless piece of land like your mama done."

"How can you say that? Mama loved that farm."

"We barely grew enough food to feed ourselves with never a dime of cash money for clothes. Sometimes we couldn't buy coal oil for the lamps." Crockett kept his face a mask, but the emotions swirled around in him licking at his insides like flames. He had never shared with either of his children the deep guilt he felt over Rebecca's death. If he had not stolen her from her family to live a harsh life in an isolated mountain cabin, he was sure she would still be alive. "You was just a youngun. You don't know …."

"I know I was old enough to have some say in what happened to me," Mallie said harshly.

"Now, hush," Riley, shouted. "You two are growling at each other like sore-tail bears and that ain't doing nobody no good. You both have a way of speaking before you think."

Crockett looked at his daughter through hooded eyes. She sat up, squaring her shoulders at Riley's words. He could see the same stubborn pride in her that coursed through his body and he knew that what his friend was saying was true.

"Laying here these last two weeks has give me plenty of time to think," Riley said. "It ain't in my nature to give up without a fight, but it has passed through my mind that I might never leave this bed again."

"Riley, you don't need to be talking that way," Crockett said. He could see the pain in his friends face. The haggard gray lines that cut deep into his ashen skin said more than the words he spoke.

"Hear me out, Crockett," Riley said, looking at his old friend.

Letting out the breath he had been holding, Crockett sat back in the chair and watched as Mallie reached over and gently touched Riley's swollen hand.

"Crockett, you may think that it weren't right that Rebecca was took from you, but you had her for fourteen years and she give you two good younguns. Most folks would be proud to have known a woman like Rebecca, even in passing. I never heard a soul say a harm word against her and that ain't true of most folks in this life."

Crockett hung his head.

"And she loved you and Mallie and Cole. Now, ain't that a blessing?"

Crockett shook his head to hold back the tears. He could see Mallie's eyes sparkling in the firelight as she strained to stop the tears from spilling over on to her cheeks.

"Mallie," Riley went on, "it weren't fair losing your mama that way. Life can wield some brutal blows. You just had to learn that lesson sooner than some folks did. Your mama would have been proud of the way you've growed up to be a fine young woman. And you made a teacher, so some good come of you going away."

With those words, the tears spilled over Mallie's cheeks and ran in torrents down her face. Crockett watched as she wiped them off with the back of her hand. He reached into his shirt pocket and handed her the handkerchief he carried. When she took it from him, their fingertips brushed and she smiled a fleeting smile. Crockett realized how tightly he had held his emotions all these years when he saw that his hand was trembling.

"I am asking a favor from the two of you," Riley said, looking first at Mallie and then at Crockett. "Promise me you'll take some advice from a crippled up old man."

"It won't be the first time you've tried to tell me what to do," Crockett said.

"Yeah, but I'm hoping it'll be the first time you listen," Riley said.

Crockett smiled at his old friend.

"They ain't no denying that life is rough. But it gets a dang site rougher when you turn away from the folks that love you."

Crockett looked at his daughter sitting on the end of the bed, her arms folded around her for protection. Having invested so much in aloneness, in keeping it all in, he hesitated even now to go to Mallie and put his arms around her. As he started to stand, she looked at him her eyes dark and bold; searching his face like Rebecca had done so often, looking for a sign. He lost the courage and sat back down.

"Crockett, you say you speak to Rebecca. That she comes to you in your dreams," Riley said.

Crockett could feel the heat spread up his face. Mallie looked at him, her head cocked quizzically. He looked away unable to meet her gaze. "Riley, that weren't meant for nobody else to hear. I just told you that because I needed you to understand about the herbs."

"What do you think she would say about you turning your back on your own younguns?" Riley said, ignoring his protest. "I know you thought you was giving Mallie a better life but here she is in front of you now."

"Riley, there ain't no call for that," Crockett said.

"I dream of her, too," Mallie said softly. "I used to cry myself to sleep and then Mama would come to me and put her hand on my forehead. She would brush the hair from my eyes and tell me she loved me. She would tell me everything would be all right and to be a brave girl."

Crockett looked at his daughter. Her face had a faraway look and she spoke more to herself than to him. He pictured her alone in bed, the covers pulled up around her for comfort. Shame washed over him as he thought of all the years he had wasted absorbed in his own grief. Rebecca was not coming back, but here was his daughter alive and needing him. Suddenly, he knew that he had wasted too much time. He rose and went to his daughter and held out his arms. Mallie looked up at him, hesitating only a second before she threw herself into his open arms. They held each other while she cried into his chest. He felt the warmth of her as he rubbed her shoulder blades through the soft fabric of her dress. "I thought I was doing right by you, Mallie. I really did. I never wanted to hurt you."

She did not speak but he could feel her nodding her understanding into his chest. He pushed her back away from him. Taking the handkerchief from her, he wiped away her tears as he examined her face so like her mamas. "Forgive me?"

"Not just yet. Maybe someday," Mallie said solemnly.

"Mallie Hamilton," Riley said his brow furrowed.

"I'm working on it, Riley," Mallie said, looking at him defiantly.

"They ain't no denying you belong to Crockett Hamilton."

They all laughed. The tension that had filled the room lifted leaving Crockett feeling awkward and unsure what to do next. The woman in front of him was his daughter, but in many ways a stranger to him. He shifted his weight from one foot to another.

"I better get you two men something to eat." Mallie said at last.

Crockett and Riley exchanged a look.

"Now what does that look mean? I can't be that bad a cook."

"I was just remembering some pretty tough venison," Crockett said.

Mallie threw her hand to her hip. "I might not have been a good hand at cooking, but you sure admired the way I shot it and dressed it in the field."

"That I did," Crockett admitted. "You could have a deer skinned and dressed out before most folks could hang one up. Are you still as good a shot?"

"I've not shot a gun since I left here," Mallie said.

Of course, she would not be shooting wild game. That was why he had sent her away so she would not have to do such things.

"Don't worry. I didn't cook it," Mallie said. "Maude left some stew on the back of the stove. I'll just heat it up."

"Crockett, you go with her and brew me up a batch of them herbs. We'll see if they can work their magic on an old man," Riley said.

Crockett followed Mallie into the small kitchen. She busied herself at the stove while he leaned awkwardly against the door facing.

"Do you want some coffee?" she asked.

"That would be nice," he said.

She set the cup on the table. Crockett pulled out the chair and sat down. "I've been here since July. I thought you might...." Her voice trailed off and she turned away.

"When I heard you were back, I wanted to see you, but I didn't know how you would feel about me."

"How do you think I should feel about you? You never wrote a letter or came to visit me in six years."

"Mallie I watched you nurse your mama. I watched you try to keep the house and tend the garden. I seen how worn down you was and all that you was missing out on. Then your Aunt Mae offered to give you a good home."

"I had a good home," Mallie said bitterly. "Every day Aunt Mae told me to forget you. She said you never loved me. She told me that you killed my mama with hard work and that she had been a fool for ever marrying you."

The words hit Crockett like bullets. He knew that Rebecca's family hated him but he never imagined that they would try to poison Mallie's mind against her own father. Anger flared up in him making his coarse red hair stand on end.

"Every day," Mallie went on, "I told myself that what she said was not true. That you loved me and you loved my mama. I whispered it to myself every night before I went to sleep. I never stopped even when I never heard from you."

Her words broke his heart. He felt ashamed now that he had not known of her suffering. "Your Aunt Mae thought it would be better if I never wrote to you."

"How could that be better?" Mallie said incredulously. "I was just a lonely little girl."

"Rebecca's family felt like if she hadn't come off up here with me, she would still be alive. I reckon at the time I felt that way too. The only way Mae would take you in was if I wouldn't have nothing more to do with you."

Mallie pulled out a chair and sat down. She put her head in her hands. "And you agreed to that?"

"They were offering you what I couldn't give you, a good life." Crockett said weakly. "But only if I swore never to see you again."

Mallie looked up, her face full of pain and confusion. "A good life. Aunt Mae reminded me every day how lucky I was that she was willing to take me and to give me that good life. She reminded me every time I sat down to eat or put on a new dress, how much it cost to keep me."

"She told you that?"

Mallie nodded.

"It never cost her a dime. I give her every penny I got from the farm. I never kept a cent of it. When I got a job with the Little River Lumber Company, I sent money every month towards your keep."

"She lied to both of us then."

They sat in stunned silence.

"I've been a fool, Mallie," Crockett said at last. "I used to sneak and read the letters you wrote to Cole. You sounded so happy. I wanted to see you so bad, but I thought you was better off without me."

"I never wanted Cole to know how unhappy I was so I made up stories about what I was doing and the fun I was having. I made it sound like everything was fine."

Crockett reached over and took his daughter's hand. "I'm sorry, Mallie. I was wrong to send you away. I can understand now if you can't never forgive me."

"I was angry for a long time, but mostly I was hurt thinking you didn't want me."

"A man can do some foolish things when he's grieving," Crockett said, shaking his head.

"I'm tired of being angry, but I don't know if I know how to forgive you just yet. I've come back to make my life here. I've come back to be near the mountains I love. I learned one thing living with Aunt Mae. Mama had a better life here than she had before. She wouldn't have traded those years of living up here for all the fine clothes in the world. I know because I feel the same way."

"It does me good to think your mama was happy."

"I think it may be time we stopped pining for something we can't have. Maybe in time, we can work things out. I think Mama would want that."

"That's the second time today I've been told that," Crockett said.

"Mama's trying to tell us to get on with our lives," Mallie said.

"So you don't think the old man is crazy?"

"Maybe we both are a little," she said. "Mama promised me before she died that she would look out for me. I believe she kept her promise. I hope she is looking out for all of us, especially Cole."

Crockett flinched at the sound of Cole's name thrown out at him so suddenly. "You heard what happened," he ventured.

"Yes, Maude told me."

"Cole will be all right," Crockett said. "He just needs some time."

Mallie got up and stirred the stew. On the way back from the stove, she brought the coffee and poured another cup for her father. Crockett looked up at her and smiled. They had fallen back into an old familiar pattern and this simple thing pleased him.

"How do you know he will be all right? I heard he was living high up in the mountains. Winter is coming on."

He did not tell her that he had been tracking Cole for months. That he knew where the boy was only because he had taught him everything he knew about surviving in the wilds.

"Do you know where he is?"

"I have my suspicions."

"Then, why haven't you brought him home?"

"He'll come down in good time. He's got some things to mull over." How could he explain to her, Cole's need to be alone? How could he tell her of his fear that Cole was too much like him, driven by a darkness that sometimes overtook him?

"But why did he have to run away? He didn't do anything wrong. Maybe he needs us to tell him that. Maybe he needs to know how much we love him and need him."

"The boy has to know that."

"And how would he know any more than I knew it? After Mama died, you went off sometimes for days at a time and left us alone. We both thought you blamed us for her dying. We thought that with Mama dead, you didn't want us around to remind you of her."

Crockett did not know how to answer his daughter, for there was more than a little truth in what she said and he felt ashamed of his selfishness.

Suddenly the stew hissed and sizzled as it bubbled over on the stove. Mallie rushed to set it off. "Cole needs me," Mallie said, without turning around.

"He knows how to find you when he's ready," Crockett said. The words, meant to give her ease, sounded cold even to his ear. She turned and gave him a bitter look, her shoulders pulled tight around her neck. Finally, she let out a heavy sigh.

"What are those herbs Riley was talking about?" Mallie asked, turning to the bag he had set on the table.

They had drawn an uneasy truce between them. "Something for his rheumatism."

"Do you want me to brew him a cup?"

"I'll have to tell you how. Lizzie Melton showed me."

"Mama's friend?"

"Yeah."

"How is she? I haven't seen her since I was a little girl."

"Getting old. Gone blind. She's got grandchildren your age."

"I'd love to see her. Mama always thought the world of Mrs. Melton."

"I'll take you over to Gatlinburg to see her one of these days," Crockett said. He felt a sudden joy that he was making plans with his daughter. The thought that he would be seeing her again and that he would be a part of her life made his chest tighten until he could hardly breathe.

Mallie poured the contents of the bag out onto the table. "I recognize this," she said, fingering the dried roots. "It's bloodroot, isn't it?"

"And skunk cabbage," Crockett said.

Opening the pouch and sniffing the contents, Mallie's face curled into a grimace. "It smells rotten. What is it?"

"Martha wouldn't tell me," Crockett said. "Martha is Lizzie's daughter. She mixed it up 'cause Lizzie can't see to do it no more." He wondered at his need to explain. "She said to boil up about two cups of water and steep about a palm full of that in it."

Mallie filled a pan with water and when it came to a boil, she dropped in the herbs. "How long do we leave it?"

"The longer you leave it the stronger it gets, Lizzie said. Ten minutes should be enough she said."

"It already looks like stump water," Mallie said, peering into the pan.

Crockett watched as she strained the thick, black concoction into a cup. "Might ort to give it to him before he tries to eat his stew. The way it looks, we'll see if he can hold it down before he tries to eat anything."

Mallie took the cup in her hands and with a doubtful look over her shoulder she went in to give the sticky brew to Riley. Crockett waited impatiently in the kitchen, wondering if he had done the right thing. Finally, Mallie came back with the empty cup. "He said it tasted like it had been brewed in a chamber pot, but he drank it all," Mallie said.

Crockett smiled. "If I know Riley, he didn't say it quite that nice."

Mallie laughed. "How often does he have to drink that?"

"Three times a day."

"You get to tell him that."

It was Crockett's turn to laugh.

"Oh, he wants you to bring him in here," Mallie said. "He wants to eat at the table."

"Is he up to that?"

"He's a proud man. This is the first time he's asked to come to the table. Usually, I feed him. I don't think he likes for you to see him like this."

"Knowing Riley, he just don't want to miss out on nothing."

"I'll set the table," Mallie said.

Crockett slowly turned to go.

"Pa," Mallie called after him. "Just try not to hurt him. I promised Maude I would take care of him while she was gone.

She may be upset enough with me when she finds out I gave him stump water."

Her voice was serious, but he could see the smile tugging at the corners of her mouth. "We may have to break for high timber if she catches us," he said, with a grin.

"I'm telling you, Riley here used to be the worse for horse trading of any man I ever seen," Crockett said, slapping his leg. "If he could get a hold of any old plug, he would trade it for a hog or mule or just about anything a man had to offer. Then it wouldn't be long till he'd traded that hog for another horse."

"It gets in your blood," Riley said, with a chuckle.

"I reckon you had it bad for a while," Crockett said. They had been sitting at the table for an hour. He had started to tell stories to call attention away from Riley as he struggled to feed himself.

"I thought I could make a living at it for a while, but I never liked to play no tricks on folks. I done it mostly for the fun of it," Riley said.

"Did you ever get tricked?" Mallie asked. She sat chin in hand, her eyes moving from her pa to Riley.

"Tell her about the time that old man come riding by on the poorest nag ever walked," Crockett said chuckling. "He was so skinny you could count every rib and his hip bones stuck out."

"Crockett and me got to laughing because it was such a sorry sight. We was laughing so hard the old man stopped."

"Riley hollers out 'what would you take for that horse'," Crockett said. Throwing back his head, he laughed at the memory.

"I had an old sow with a litter of piglets," Riley picked up the story. "They was rooting around under a tree not far from where we was standing. So the old man says, 'I'll take me one of them piglets.'"

"And with that, he just gets off that nag, ties her to the fencepost, tucks one of them piglets under his arms and walks on off," Crockett said, howling with laughter.

"What did you do, Riley?" Mallie asked.

"Well, it struck me after a while that the man was serious about trading. I said to Crockett, you reckon he meant it. Your pa was rolling on the ground a laughing. He said, 'Dang right, he meant it. You done got yourself a horse.'"

"Riley took that horse to every settlement trying to get rid of it. He finally had to give a feller a dollar to take her." Crockett slapped the table and threw back his head.

Mallie held her sides and rocked with laughter.

"I felt bad about that deal till about a year later the man come bringing that horse back," Riley said. "He give me that dollar, said if he had knowed that horse was going to live so long he never would of took it."

"What did you do with the horse then?" Mallie asked.

"I put it out to pasture. I had to feed it every winter. That ole swayback nag lived another ten years. Cost me a fortune to keep it."

"Surely you're not still begrudging an old man his pig," Mallie said.

"If I'd a knowed then what I know now, I'd of give him two pigs to take the horse with him," Riley said, grinning at them.

"Stop it, Riley," Mallie said through tears of laughter. "My sides hurt already."

Mallie stopped laughing suddenly. Crockett followed her eyes to the kitchen doorway. Maude and Rose stood looking at them. He had not heard them come in. Their eyes were wide and questioning.

"Riley, what are you doing out of bed?" Maude asked. Her eyes searched the room taking in the surprising scene.

"Maude come and join us," Riley said cheerfully. "Crockett's come to visit."

"I can see that," Maude stammered. "Good to see you Crockett." Maude fidgeted with her hair and smiled nervously at the group.

"It's all right Maude. They've done made up," Riley said.

Crockett's eyes flew to Mallie, but before she could react, Maude clapped her hands. "Hallelujah, it's about time. Rose, set a pot to boiling and Mallie, you stir up the fire. I'm a fixin' to make us a sweet potato pie. We've got something to celebrate."

Rose and Maude went to work in the tight little kitchen. They moved about each other with practiced ease while Mallie added more wood to the fire. Crockett's heart felt so light and free he thought it might float out of his chest just watching his daughter.

A noise out back made Mallie's eyes fly to the back door. Crockett turned to see a young man struggling to bring in an armload of packages. He could see Mallie's eyes light up at the sight of the young man. Jumping up to help the boy, he almost bumped into his daughter who was rushing toward the door. They all laughed.

"Pa, this is Will Stenson," Mallie said. "He stays here sometimes."

"Crockett Hamilton," he said, taking a load of the bundles. Will greeted him with a huge smile. When he put down the bundles, Will took his hand and shook it vigorously.

"I am delighted to meet you Mr. Hamilton. I must say I am surprised and delighted," Will said, enthusiastically.

"Well, thank you son," Crockett said, somewhat puzzled. "Call me Crockett."

"Thank you sir," Will said.

Crockett watched as Will turned his smile on Mallie. She blushed up her neck and into her hair.

"Will was kind enough to take Maude and Rose to their farm in Wears Cove," Mallie explained.

Crockett nodded.

"Joe has done a fine job with the farm," Maude said, with obvious pride in their son. "The fall harvest is in. He sent a bushel of sweet potatoes and a bushel of Irish. And Riley, Becky sent you some leather breeches. Said to tell you they was especially for you 'cause she knowed how much you love them."

"Well weren't that nice of her," Riley said, obviously pleased that his daughter-in-law had thought of him.

They talked on until late into the night, eating sweet potato pie and reliving old times. Finally, weary from the excitement of the day they said goodnight. Crockett laid a pallet by the fire, closed his eyes and fell fast asleep for the first time in years.

Just before dawn, he rose, looked in on his daughter sleeping, the quilts pulled tightly around her like when she was a little girl. Softly he closed the door and headed back up the mountain to work.

14

As soon as Mallie heard the front door close, she threw off her quilts and pulled on the clothes she had stashed earlier. There would be no fancy outfit for her ride today, she thought, as she laid out the overalls and work shirt. Will had left her a pair of boots and a jacket in the loft and she would have to climb up and get them before leaving.

She had pretended to Rose to have the curse. She hated lying, especially when Rose brought her a hot water bottle and was so solicitous, but she knew the family would not question her further about female problems nor beg her to go with them.

Riley was much better after only a week of drinking the herbs. He had wanted to go back to work as soon as the swelling had gone down in his joints, but Maude would not hear of it. She told him the cold weather on the mountain would send him right back to bed. Riley had reluctantly agreed to wait.

In high spirits over Riley's improved health, they had decided to spend Saturday and Sunday at the farm with Joe and his family. Mallie had seized the opportunity to go looking for her brother.

Her fingers fumbled with the unfamiliar buttons of the man's shirt. It belonged to Will and she found herself raising her arm to smell the sleeve. The musty smell of earth and wild plants filled her senses. She shook her head to clear her senses. Her feelings for Will confused her. At times, she had talked herself completely out of them, only to be overwhelmed by them in the next moment. She had made it clear to him after that first night that she was not interested in falling in love and yet sometimes as they sat by the fire in the evenings, Will so completely absorbed in his journals and sketches he seemed unaware of her, she found herself longing for his attention.

Climbing down from the loft, she hurriedly laced up her boots and slipped into the rough work jacket. Then she remembered she had not made her bed. Quickly she smoothed the covers as she laughed to herself. She would be spending the night in the mountains with a man she hardly knew but at least her bed would be properly made, she thought. When she stopped to bank the fire and prayed an errant spark would not burn the cabin down while she was gone, she knew her nerves were getting the better of her.

Grabbing a cold biscuit from the stove, she headed out the back door. Excitement drove her steps as she headed along the path. Picturing herself throwing her arms around her brother, she smiled. They would talk for hours just as they had as children. Then she would bring him home.

Will had been waiting for her with the horses since before dawn. He smiled when he caught sight of her and she waved to him. "I came as soon as I could get away. Maude decided to bake another pie at the last minute, as if five wasn't plenty," Mallie said, exasperation in her voice. "I reckon we better get going. I want to cover as much ground as we can."

"Good morning to you too," Will said.

Mallie looked at him. His body was lank as he leaned against a tree, his face showing no signs of hurry. He had reluctantly agreed to take her along on this trip into the mountains and she truly was grateful. "Good morning," she said smiling. "Did you have any trouble getting the horses?"

"No, Dan Cannon is a friend of mine. I just told him me and my gal, Mallie Hamilton, was going camping for a few days and I needed to borrow Pierce Gerard's best saddle horses."

"Will Stenson, you did no such thing!" Mallie said, swallowing hard.

"I didn't take you for the kind of girl who was all that concerned about what folks thought," he said, glancing up and down at her outfit.

"First off, I lied to my best friend, and I used a man's good will for a horse, so I'm not feeling too good about myself. Second off, I don't need the whole town thinking I'm your gal."

Will handed her Lady's reins. "Dan didn't ask me a thing," he said simply. "Just let me take the horses. He's a good man."

Mallie let Will help her up without a word. Regretting her outburst, she said more gently, "Where are we going?"

"I thought we would ride up Jakes Creek, cut over to Huskey Branch and then we will head on up the ridge."

"I thought we might ride up to the ridge right away."

"Mallie, I do have work to do. I am collecting native seeds from maturing plants. This may be my only chance. I agreed to take you along, but my work comes first." He mounted his horse, glanced back at her once, and then headed out. He rode ahead and she quickly lost sight of him in the thick morning fog.

She had seen Will working with his plants, dried and stuck to thick papers. He could look at one small stem for hours, studying each tiny leaf. She thought it might take all day to reach the ridge. She might be better off heading out on her own, but Will had all the supplies and the thought of sleeping on the cold ground in the open was none too inviting. She kicked Lady in the sides and caught up with Will as they neared Jakes Creek. "All right, I accept," she said as she rode up beside him.

"You accept what?" Will asked puzzled.

"I accept your terms. We look for seeds along the creek and then we head up the mountain. Isn't that what you said?"

Will let out a whooping laugh, the sound echoing through the valley. "Mallie you are something else. Given your kind consideration, I'll try not to take up too much of your time."

Mallie nodded solemnly.

Will let out another whoop.

Mallie started to protest, when Will jumped from his horse and ran into the woods. She watched as he knelt by a rotting log. She waited impatiently until her curiosity got the better of her and she jumped from her horse to join him. When she walked up behind him, she saw that he was examining a cluster of mushrooms on the side of a rotting log. They were bright yellow and looked like fingers reaching to the sky.

"They are of the species Calvarias," he said. "They look like ocean coral."

"You see them all over the woods, this time of year," she said sighing to show her impatience. "Have you never seen one before?" Mallie could only think that it would take them forever to reach the ridge if Will stopped to examine every mushroom along the way.

"I have seen hundreds of them, but never this one."

Just then, the fog parted and the sun sent a shaft of light racing down to light up the golden mushrooms. She squatted down by Will. "They look like a choir getting ready to sing," she said.

"Such beauty," he said and his eyes sparkled.

Mallie was struck by the pleasure Will found in everything in nature. Even she, who loved the mountains so much, could not understand the depth of it. For nearly a minute they did not move, but merely took in the beauty.

"I'm surprised to see them so beautiful since we have had so little rain," she said finally.

"We are just so fortunate."

"Yes," she said. Suddenly, she felt it, a letting go of all that was binding her. She took a deep breath and felt the crisp air as though for the first time. The freedom and joy of the day worked its way down her arms and made her fingers tingle. The sense of urgency that had pushed her since she first promised herself she would come back someday eased its talon hold on her.

"Are you ready to head out?" he asked.

"When you are," she said and meant it.

They stood up and he took her hand. She did not protest as he led her out of the woods and back to the trail.

"It's going to be a warm day once the fog burns off," Will said. He let go of her hand and motioned toward the sky. "The sun is already trying to break through."

"I think I'll keep my jacket on a bit longer," Mallie said, hugging herself with her arms.

"Are you cold?" he asked. Stepping toward her, he rubbed her arms to warm her.

She looked up at him and smiled. He bent to kiss her but she turned her head away and his lips brushed her hair. "Where does that come from?" she asked.

"What?" he said genuinely puzzled by her question. "A kiss?"

"No," she said shaking her head. "That look you had when I walked up on you in the woods. You were in a world of your own. I could see it in your eyes. There was such joy there. Where does that come from?"

"When I look at something so beautiful, everything else falls away," Will said simply. "I don't worry about tomorrow nor dwell on the things that happened to me in the past. When I am here, all I think about is wandering these woods forever discovering new and wonderful things each day."

"I wish I could do that and think only about this moment."

"I've heard you crying at night."

"Oh," she gasped.

"Often, I lay awake at night. I like to think about the day and what wonders the next day will hold. You should forgive your father, you know."

"I'm not sure I can."

"You want him to suffer more for what he's done?"

"I see him sitting in the kitchen laughing with Riley as though all those years had not happened and it makes me angry."

"Mallie, one thing I have learned up here in the mountains is that nature has a lot to teach us. With each changing season, the past is swept away and makes room for the splendor of the next. Each plant's destiny is in the nature of the seed. Only people have a choice. Why do we so often fail to choose happiness?"

He looked at her and his gaze was kind, but she felt trapped by his words. Her anger and hurt was a wound she had picked at so long, she was reluctant to let it heal. It had become a part of her and yet she knew he was right. "I don't mean to hurry you," she said, her voice sticking in her throat, "but I think we need to get going."

Will cupped her chin in the palm of his hand. "I don't mean to hurry you either Mallie."

She felt the heat of his hand on her cheek and she wanted to lean into it. Instead, she gently pushed him away and headed for her horse.

They followed the trail along Cucumber Gap all the way to the base of the mountain. The white trilliums and lavender lilies of spring had given way to the scarlet berries of the jack-in-the-pulpit and the purple fruit of the Indian cucumber. The dogwoods, whose spring show of white flowers had lighted hillsides, now presented crimson flowers and red berries. With the forest more open, the mountains became visible in the background stretching starkly upward toward the sky.

As soon as they reached the ridgeline, Mallie jumped from her horse and found the old paths as though she had never been away. She left Will behind and walked as fast as her legs could carry her. She did not slow down, even though the stony path bruised her feet, until she was up the ridge.

The place where she had grown up was as familiar to her as the back of her hand. Memories flooded back through her mind and she did not know how long she had been on the path when she burst through the trees and saw the cabin. Freezing in place, she took in the sight of the farm. The land all around had grown up. The cabin wore a sad and lonely face. Not prepared for the shock of it, she felt her knees grow weak. There was a sound behind her but she did not turn. Feeling warm arms around her, she leaned into them. "Will," she whispered.

"I'm here."

"It's not as I remember it."

"You remember the way it was when you were a child."

She nodded and the tears came into her eyes blurring the cabin. Without moving, she stood with the tears running down her cheeks. "The cabin looks so lifeless and empty."

"No, that isn't true. Come and I'll show you."

He led the horses to the cabin. She could hear his voice fade as he walked around back. He continued to talk to her in soothing tones even when she could not hear his words.

She stood before the doorway of the cabin trying to muster the courage to go in, when Will came around the corner. "Look, the last of the goldenrods," he said handing her a bouquet. "They were growing in the garden."

Her tears had finally stopped and she took the flowers from him. He smiled his radiant smile and she was struck once again by the tenderness in his face. "Thank you," she said.

A chipmunk ran out from under the porch and quickly disappeared behind a log. It popped back watching them for any alarming movements. "See the cabin is not empty," Will said, with a chuckle. "He's a curious little guy. He is afraid but he wants to know what we are doing here."

"His cheeks are stuffed," Mallie said.

"He's probably been gathering seeds and nuts. He will be hibernating for the winter soon. "

Mallie moved toward the door and with a flick of its tail, the chipmunk disappeared behind the log and was gone. "I scared him off," Mallie said.

"Not for long. His curiosity will get the better of him and he'll be back."

Without hesitating, Mallie pushed open the door. She was surprised to see the furniture still there. Two ladder-back chairs sat in front of the fireplace. Her pa had made the chairs and she had soaked the white oak splits and woven the seats into a herringbone pattern. A black cook pot hung from the iron bar. She could picture her mama there cooking soup on the hot coals, sliding the pot along the bar to the side when the fire got too hot. "My mama had a Dutch oven she used to make cornbread," Mallie found herself saying. "She used to put it in the fireplace and cover it with coals to bake the bread. On my birthday she would make me an apple cobbler in it."

Will looked down into the fireplace. He ran his hand along the mantel. He said nothing but waited patiently for her to go on.

"She never even had a wood stove," Mallie said as though she had just realized it. "Sometimes the wind would blow down the chimney and ashes would fly everywhere. You would have to wipe off everything. And of course, you had to gather wood all the time. It was Cole's job to keep the fire going."

'That must have been a big job," Will said.

"Pa cut most of the wood from the farm," Mallie said distractedly, looking around the room. A four-poster rope bed filled most of the room. Some of the ropes had rotted through and the shuck mattress hung precariously. A dusty, threadbare quilt covered the mattress. "It's as though he just walked out and left everything," she said at last. "Why would he walk away and leave everything?"

"He was grieving," Will offered.

"It was like he had no use for any of it without Mama."

"He's just a man, Mallie. We all do things that don't make sense when we are in pain."

"I thought he loved this farm."

"I think he did," Will said kindly, "but it couldn't have been easy living here. It would have been hard work for even a dozen men to turn this farm into anything productive. Did you ever think, it might have been your mother who wanted it? Maybe she was the one who gave him the courage and determination to keep going."

"She never complained. I think she felt free here. I think she could be herself here. There was no one here to tell her to act like a lady."

"No one here to tell here she couldn't wear men's overalls," Will said looking at Mallie's outfit.

Mallie laughed a hearty laugh. "Oh, Will. I'm more like my mama than I ever knew."

"You are a brave woman, Mallie. You have a good mind and a strong will. Use those qualities your mother gave you to find your own happiness."

"Will, you are the dearest man," Mallie said looking into his eyes. She put her hand on his chest and she could feel him tremble. She backed away.

"I can fix you a pallet in here for the night," he said. "I'll sleep outside on the porch."

She nodded, unable to speak.

"I'll gather some firewood," he said. "It could get cold tonight."

He walked outside and she followed him. "Would you care if I go down to a stream where I used to fish with Pa?"

"I could go with you?"

She gave him a look. "Do you have a hook and some string in your pack? I'll catch us some supper."

Will looked at her with one eyebrow raised, but without a word he left to get her what she wanted. "Be careful," he said.

Walking away, she could feel him watching. She turned to smile at him. "Build a big fire out back, so Cole will know we are here."

"It doesn't mean he will come."

"He'll come," she said walking away. The sun was warm on her back and it burned away everything but the memory of fishing with her pa. An occasional breeze stirred the remaining leaves on the trees causing them to shower down on her. She laughed and danced about kicking them with her boot. As she walked deeper into the woods, the path to the stream became more overgrown. Twice she lost her way and had to backtrack. Then she heard water and the woods opened up to the very spot where she had fished as a girl. She had come to it more by instinct than memory. Stopping only long enough to collect some bait, she found a stick and tied the line to it. She laughed to herself, when on the first try she caught a trout. She saw now, how the rocks formed a dam causing the trout to collect in a pool. It was no wonder she had been so lucky fishing as a young girl. Even now, she could almost reach down into the clear water and grab a fish with her hand.

When she had caught half-a-dozen small trout, she slipped them onto her rod to carry back to camp. Walking to where the stream bubbled over the rocks forming waterfalls, she rolled up her sleeves. She washed her hands and face in the icy water, crying out from the cold. Turning suddenly, she thought she heard a noise behind her, but there was no one there. Then she thought it might have been the echo from her own voice. She shook her hands dry and rolled down her sleeves, picked up her trout and headed back to camp.

Before she had walked a hundred yards, a rattling in the brush stopped her. "Cole," she called out. A doe walked out of the shrubs and froze when it saw her. She held her breath not wanting to frighten it. It cocked its head at her and then headed back into the woods. As beautiful as the doe had been, she could only feel disappointment that it had not been her brother.

Will met her at the edge of the woods. "I was getting worried."

"Was I gone that long?" Mallie asked, surprised at his concern.

"Two hours," he said. "It's starting to get dark."

She had not noticed the sun going down. She had been so engrossed in her memories the two hours she had been gone had seemed like minutes. "I caught enough fish for all of us," she said proudly.

"Mallie there is only the two of us."

"Cole will be along shortly," she said, handing him the fish.

"Aren't you going to clean them," he asked.

"I caught them." She walked on toward the cabin, a grin splitting her face.

In the end, Mallie had cleaned the fish. She put them on sticks to cook over the fire outside while Will made hoecakes to bake on a stone.

"It took a lot of convincing to get Maude to teach me how to make these hoecakes," Will said, his back to her.

"She doesn't think it's proper for a man to cook," Mallie said, gazing up at the stars. "I'm glad we decided to cook outside. It's such a beautiful night."

Will nodded.

"How did you get her to teach you?"

"I told her it would come in handy when I was camping out."

"I bet she didn't think you would be making them for me over a camp fire."

"She'd skin me alive, if she knew."

"That even sounds like something she would say."

"Well, that's because she has threatened it more than once."

"That just means, she thinks of you as one of her own."

Will grinned. "Then it would be worth it."

"Are they ready yet? I'm starved."

"Get the plates and utensils from my pack," Will said. "I think these are about done."

She held the pressed tin plates while Will placed the steaming hoecakes and crispy trout on them. Mallie's mouth watered.

They ate in silence for a long time. "I didn't think anything could taste this good," she said her mouth still full. "You done Maude proud."

"Kind of you to say so," Will said, bowing his head in a gentlemanly fashion even as he reached for another trout.

Mallie looked at him.

"I'll save some for Cole," he said, lifting the fish from the stick.

"You don't think he will come, do you?"

"I just don't want you to get your hopes up."

"Hope is what I live on."

"Then, he'll come. I'm sure of it."

"You're not just saying that to make me feel better," Mallie said. The fire light danced in his eyes making them hard to read.

"No matter what, Mallie, Cole loves you."

"I know," Mallie said. She watched as Will finished his supper. He relished every bite stopping to savor each tiny morsel until it was all gone. Then he leaned back and closed his eyes. She had never known anyone so perfectly content with whatever he was doing. He seemed to long for nothing more than to be alive at that moment.

Taking the plates and forks, she wiped them clean and put them back in the pack before she sat down by the fire. Will sat reading by the firelight. He looked up to catch her watching him and smiled. "What are you reading?" she asked.

"A journal of William Bartram. He was a naturalist. He spent five years in the South studying the plants."

"You admire him?"

"I envy him. Like me, he followed in his father's footsteps to become a naturalist. Imagine traveling this land when it was yet unspoiled, seeing the virgin forest, discovering new plants. Sometimes, I feel I was born too late."

"Are there not new discoveries to be made?"

"I can only hope, Mallie," Will said pensively.

"Will you be so disappointed if you don't make a great discovery?"

"I have already made many great discoveries here."

"You didn't answer my question."

"It's time you got some rest," Will said, closing the book and putting it away in his pack. "I made you a pallet in the cabin. I'll build a fire to keep you warm."

Mallie searched the dark. Cole had not come as she had hoped. Wearily she got up and dusted off her pants. She still had tomorrow, she thought. Will collected some firewood. She followed him into the cabin and watched as he deftly built a fire.

"This should hold most of the night," he said.

"Stay with me a while," she said hesitating. "Until I fall asleep."

Will sat down in the ladder-back chair.

"No, here on the pallet," she said motioning to him. "Lie down with me."

"Are you sure?" he asked.

"I trust you," she said.

He lay down beside her and wrapped his arms around her. She rested in the crook of his arm. “Cole will come,” she whispered.

“I know,” he said.

She could feel him gently stroking her hair and then she fell into a deep sleep.

15

Good Morning," Cole said. He sat across the room in a ladder-back chair and watched as his sister opened her eyes and stretched her stiff limbs. Finally, her eyes sought out his voice. When she saw him, she jumped up rolling Will's body away from her.

"Cole!" Mallie screamed throwing herself into his arms and nearly knocking him over in his chair.

"Mallie," he said into her hair with a deep-throated laugh.

"I knew you would come," she said.

"Whoa," he said pulling her away to look at her. "You're hugging me so tight I can hardly breathe. Let me have a look at you. Could this be my baby sister? Look at you all growed up. I see Aunt Mae sure managed to make a lady out of you."

She blushed and looked down at her overalls dirty and smelling of horse. Her hair had come loose from its pins and fallen down her back. The way she deftly pinned it back into place, struck Cole as such a womanly gesture. The years they had lost were in the soft curve of her arm and the practiced way she straightened her hair.

"I must look a sight," she said shyly.

"You are the prettiest thing I've seen in years."

"Cole," she said, "now don't you tease me."

He could tell by the way she said it, that she too was thinking of when they were children and he had tormented her at times for sport. He could not explain to her how beautiful she looked to him after all his months of lonely wandering.

Examining him closely she said, "I have missed you so much. I wouldn't have known you except you look like Pa." She stroked his wild red beard and giggled. "Your clothes are a sight, ragged and torn. I wish I had brought you some things to wear."

A noise behind them made them both turn to see Will standing at the fireplace grinning sheepishly.

"Will, good to see you again," Cole said. Even in the dim light of the cabin, he could see Mallie blush.

"Will brought me here," she said. "He's been looking out for me."

Cole raised an eyebrow and looked at Will. Before he could speak, Will said, "I know you asked me not to tell her where you were, but as it turned out Mallie is teaching in Elkmont. I ran into her by accident when I went down the mountain."

"And she forced you to bring her up here?"

Will shrugged. "You know your sister better than I do," he countered.

"Mallie, why did you come back, I thought you were happy living in Knoxville."

"That's what I wanted you to think," she said with a self-satisfied tone. "The truth is I always meant to come home."

Cole looked around him at the ramshackle cabin. He looked back at Mallie a questioning look on his face.

"To the mountains, Cole." She searched his face for understanding.

He gave her a closed mouth smile and touched her face with his rough hand. They sat in silence looking at each other as though they were unable to believe it was true that they were finally together.

Will cleared his throat. "I'll leave the two of you to talk."

"You don't have to leave Will," Mallie said.

"I've got work to do, Mallie. I'll be back by noon. We'll need to head back down by then."

Mallie's face fell and then she smiled and said, "Thank you, Will."

Will turned and walked out without another word.

"He's a good man," Cole said. Mallie would not meet his gaze and finally he looked away. When a moment had passed, he said, "Are you in love with him?"

"Cole nothing happened between us. I just asked him to stay with me because I . . . I was upset when you didn't come."

"I wouldn't stand in judgment of you."

"I know," she said, turning away from him.

"What's wrong?"

"It's just you can't ask me that," Mallie said, slinging her head until tears came out the corners of her eyes.

"Why does that make you cry?"

She turned to face him. "Because I'm afraid I do love him. I'm afraid I love him the way Pa loved Mama."

"Would that be so bad?"

"That love has nearly destroyed him. It has nearly destroyed us all."

"We're still here," Cole said simply. "I reckon we must be stronger than we know."

"You are Cole," Mallie said. "You are strong and brave..."

Cole chuckled and held up his hand to stop her. "That's just what I would expect my sister to say."

"Maude told me what happened, about the accident. I can't see why you are blaming yourself. Why did you have to run off? When you didn't write, I was so worried."

"I'm sorry, Mallie. Things had been piling up on me for a while. When the accident happened, it just got the better of me."

"Then you lied to me too, in your letters. You said you liked logging."

"I liked it 'cause Pa seemed to think better of me. He can be a hard man to please," Cole said bitterly. "Fact is I don't think I ever did please him."

"Oh, Cole you are wrong," Mallie said.

Cole gave a harsh laugh. "I run off thinking I could do better for myself somewhere else," he said. "That, away from here, I could do as I please."

Mallie smiled at him. "In Knoxville, it just seemed there were more people to tell me how I was to behave."

"I reckon after a while that's why I found myself back here. Now, I've come to like it. I feel like I can be myself up here. I don't have to answer to a soul but me."

"But you can't live here forever," Mallie reasoned.

"I don't think about forever," he said honestly. "I just take it a day at a time."

"Still it makes me sad that you've chosen such a lonely life."

"It only looks lonely. Living around other folks can be more lonesome. Here, I'm part of a world where every plant and animal knows its purpose. They don't get up every morning and question if they're living their lives right and to the best they know how."

"And you do?"

"I have many times in my life, but not now."

"Is that enough for you Cole?"

"It is for now," he said. He realized for the moment he meant the words he spoke. Perhaps, tomorrow the darkness would visit him again and he would find himself running blindly through the woods the madness chasing him. His happiness was always tempered by the fear of the sadness that crept up on him swallowing him whole just when he thought, he had conquered it forever. Of course, he did not say these words to his sister. It would only make her unhappy and he could not bear that. He looked at Mallie, her dark eyes wide and searching. He smiled at her reassuringly. "It's what I want, Mallie."

"All right Cole," Mallie said, doubt in her voice. "As long as this is what you want, but I still think you should come down to Elkmont and live with me."

He kissed her on the forehead. "Well, now I appreciate that and I know in your mind you have it all worked out, but I'm fine right here."

Mallie shrugged her shoulders. "Then let's build a fire and get some breakfast started. I'm starved."

"I've got two squirrels, skinned and cleaned, tied to my pack out back," Cole said.

"Will brought you some supplies, coffee and bacon," Mallie offered.

"Why didn't you say so," Cole said. "The squirrels can wait."

After breakfast, they strolled around the farm reliving childhood memories. The sun was warming up the crisp morning as they headed up the slope to the cave. "The farm looks so small. I remember the cleared land stretching out for miles," Mallie commented.

"It's grown up a might," Cole said. "It was a fight to get it back even then."

"It was hard work wasn't it? I didn't think of it that way when I was young."

"We didn't know no different."

"Do you think they'll be logging up here soon?"

"I suspect."

"What will you do when they come this high?"

He could feel her eyes on him searching his face. "Decide then, I reckon," he said with a shrug.

Instead of going into the split in the rock, they scrambled up and sat on a huge boulder. Mallie stretched out and sunned herself looking up at the sky. "Remember how we used to sneak off up here at night and count falling stars?" she said.

"What was the most we ever counted in a night, fifty?"

"No, more. A hundred," Mallie said excitedly. "The sky was so clear, I thought I could reach up and catch a star as it was falling out of the sky. We were happy then weren't we Cole?" She looked at him to confirm her memories.

"Yes, we were happy then," he conceded, at last unwilling to taint her joy with any melancholy he felt.

They sat in silence enjoying the morning. Mallie pointed to the sky as a red-tailed hawk swooped overhead. "Look Cole, it's a hawk," she said.

"She doesn't like it that we're here. Must have a nest nearby."

Mallie sat up and scanned the sky, hand to her forehead. "She'll soon realize we don't mean her any harm."

"I'm not so sure."

"What do you mean?"

He hesitated. "The accident wasn't the only reason I quit logging." He looked around uncomfortable with what he needed to say. "I just didn't like cutting down the trees. Some of them hundreds of feet tall take half a dozen men to span it. Been growing for a hundred years and we'd cut it down in a day. The truth of what I was doing just seeped into my bones after a time and formed a knot in the pit of my stomach."

"Oh Cole," Mallie said her brow knotted. "I wish I had known."

"By the time we got through working a mountainside, there was not a sapling bigger than my arm left standing," he said, afraid to stop now that he was telling his story. He scanned the skies and waved his hand toward the hawk flying low over their heads. "Where do you think a hawk like that is going to build her nest when the trees are gone?"

"What about the jobs logging has brought here? I've heard Maude and Riley talk about how much better off they are?"

"Are they better off because now they buy what they need at the commissary instead of growing it? What happens if Riley loses his job? When the trees are gone, the lumber company will be gone."

"How long will it take," Mallie asked, "to cut down all the trees?"

"Another ten years, I suspect. Who knows with all the equipment they are bringing in? By then the animals will be gone. The plants will have died off, the ones that need the shade of the trees. Then the rains will have come and washed the whole hillside away, if the fires don't come first burning the slash and the last of the shrubs."

"That's why Will is working so hard to find the plants, isn't it?"

He nodded.

"Can't he stop them from cutting down the trees until he has more time? Until he can show them what they need to do."

Cole laughed. Mallie looked offended. "Not when there is money to be made," he said simply.

"I understand now, why he works so hard. All the way up here he was collecting seeds and writing things down in his journals."

"Will was the one who helped me name what was bothering me. I thought it was just a weakness in me that I couldn't be a logger. You know Pa saw the trees on the farm as a nuisance. We would just girdle'em off and let'em die to clear a field. I reckon that is why he took to it easier than I did. But clearing a field is different from cutting down a whole mountain range."

"Couldn't you have told Pa how you felt?"

He looked at her and he could tell she regretted the question. "Besides I didn't even have the words for what I was feeling."

"Until you met Will?"

"He allowed that everything I was feeling was true. He says there is a better way. He says there are new ideas about forestry, leaving trees behind and not cutting everything, reseeding when the logging is done. Even sometimes setting aside whole forests that can't be touched for nothing."

"I remember him talking about it at dinner at the hotel. There was a man there from the Forestry Service. And I know Pierce was interested in what he had to say."

"Pierce?"

"Mr. Gerard. He's an investor in the lumber company," she said hesitantly.

Cole knew his face registered the surprise he felt. "You had dinner with an investor in the lumber company?" He realized how little he knew of his sister's life and the young woman she had become.

"I met him on the train when I came to Elkmont," she rushed to say. "Those are his horses we rode up. He said I could use them whenever I wanted," she said more slowly. "He's been very kind to me."

"I can see that."

"It's not like that Cole. Pierce is a very kind and intelligent man. He is open to new ideas. I'm sure if you came back and talked to him about what you've been thinking about, you know, not cutting all the trees, reseeding, he would listen."

He waved her off. "I'm done with that Mallie." Hurt showed on Mallie's face and he regretted his harsh manner. "I may not be able to stop them, but I don't have to be a part of it," he said more gently.

"You can't just shut yourself away from everybody, Cole," Mallie said, her voice questioning. "That's no way to live."

"What about you, Mallie?" he asked, to turn the conversation away from him. "Are you happy now? Are you happy teaching school?"

"I like teaching and I love the children but I like earning my keep the most. I like not being beholden."

Cole shook his head. "I reckon that's something we got from Pa."

"Mama too, I think. We get it from both sides."

"Have you seen him?"

"Pa?" she asked, but then before he answered she went on. "He came by Maude and Riley's. Mostly to see Riley. He's been sick."

"Is he bad off?"

"He's better. Pa went all the way to Gatlinburg to get some herbs from Lizzie Melton. Do you remember her?"

Cole squinted trying to remember. "She was a friend of Mama's."

Mallie nodded.

"What did Pa have to say to you?" A shadow passed over Mallie's face making Cole regret his question.

"He thinks he did the best he could by us."

"And what do you think?"

"I don't know anymore. I've been angry with him so long, I don't know any other way to feel. Being up here, I can see where I've been looking at everything through the eyes of a child. I don't know if I have the right to judge him for his struggles."

"Did you get that from Will Stenson?" He could tell Mallie was taken aback by his question.

"Why do you say that?" Mallie said uncrossing her legs.

"Well for one thing, the girl I remember could hold on to a grudge better than anybody. You wore me plumb down many a time and I had to give in to your stubborn, unyielding nature," he said teasingly.

"That is not true, Cole Hamilton." Mallie said throwing her hand to her hip. "Just because I happen to have a mind of my own, does not make me stubborn."

"Besides, that just sounds like him," Cole said ignoring her anger. "I swear that man would forgive a blackguard devil."

"And is that so wrong to forgive, Cole?" Mallie asked, softening. Leaning into him, she put her hand on his arm.

"No, Mallie, it's not wrong to forgive," he said, covering her hand with his. "It's just hard."

16

You take care of yourself, Cole," Mallie said. She kissed his cheek and peered into his eyes. They showed the same mixture of peace and wildness his words had confirmed. "I hope you'll come home soon."

"I am home, for now." Cole said, not unkindly.

"I mean home to be with me," she said, shaking her head. "I can get us a place."

"We'll see," he said, kissing her on the forehead.

She could tell he was mostly humoring her. "It was good to see you," she said holding on to his arm. "I'll be back next week if I can."

"I don't know that I'll be here," he said, putting his hand over hers. "I don't like to stay in one place too long."

He eased her arm from his and backed up. Hurt spread through her limbs and she tried not to tear up. "Well, anyhow, I'll be back."

"You watch out for her, won't you Will?" Cole said.

"You know I'll do my best," Will said, with a nod.

Mallie bristled at Cole's words, but she let it go and gave her brother one last hug. He helped her up on Lady.

"Mallie, it would be best if we could get going," Will said gently, mounting his horse. "Cole, I left what supplies I could at the cabin."

"I thank you kindly, Will," Cole said. With a wave of his hand, he turned and walked away.

Mallie watched him go, expecting that any moment he would change his mind and come back to her. Finally, Will signaled that it was time for them to head back. She rode only a few hundred yards when she stopped. "I forgot to tell Cole, I love him."

"He knows, Mallie."

"No, I have to go back," she said, turning and riding back up the trail. When she entered the clearing, there was no sign of Cole. She rode to the cabin and called out his name, but it was as though he had vanished.

When she met back up with Will on the trail, he smiled at her but said only, "He was gone wasn't he?"

She nodded her head. They rode in silence for a long time. When they came to a stream, Will stopped and helped Mallie down from her horse. "We can stop here for a bite to eat."

He took a cup from his pack and dipped water from the stream. When he had drunk his fill, he brought the cup to her. She drank fast, the water spilling out the sides of her mouth and down her chin. She felt the coldness of it in the back of her throat and down to her stomach. "Ah," she said, wiping her face with her sleeve, "that was good." Will laughed and she could not help but laugh back. "Well, I'm out here in the middle of the woods with a man I hardly know wearing his overalls, it's a little too late to pretend to be a lady, I reckon."

Will laughed heartily and, grabbing her up, twirled her around. "Mallie, you are a treasure, a joy. That is what you are, Mallie, a joy."

When he put her down, he surprised her by kissing her full on the mouth. This time she did not stop him or pull away. "It's your eyes that see the treasure Will. I'm afraid you see more to me than truly exists."

"What I see, Mallie Hamilton, is a rare, undiscovered plant luring me deeper into the mountains and daring me to find you, testing me to see if I am indeed worthy of finding such rare species. Do I have the words to describe what I have found, am I capable of understanding all the adaptations you have made to survive in this environment?"

"Is that what I do Will, test you?" she asked, folding herself into his arms.

"Ah, as though you don't mean to," he teased.

"I really don't," she said solemnly. "If I wanted to fall in love, you would be an easy man to love, Will."

"I believe that's what I have been trying to get you to do since the day we met. I have been trying to get you to love me since the moment I laid eyes on you. And you have tested me at every turn."

She could feel his breathing, his chest rising and falling. Her body began to tremble, tears pooling in her eyes. "Will, I...."

"What is it you fear might happen if you follow your heart?" he whispered into her hair.

"I have seen so much hurt and sorrow come from love," she said honestly.

"It seems to me there's more sorrow in not following your heart."

"Could that be, Will?" she said looking up into his eyes. A strand of his hair had fallen onto his forehead. She brushed it aside with her hand.

He reached up and held onto her hand caressing her fingers with his lips. "I'm certain of it," he said. "What if love turned out to be a gift?"

She felt her resolve weaken.

"Marry me, Mallie and I will show you," Will said.

Slipping her hand from his, she turned and walked to the stream. "The water is so clear." He did not answer her, but she could hear him fumbling with the pack.

"I left most of the supplies with Cole, but I have some venison jerky and dried apples."

"Good, I'm starving," she said, relieved to be talking about something as ordinary as food.

"You are always starving."

"That's the truth if you ever spoke it," she laughed. He handed her some jerky and they sat down by the stream to eat. She stretched her arms behind her head and took a deep breath. The musky smell of rotting leaves filled Mallie's senses and the sound of the stream eased her mind. "Thank you, for bringing me to see Cole," she said at last.

"You would have come on your own at some point," Will said.

"Still, I'm grateful to you."

"Do you feel better now that you've seen him?"

She nodded. "I still wish he would come home to live with me."

"Well, what would life be if we weren't hoping for something all the time." He looked at her his brow furrowed his eyes squinted.

"Is there something wrong?" she asked. He rubbed his hand across the stubble that covered his face. She watched and waited for him to speak.

"May I tell you something very important? It is important to me anyway. I haven't shared it with anyone except a few other scientists." His body tensed, his eyes sparkled with excitement.

"Will are you sure you want to tell me?"

"Yes," he said. "I need to share this with you."

"Please, tell me then."

"My father was a botanist. He died before I was born, here in the Smoky Mountains."

"Oh Will, I'm so sorry."

"I uh, I had access to his papers," he said, "when I was growing up. He had collected and described a number of specimens one of which I believed to be rare if not completely unknown to the outside world. I came here hoping to retrace his steps and find that trillium."

"You found it didn't you?"

He nodded. "I believe that I have indeed found the one he described. In the spring, I collected a specimen and sent it off to a fellow I know at the Herbarium at the University of Tennessee."

"Will how wonderful! You are going to be famous."

"If only it were that simple. Classifying even a single new species is a very arduous process dependent on the aid of many people and sometimes the good will and finances of a great many more."

"Have you told Pierce?" she asked. "I am sure he would help you." She could see him wince.

"I will have to soon enough. Selfishly, I have held on to this as long as I could."

"But why? Wouldn't he be pleased to know you have found something? Isn't that one of the reasons he supports you? I know from his conversation that he has a great interest in plants and in what you are doing."

"I was going to tell him that day at the hotel."

She waited. Will looked away studying the sky. "Why didn't you?"

"I could see that he was in love with you."

Mallie gasped. "Will that's crazy. Pierce is just a friend."

"Pierce Gerard does not have friends. Everyone in his life serves a purpose or he simply brushes them aside and goes on."

"What purpose do I serve, Will?" Mallie asked.

"That's the part that scares me. I think for the first time since my mother, he is actually in love."

"What about Christina? Surely he loved her."

"He admired her."

"He seems so lost without her."

"Oh, they were a perfect match. She was beautiful, gracious, charming. She was the perfect hostess."

"Then you are wrong Will. He could not be in love with me for I am none of those things. I am nothing like Christina."

"Maybe that is why he is in love with you."

"You forget one thing. I am not in love with Pierce Gerard."

"You underestimate him."

"You've told me that before, but he's shown me only kindness. He's never done anything out of turn."

Will shrugged.

"What does telling him about your discovery have to do with me?"

Will hesitated, running his fingers through his hair. "Before you came along, I didn't mind taking money from Pierce. I thought if it served to ease his conscience, so be it. I was only interested in following the dream that I had carried so long."

"I don't understand."

"I don't want to be any more beholden to him."

"You think he will stop funding you if he finds out you are in love with me?"

"No, I think he will stop funding me, if he finds out you are not in love with him, and that you are in love with me. I am hoping you already love me," he said pausing. "I want to give you time to find that out for yourself," he went on. "If I stop taking money from him, then he has nothing to hold over your head. I want you to be free to decide."

"Please don't do this Will. Your discovery is the most important thing in your life. You can't give up the chance you've waited your life for."

"You are the most important thing in my life Mallie. I'll just find another way to fund my work."

Mallie rubbed the crease from her brow. She let out her breath and her shoulders sagged.

"Don't look so glum," Will teased. "The work is going well. Word has come from my friend that he has been unable to locate any such species in his research."

"Is that not good news?"

"It is, but it is only the beginning. Now I must hire other researchers to check a larger number of books to see if anyone might have described the plant here in America or in Europe. To be sure, someone must also search the latest scientific journals."

"You will need money."

"I'll find it Mallie," Will said. "It may take time. Even at best, it's a slow process."

"How long could that take?"

"A year or more," he said with a shrug. "Then if nothing is discovered, I must write up my findings, describing my new species, naming it and, if possible, making an illustration that is wholly recognizable."

"I have seen your illustrations and they are quite remarkable."

"Ah, then if I only had you to please," he said with a warm smile. Then his mood turned more solemn. "I must, however, convince someone in the scientific community to publish my findings so that other botanists might pass judgment on them."

"You can do this Will. I have seen the dedication with which you work."

"There was a time not long after I came here when I doubted myself. I had been walking through the forest for weeks alone. I had lost track of the miles I had walked and I had not met a single human in all that time I had been in the forest."

She had not imagined him so lonely here in the forest he loved, among the plants he studied. She realized that he was by nature, a companionable man who enjoyed the company of others. His passion forced him to sacrifice that part of himself. "You were just weary," she said.

"It is true, I was tired, sore from sleeping on the ground, and sick of eating salt pork, when it started to rain," he said with a wry grin. "My body was shaking with the damp and the cold when I turned my ankle on a rock scrambling for shelter.

Just as I started to take a step, a tree crashed down in front of me. I thought, 'Will you are some kind of fool.'"

"I grew up in a world where men faced such dangers everyday just trying to feed their families," she said, simply stating what she knew to be true.

"If they die doing something so noble surely the world can understand and applaud them. Can the world ever understand a man's obsession to find and put a name to the natural world around him?"

"I understand," she said kindly.

"That is why I had to share it with you. You understand how fragile and tenuous the things are that shape a life."

"That you might have chosen to turn and leave the mountains and your dream at that moment?"

"Yes, indeed, I was at that point. Instead, I took shelter under a limb of that fallen tree. As I sat there contemplating my misery, the rain stopped and the sun came out shining like a beacon down through the dense forest. That was when I spied it not twenty feet away, a trillium in full bloom. I walked over to it and bent down, afraid to touch it for fear I was imagining this perfect flower. It was just as my father had described it in his journals and sketched it out in his drawings. I was overcome by a sudden joy, I can hardly describe to you now."

He looked at her, his body tense and leaning forward. His eyes were pleading with her to understand the meaning of what he was trying to tell her. Mallie wondered how she could find the words he needed to hear. Finally, she said, "Will, your father would have been so pleased."

He smiled and relaxed. "When I looked at it I was struck by how easily it might have been mistaken for a trillium erectum, with its characteristic three leaves radiating from the top of a slender stalk and the usual three petal flower had it not been for the color," Will said excitedly.

Mallie looked at him puzzled.

"A Wake Robin, folks around here call them. It looked like a common Wake Robin, but you see it was not, because down the center of each petal ran a yellow line. Now usually a Wake Robin can be yellow or deep maroon. Sometimes I have seen both colors together in one plant, but never one with a yellow line spreading out from the heart of the petal."

"I've never seen anything like that, either. I have never even heard anyone speak of such a thing. You must have been so excited."

"Time meant nothing to me," he said waving his hand. "I sat sketching and writing in my journal until it was too dark for me to see and then I quickly made camp. The next morning, I woke up thinking I might have dreamed it all, but the trillium was still there. I searched the woods for hours, but found only five more of its kind. I noted them all and finally took my specimen."

Will's eyes were ablaze with a fiery excitement she could only begin to understand. She had always felt great joy from being in the woods. Her mind had always sought the peace that such beauty brought, but Will's excitement charged the air like a thunderstorm. She rubbed her arms to take away the tingle.

Will laughed. "I tell you Mallie, I was drunk for days on my own joy. I could hardly contain myself until I could travel to Knoxville where I had the use of a fine microscope at the Herbarium and I could examine the trillium more closely. It only served to confirm my belief that I was looking at a new species."

"What will you call your new species?" she asked.

"It is customary to name the plant after the person who discovers it, but if I use my name it will be in honor of my father who first discovered it and did not live to claim it."

"That would be kind of you."

"No, he's given me so much and I never even knew him. He brought me here," Will said looking around. "And here is where I met you. That debt could never be repaid."

"Ah we'll see. There may come a time you'll wish him back just so you could take him to task for that."

He came, took her hands, and lifted her up. "I'm willing to take my chances that I will never regret meeting Miss Mallie Hamilton."

"You are a special man Will Stenson. I have never met the likes of you in my life."

"Now you are coming around to my way of thinking," he said teasingly.

"Will it's getting late. Shouldn't we be getting home?"

"I'm so sorry Mallie. I forget the time," he said apologizing.

"It's all right, Will and thank you for sharing your discovery with me."

He kissed her briefly and they quickly gathered up their things. "I brought my clothes," she said. "I can change after we bed down the horses and then I will walk home. I don't think the Combs will be home before dark."

They rode in silence. It was dusk when they reached the stables. Will jumped down quickly and helped Mallie off. "I'll take care of the horses," he said. "You head on home. I need to see Dan and let him know the horses are back safe."

She nodded. "Thank you, Will." She turned to go when she saw the shape of a man framed by the barn door. Pierce stepped out from the shadows and came toward her.

"Mallie, I see you have been riding?" he said, his voice low and steady.

"Pierce, you're back," she said feebly.

"I got in last night. I came early to take you riding, but you had already gone out and without your beautiful riding habit," he said looking her over.

"Will took me," she said, looking down at her overalls stained with mud and smelling of sweat. If the light had been better, he might have seen her blush. Why she had not changed into her skirt and blouse earlier, escaped her.

Will stepped forward to shake Pierce's hand. "I was happy to escort Miss Hamilton," Will said.

"Very kind of you young man," Pierce said dismissively. "I'm sure you won't mind caring for the horses while I see Miss Hamilton home."

Mallie's mouth dropped open and she looked at Will. She wanted to protest but her mouth would not form the words. Will looked directly at her, "I hope you enjoyed your ride today, Miss Hamilton. If you ever need my assistance again, don't hesitate to ask."

"You are too kind, Mr. Stenson," she said, offering her hand.

He shook her hand and held it a moment too long. "Don't forget your things," he said handing her a pack.

"Yes, thank you," she said. She hesitated to leave him, but before she could say another word, Will turned and walked away.

Pierce took her by the elbow and led her away leaving Will to tend to the horses.

17

Men, today we are going to build a schoolhouse," Crockett said proudly. "The company has given you men the day off from logging to build a place for the families to hold church and give the younguns a place to go to school. Colonel Townsend said to see to it that you're paid your regular wages."

A cheer went up from the crowd.

With so many families moving into Fish Camp, the wives had been pressing for a school. Crockett knew that the Colonel's investment of a day's wages would pay off tenfold if it made the wives happy and kept families together. "The building is to be used for a church on Sundays," Crockett said. "I suspect they'll be sending a preacher up this way soon."

The men shuffled about, eager to get to the job at hand. Crockett, wasting no more time with talk, quickly picked the best-qualified men from his crew to lead in building the simple box structure. He had drawn out a plan on paper the night before and he showed it to the men he had selected. The building was to be located behind the commissary along side the main rail line. The sawed lumber and supplies, brought in by train and unloaded, set waiting for the men to be quickly set to task. "We only have a day to get the job done men, so let's show'em what we've got."

The men nodded, asked only a few questions and then went to work. Crockett looked up when he heard the noisy exhaust of the Shay engine and the scream of its whistle. He was surprised to see Riley waving to him from the engine. Crockett could not believe what he was seeing, when his friend hopped down and came walking toward him. Rubbing his hand over his eyes, he shook his head to clear his senses. "Am I seeing a ghost or am I looking at Riley Combs for sure?" he said.

Riley grabbed Crockett's outstretched hand and shook it vigorously. "It's me for sure, Crockett. I'm no ghost, but I come close to it. Thanks to you, I'm standing here before you right now ready to get back to work." He slapped Crockett on the back with his free arm.

Crockett was surprised to see tears gleaming in his friends eyes. "I thought I was a man passed believing in miracles, but I can't deny what I'm looking at."

Riley smiled showing all his teeth and then danced a jig, jumping into the air and landing with a spring in his feet. His once beefy frame had fallen away and he appeared shrunken as though his weight had made him taller, but he moved like a man years younger. "Maude sends her love. She wants you to come as soon as you can. Says she wants to cook you a fine dinner to thank you for getting me outta the house and out from under her feet."

Crockett laughed aloud to see his friend so sprightly. "Well, if you're so fit, quit lollygagging and get to work."

Riley let out a roaring laugh that shook his whole body. "Nothing could please me more."

"Then see Carl over there and he'll put you to work. You picked a fine day to come back. We're not logging today. We're building us a schoolhouse," Crockett said.

"A schoolhouse?" Riley said with surprise. "You seem mighty pleased by that."

"Well, it's good for the camp, I reckon," Crockett muttered. "Now do you want to work or not?" He could not tell his old friend that he knew who the teacher would be or that he had talked to Colonel Townsend personally and asked for Mallie. It had taken some convincing to have her sent to Fish Camp instead of the young man they had recruited, but if he was to have a chance to get his family back, he had to start somewhere.

"I want to work in the worst way," Riley said earnestly.

"Then you best see Carl before the good jobs get away from you. Tell Carl to put you to framing. Don't you try no digging today nor nothing ...." He stopped talking unsure of what he meant to say. He could not be sure Riley heard his words for he was already walking away at a fast stride his arms pumping as he moved.

He thought again about his promise to return to Gatlinburg and tell Martha how Riley made out from drinking her tea. It was not the first time he had thought of Martha in the last weeks. Her face had come to him unbidden many times, her dark eyes looking deep into his face with a kindness that made an ache spring up in his chest. Once he had awakened in the night and realized she had been walking through his dreams. The shame spread through him like a flame and he found himself begging Rebecca to forgive him. Still, thoughts of Martha wandered in and out of his day and each time it was like his feet hitting a familiar path. He shook off his thoughts and reminded himself that it would only be polite to see her again and thank her for all she had done for his friend. Maybe, he would even take Riley with him. Yes, that was what he would do. Wouldn't that prove that it was just an act of gratitude for, what was after all, a miracle? Satisfied, he threw back his shoulders and joined Riley already hard at work.

"It's a letter from Reverend Thomas," Mallie said, standing in the doorway to the kitchen.

"Well, open it," Rose said. She sat at the table helping Maude peel apples for pies.

"Why would he be writing me a letter?" Mallie puzzled.

"We're not likely to know if you don't open it," Rose said impatiently over her shoulder.

Mallie tore off the end of the envelope and poured the letter into her hand. She examined the ornate scrip before her mind took in the words.

"Why Mallie," Maude said. "You are white as frost. Sit down here and tell us what it says."

"They're sending me to Fish Camp to teach school," Mallie said her voice a whisper.

Maude's hand went to her mouth and she let out a gasp. "Honey, are you sure?"

"It says right here that a teacher will be here to replace me in a week's time. I'm to take the train up as soon as he arrives."

"They're sending a man to take your place. Why don't they send him to Fish Camp? Things up there is as sparse as they get in a logging camp. It don't seem right to send no young girl up there."

"The Reverend thinks because my pa is foreman up there, he can act as chaperon for me while I'm there."

"Mallie I just can't stand the thought of having you gone," Rose moaned. "I've got used to having you here. You're like having one of my sisters home with me."

"I don't want to go, Rose," Mallie said, still unable to believe what she had read. "I'm happy here. Besides, I thought the Reverend understood about Pa. At least his wife had heard from Aunt Mae that we didn't get along."

"I thought you had put that behind you Mallie," Maude cautioned.

"That does not mean I'm ready to live with him." Mallie snapped.

Maude looked at her with tight lips. "I'm sorry Maude. I shouldn't have said that as I did. You've been so sweet to me."

Maude patted her hand. "Don't you think no more about it. The news has got you rattled. Do you think if you wrote to the Reverend he would listen to what you had to say?"

Mallie shrugged her shoulders, but she could find no words. After all her years of hoping, she had found a measure of happiness in her life. The thought of giving it up to move to Fish Camp made her stomach turn over. "They're building the school this week. He has already had it announced that I am coming. He says the camp is very excited to have a teacher for the children. They are giving me a boxcar so I can have a place of my own. They never asked me a thing about it."

"Maybe you could ask Mr. Gerard to help you," Rose insisted.

Mallie squirmed at the thought. Pierce's growing interest in her left her uncomfortable. His reaction to seeing her with Will had told her that he might want more from her than friendship. "I have asked enough from Mr. Gerard. I wouldn't want to impose on his kindness."

"Do you think they told your pa?" Rose asked.

"It's not his concern where I go Rose. I can take care of myself," Mallie said throwing her hands to her hips.

"Mallie Hamilton one of these days you are going to fall off that high horse you ride," Rose shot back.

"Girls," Maude said firmly, the way she had done when they were children. Mallie and Rose looked at her with surprise. "Did I ever tell you the story of my friend Arlene?" she asked.

"Mama," Rose protested.

"Rose, honey, you just let me talk," Maude said.

Mallie exchanged a knowing look with Rose. Maude was going to tell one of her stories. Rose gave her a pained expression. Knowing that Maude always took her time when she told one of her stories and that nothing could stop her when she was wound up, Mallie pulled out a chair and sat down. "No Maude you never did?" she said winking at Rose.

"Well Arlene was married to one of meanest men ever walked the earth. From the day they was married he told her that she was to cook pinto beans for him everyday. He didn't want no warmed over beans neither. She was to cook'em fresh everyday. She done just what he said for years. Then before long she had a passel of younguns to take care of and always a baby on her hip. One day she was just so tired she thought she just couldn't cook one more pot of beans. So she warmed over the beans from the day before thinking Joe would never know."

Rose got up and poured them all a cup of coffee. Her mama sat sipping her coffee tracing the patterns in the tablecloth until Rose said, "And did he know?"

Maude looked up. "Did he know what Rose?" she asked.

"Mama, did he know the beans was warmed over?"

"Noticed it right off and with the first bite, he throwed his plate up against the wall. Screamed at poor Arlene and then, he throwed her and the younguns out of the house. 'I told you never to feed me warmed over beans,' is all he said."

Mallie's mouth dropped open. "He threw her out for that?"

"She come to my house a crying and dragging them poor babies. Stayed nearly two weeks with us before she went back."

"She went back," Rose said astonished.

"All men ain't like your daddy, Rose," Maude said. "Why I remember the first meal I every cooked for your daddy. It was just fried potatoes and cornbread, but I burnt the bread. He never said a word just eat around the burn and said it was the finest meal he ever had." Maude chuckled to herself at the memory. "They ain't many men that would do that. Come to think of it, your daddy never complained about a thing, I ever done."

"Mama," Rose said. "Why did she go back if Joe was so mean?"

"The way she seen it, it was her fault. He'd asked her to cook beans fresh for him every day and she hadn't done it. She begged him to take her back and he done it. She's cooked pinto beans everyday since then and I reckon that's been a good twenty-five years ago."

Maude sat back in her chair, her hands clasped over her belly, satisfied with her story. Mallie wondered what any of this had to do with her, but her mind raced ahead to the move to Fish Camp and the possibility of facing her Pa everyday.

"I don't know what that story has to do with Mallie having to move," Rose said.

"Didn't I tell you?" Maude said as though it was all perfectly clear. "Joe died not more than five years after Arlene went back. She kept right on cooking those beans everyday though just like Joe was still there. She never was able to change her ways. Sometimes folks just get in such a habit of seeing things the same way, they're afraid to see it any other way."

"You think I'm stubborn," Mallie said with a chuckle.

"I think you can be willful, but I wouldn't use that word against you the way men sometimes do with a woman who knows her own mind. I'm just saying that change is hard for most folks, but it can turn out to be a good thing." She looked at Mallie and smiled her kind smile.

Will had been telling her the same thing, but she had thought of it as just his way of always looking on the bright side. "I'm just getting to know the children here," Mallie said sadly.

"And in no time, you'll learn the children at Fish Camp," Maude said confidently.

Mallie wanted to believe Maude, but she was still confused. She felt she needed to talk it over with Will, but he had taken off to Knoxville right after their trip up the mountain. He had said nothing about Pierce escorting her home. He had only said that with him gone, she would have a better chance of sorting out her feelings. As though her feelings were, just laundry and she need only be careful not to put her scarlet blouse in with her dainties. She knew, when he came back, he would be expecting an answer to his question.

She had not told Will that Pierce had questioned her endlessly about him. Every time she had tried to tell him about finding Cole, he had brought the conversation back to Will. His questions had been deep and accusing. Finally, he had told her that he was concerned about what people would think about her riding alone with a man such as Will. When she questioned what he meant, he had simply said, 'someone might get the wrong idea. A young woman, a teacher, has to protect her reputation.' What he said was true, still his words had chilled her. Worried about Will, she had said nothing to reproach him.

The more she thought about moving to Fish Camp the more reasonable it seemed. It would give her a chance to get away from Pierce's' attentions. It would give her time to think. Her pa would be working twelve hours a day and in the meantime, she would be higher in the mountains. Somehow, she thought she might see things more clearly there.

In just a few months, she had come from her Aunt Mae's stuffy parlor to earning her own keep and living in the mountains. The thought was exhilarating and frightening. "You are right, Maude. I will get to know the children of Fish Camp. Maybe it will turn out to be the best thing."

The woman who met the train wore a solemn expression. She was thin, her hair pulled back severely. On her hip perched a baby of seven or eight months. Clinging to her dress tail was a girl of about four. When the woman stepped forward, the girl moved with her without letting go.

Mallie sat down her suitcase and walked toward the woman. Her face lit up and she gave Mallie a shy closemouthed smile.

"Miss Hamilton, we are so proud to have you," the woman said nodding. She did not extend her hand to shake.

"I'm very pleased to be here," Mallie said, nodding back at the woman.

"I've come to see you to your place. My name is Nadine Ward. This here is my little girl, Velma and the baby is Chester. Velma is just four, but we've got two boys back at the house that will be going to school. They've not been to school in a while, so they're pretty excited. Most of the younguns in camp is excited to be going to school."

"I'm so glad to hear it," Mallie said. She towered over her by several inches and yet Nadine reached for her suitcase. "Oh no, I can get that. You have the children," Mallie said gently, hoping she had not offended the woman.

"Do you have anything else?" she asked.

"I have my books and a few things on the train."

She waved her hand at the engineer and he nodded back. "Frank will leave them at the commissary for you and my husband will bring them up later."

Mallie wondered how she had conveyed all of this with one wave of her hand. Most of the buildings of Fish Camp clustered around the one flat area around the commissary. A newly constructed box building sat near the store. "Is that the school?" Mallie asked.

Nadine nodded. "When we get you settled in, you can come down and look things over," Nadine said.

Mallie wanted to look at it now, but she had little time to think about it for Nadine took off up the tracks toward a row of boxcar houses. Even with her long legs, Mallie had to walk fast to catch up.

The portable houses had been set off on a passing track within a few feet of the rails. The roofs were slightly slanted and covered with tarpaper. As they walked by, Mallie could see curtains part. Women and children peered at her through the windows.

"This here is Miss Mallie Hamilton," Nadine called out.

Some of the women waved shyly while others flung open the door and boldly stared at her. Nadine called out the women and children's names. Mallie would never remember them all but she spoke politely to each of them. Their eyes followed her up the long walk. When they stopped in front of one of the houses, Nadine motioned for Mallie to go in. The box structure still setting on its pallet and propped on blocks needed three steps to reach the door. She sat down her suitcase, climbed the steps and opened the door.

Fresh starched curtains hung on the windows and in one corner, the bed was covered in a beautiful quilt. "Why Nadine, where did all this come from?" Mallie said with genuine surprise.

"All the womenfolk got it together for you. They all give something. Marcella give the quilt. Ethel and her girls made the curtains. We all give a cup or a plate. Folks give what they could. We wanted you to feel at home," Nadine said, pride in her voice.

"Oh I have to thank them all," Mallie said, her eyes searching the room again. "You'll tell them for me, how pleased I am."

"They'll be happy to hear it," Nadine said.

"Is this all to be mine?" she asked.

"Yes, ma'am," Nadine said.

"But I understood that houses were in short supply here. I thought that anybody that had an extra bed boarded it out."

"But Miss Hamilton, you've come to teach our younguns," Nadine said as though that explained it.

Mallie did not know what to say. "Tell everyone how pleased I am at such kindness," she said.

Nadine blushed. She turned suddenly shy at the praise. "Your pa's place is right next to this one, so you'll be safe. Some of the single men can get rowdy, cussing and fighting, but folks here will look out for you."

The room was warm and she felt a blush rise to her cheeks. A pot sat on stove in the center of the room. She lifted the lid and smelled the delicious aroma.

"The womenfolk thought you'd be needing something to eat."

"Pinto beans," Mallie said.

"Fresh cooked today," Nadine said.

Mallie almost laughed aloud. She could only think of Maude's story. She hoped Nadine took her laugh for the simple pleasure she felt.

She loved the way the men pounced on their food like a hawk on a rabbit. They went after it all elbows and mouths until they finished at least one plateful. Mallie sat along side her pa and Riley, her usual hearty appetite unable to keep pace with the loggers. The clang of forks against plates filled the small room making conversation hopeless, even if the men had been inclined to stop chewing long enough to say anything.

At first, her pa had brought her a plate of food each night knocking softly on her door and handing it to her with hardly a word. One night she had invited him in for coffee. He had sat with the cup to his lips pretending to drink while he watched her up through his lashes. They had talked little that first night and he had left early, but he had come again each time staying a little longer, relaxing more into his chair each time.

One night she had shown up at the house where Grace Field and her husband, Tom, fed eight loggers that included Crockett and Riley. Her pa had been surprised, but Grace had acted as if she had been expecting her, pulling up another chair and setting a plate for her with little more than a nod and a smile.

She offered to pay Grace for her meals, because she knew that, as sweet as the woman was, feeding the men was her way of making a living. Grace told her that her pa had taken care of it. Against Grace's protest, Mallie would help clear the table and sometimes even wash dishes. Grace seemed to enjoy the company and so did Mallie. There was little else for her to do in camp

The men had been polite but reserved around her at first, but soon they were unable to control their good-natured rowdiness and they came to treat her like everyone else. At first they talked little at the table, as was their custom, but she found they could not resist entertaining her with stories. She soon discovered that the truth of the story told was not as important as the entertainment it provided. They could make an evening arguing about the biggest log they had every hauled out or the most rattlesnakes killed in a day. In the time Mallie had been eating with them, the size of the tree had grown to eleven feet across and three thousand board feet from one tree and the number of rattlesnakes was up to twenty.

"If you have a good working buddy, you can come out all right," Hayes Brown, a wry little man who worked saw crew, said continuing his story from the night before. "If'n you don't, it can get you killed in a minute."

He looked right at Mallie and winked as though he was imparting the wisdom of the ages just for her benefit. Mallie learned that despite the harsh conditions many of the loggers enjoyed their work. The daily dangers forced the men to form bonds they found nowhere else.

"Your pappy here is a good man to work with," he went on, "'cause they ain't nothing he can't do nor won't do."

The men at the table heartily agreed. Her pa squirmed uncomfortably in his chair.

"I've seen him shimmy up a tree had to be seventy-five feet to the top," Russ Ellis said proudly, as though it were his own accomplishment of which he spoke. He was a long, lanky man of undetermined age. His front teeth were missing and he looked directly at Mallie and smiled a big mouth smile.

"That was just to save one of you fools from killing your dang selves," Riley spoke up.

"Show her that gash in your head," Hayes said pointing to Crockett.

Her pa did not make a move. She could tell he was trying mightily to tolerate being the center of so much attention. Slowly she reached up, parted his hair, and almost gasped aloud at the ugly, ragged scar that ran the length of the top of his head.

"You remember how you got that don't you Crockett?" Hayes asked.

Crockett nodded but said nothing.

Mallie thought it a foolish question for what man could forget whatever had caused such a gouge. "What happened?" she asked even though she knew Hayes would tell her if she waited.

"He was working with a new man, just a little drip of a boy, really. Crockett was trying to watch out for him and show him what to do at the same time. That weren't an easy job, 'cause this little feller didn't know a thing about logging. He just needed to work. What was that boy's name? I swear, I never thought that name would leave me," Hayes said studying on it.

"Kilby," Crockett said, his voice low. "Kilby McClure."

"Kilby," that's right," Hayes agreed. "He was killed not more'n a year later logging for Ritter over in North Carolina. Tree fell on him."

Hayes said the words so matter-of-factly, it made Mallie realize how much death and injury were a part of the loggers lives. Still she felt sad for a boy lost so young, just trying to make a living.

"Hayes, am I going to have to tell this story or are you going to get on with it," Riley joked.

"I'm a gettin' to it. What's your dang hurry. You got some place else to be. You don't never go to the lounge car no way."

"Bed," Riley said simply.

Mallie knew that after supper most of the men went to another boxcar they referred to as the lounge car. That was where they smoked, drank whiskey and played cards to all hours. Or as Grace Fields had explained it, they 'acted a fool' and she had cautioned Mallie against ever going there.

"The boy was sawing limbs," Hayes said, taking up the story again where he left off, "and one of them must have been bound up 'cause when it let go it struck your pa right in the top of the head. Blood come gushing out, running down his face as fast as he could wipe it off."

"What did you do Pa?" she could not stop herself from asking.

"Went on working," the men chimed in.

"It was near quitting time," Crockett said by way of explanation. "I sewed it up when I got back to camp."

Hayes sat back with a satisfied look on his face; his arms folded in front of him and grinned at Mallie. "Sewed it up hisself," he said finally.

The men nodded all around. Watching the men, Mallie could see the respect they held for her pa. They were men as rugged as the jobs they did, taking each day as it came and yet still impressed by her pa's courage. They respected him and he watched out for them, tolerating their endless practical joking. He was not the man she had known as a small child or even the man who had sent her away. He was someone completely different seen through their eyes. Grudgingly she found she was beginning to like him. The men went on talking, their words slipping in and around her until finally, she said goodnight and went out into the cool night air.

As she walked along the tracks, she realized Maude had been right about one thing, she had quickly come to love the children of Fish Camp. They were glad to be in school and eager to learn. Many of them had never attended school for more than three months each year. They moved often and sometimes lived in places where there was no school for miles. The girls pulled at her skirt, overwhelming her with offers to sweep the floor or clean the blackboard. The young boys took turns keeping the fire going and the lamps filled.

Instead of rushing out to play after school, many of the children would wait for her to finish her work so that they could walk her home. She would stop to talk to the mothers who would pin back fallen strands of hair and straighten their dresses as they saw her coming. She loved talking to the women who worked so hard and seemed not to notice their rugged, dreary surroundings. She was not surprised to learn that many of the families had grown up in and around the Smoky Mountains. They all knew her pa and it pleased them to have a teacher who was one of them.

As much as Mallie loved the people, she could not say the same for Fish Camp. It was the nosiest place she had ever lived. The quiet of the mountains was shattered by the endless stream of trains, loaders, skidders and supply cars that rumbled by rattling the windows. The screech of brakes and the scream of the train whistle tested her nerves everyday.

The weather had turned off cold and at night, the wind howled in and around the ill-fitting roof of her little house. She missed Rose, Maude and their endless chatter.

Will had written to say his work was going well. There was some enthusiasm about his discovery among the botanists at the University. He would need to stay longer to build more support. She missed him more than she cared to admit, even to herself. In the bleakness of Fish Camp, she missed the way he had of making everything magic. It was as though he woke up every morning, to a new world, where ordinary things became delightful. She tried to imagine what a lifetime with Will would be like, but her mind stopped her. Everything seemed possible when Will was with her and she longed to have him there.

When Mallie opened the door to her house, she saw that someone had left her a pie. She was always coming home to find fresh baked bread or fried apple pies wrapped in a clean dishtowel setting on her table. The women had learned that Mallie was not much of a cook and even though they had clucked their tongues and offered to teach her, they soon gave up and simply shared what they had made.

She always thanked the women, but often found herself with more goodies than she could eat. Cutting a large slice of the apple pie, she decided to take it next door to leave on the table for her pa and Riley to find when they got home. They could always put it in their dinner pails for the next day. Grace had told her she could never bake enough pies to fill the men up.

Knocking tentatively on the door, she waited even though she knew that no one was home. When she opened the door, she was pleased to see that it was sparsely furnished but neat. A bed filled each end and a small table with chairs sat in the middle of the room. She set the pie down on the table.

She recognized her pa's shirt hanging on a nail by one of the beds. Walking over to it, she fingered it gently. It gave her an odd feeling thinking that this was where he lived and slept. A shelf above the bed had a tiny lip to keep things from falling off as the trains rattled by daily. On the shelf was a blue cup. Drawn to the cup, she picked it up holding it in her hand gently as though it were a robin's egg. It had once been broken, but someone had carefully glued the pieces back together and she remembered one like this that had belonged to her mama but it had a piece missing. Her mama had loved it and refused to throw it away. If this were the same cup, it would mean that her pa had kept it all these years. It would mean that he had continued to search and finally found the missing piece, she thought. What did it mean to love someone that much, she wondered. The thought made her feel pushed out, excluded by the power of it. She doubted that such a love could leave room for anyone else. Placing the cup carefully back on the shelf, she felt like she had trespassed on a very private place and it shamed her. She picked up the pie leaving no trace that she had been there.

18

Maude, I can't remember when I've eaten such a good meal," Crockett said, patting his stomach.

"Why Crockett it was the last time you eat at my table," Maude teased.

Crockett chuckled. "There's no denying that," he said. He and Mallie had come down from Fish Camp the night before to join the Combs' family the next day for church and Sunday dinner. Crockett could not remember the last time he had been inside a church, but he had a lot to be thankful for and it seemed a place to start. Looking around the table at Mallie, Rose and Riley laughing and talking, he felt like a man let out of prison. He had Mallie back and if she had not completely forgiven him, she seemed at least not so quick to judge him. Having her at Fish Camp had been one of the best things that could ever have happened. He had been worried about having Mallie come to live in such a rough place as Fish Camp. Seeing how she got along with the men, holding her own against their constant joking, how see held up against the harshness of camp life and how the children loved her, gave him a respect for her that he could not have had before. He could see now what a fine woman she had grown up to be, with courage and strength, he knew she had earned during their years apart.

Crockett pushed back from the table. "I hate to leave such fine company, but I promised to see a man about some work."

"It's Sunday," Maude protested.

Riley looked at him puzzled. He had mentioned nothing of his meeting with Pierce Gerard. The call had come yesterday to the commissary. It was a message from Colonel Townsend asking him to meet with the man. Crockett did not know Gerard but he could hardly refuse the Colonel. "Riley, this won't take long," he said. "Thanks for the dinner Maude."

"Pa, who are you meeting?" Mallie asked.

"Just a man, Mallie, I doubt if you know him. I'll be back before dark. We can take a handcar back up the mountain." He put on his hat and walked out without looking back but he could feel Mallie's eyes on his back. He did not mean to worry his daughter but he had been asked not to mention the meeting to anyone.

Walking up toward Jakes Creek, Crockett could see where construction on a number of summer homes had begun. It was a wonder to him how the rich could always get richer. After taking out all the usable timber, the lumber company had been able to sell the land in small parcels to the tourists at a huge profit.

Just east of the Appalachian Club, Crockett could see a man about his age, wearing a black topcoat against the chill air. He stood with hands behind his back gazing at a partially built house. He turned and looked at Crockett, but made no move toward him until he was almost to the man, then he extended his hand slowly and introduced himself.

"Yes, Crockett," the man said shaking his hand. "I'm Pierce Gerard."

"Mr. Gerard, you asked to see me," Crockett said.

"What do you think of my house, Crockett?" Pierce asked waving his arm.

"It's right nice." The house was little more than a foundation with some framework in place.

"Yes, well. I admit it is hard to tell with little more than a foundation completed so far. Let me show you around."

The house backed up to the creek and as they walked around, Pierce pointed out things done and what needed to be done. "You see the porch will span the entire length of the back of the house so it will be possible to sit and listen to the creek in the evening. It will have small windows in the front for privacy and large windows in the back for a view of the mountains. What do you think of the plan?"

"I reckon, I couldn't of planned it better myself."

Pierce laughed aloud, taking Crockett off guard. "Yes, well, I had a little help. I hope to have the house completed by spring," he concluded. "What do you think?"

Not sure, what Gerard expected of him he said, "If you've got good men and the weather don't stand in your way, I reckon you'll have no problem getting it done by then."

"That is why I have asked Colonel Townsend to loan you out. He has agreed to allow you to work as supervisor on the house until it is completed. You can put together any group of men you want for your crew."

"Mr. Gerard, I appreciate the offer, but I'm not a builder. I'm a logger."

"You come highly recommended. Colonel Townsend tells me you are a man of considerable skills. I am sure you will do a fine job."

"Well, thank you kindly, Mr. Gerard, but I'm right happy doing what I'm doing."

"This is far less dangerous work, I assure you. And with winter coming, Elkmont would be a more comfortable place for you than Fish Camp."

"You may be right there," Crockett said noncommittally.

"I am sure that I can find others who would be interested in employing you to build their homes after this one is complete if that is what is worrying you."

Crockett stood idly kicking a rock with the toe of his boot, a nagging in the back of his head. The thought of the work did not bother him. He was curious as to why this man had come to him. He did not really believe that Colonel Townsend had recommended him since he had no experience in building a rich man's house. Something more bothered him, the thought that his life had started to come back together after all this time. He was just beginning to know his daughter and he did not want to do anything to endanger that. "I don't think I am the man for this job, Mr. Gerard. Thank you kindly though," Crockett said at last.

"Is it your daughter you are worried about?" Pierce asked.

"What do you know about my daughter?" Crockett asked, unable to hide the surprise in his voice.

"I understand she was away for some time. She has just recently returned to teach. You asked that she be sent to Fish Camp."

"You seem to know a lot about my family," Crockett said bristling.

Ignoring his remark, Pierce said, "I can arrange to have Mallie sent back to Elkmont."

The shock of his words hit Crockett like a blow. All he could manage to say was, "You called my daughter by her given name."

"She asked me to call her Mallie," Pierce said.

"You've met my daughter?"

"I know her quite well. I took her to lunch at the hotel. I loaned her my horses to ride."

"Did she ask to come back to Elkmont?" Crockett asked hoarsely. He wondered if all this man was saying could be true. He wondered if these last weeks had all been a dream. He wondered if Mallie had been miserable at Fish Camp and only pretending to enjoy her time with him.

"I haven't asked her, but then neither did you. Am I right about that Crockett?"

"That doesn't concern you," Crockett said angrily.

"Maybe you should think of your daughter. I understand that you want to be close to her but, surely, she cannot find living conditions in Fish Camp to her liking after the life she has known for the last few years."

"How do you know so much about her life?" Crockett demanded.

"We are good friends, perhaps, more than friends, if I might say so."

Crockett could not believe what he was hearing. He could not picture his daughter with this arrogant man, but then how well did he really know his daughter, he thought. "Like I said before, I'm going to have to turn down your offer, Mr. Gerard. I think I like the way things are at Fish Camp just fine."

"I'm sorry to hear that Mr. Hamilton. I hope you don't come to regret your decision." Pierce said.

Pierce Gerard scanned the skies as though he had merely said it was a fine day, but Crockett caught the meaning of his words. "I'm tired of regretting things Mr. Gerard. I am tired of doing what other folks tell me is the right thing for me to be doing. That way of thinking has brought me a heap of misery. I've just got to do what I think is right from now on."

"Suit yourself," Pierce said, "but let me give you a piece of advice, I will only make this offer once. You would be wise to think about that."

"Let me give you a piece of advice," Crockett said throwing his shoulders back. "If you've got good sense, and I'm beginning to wonder, you won't make the same mistake I've made."

"And what mistake was that Mr. Hamilton?"

"You won't go deciding for Mallie what's best for her. You'll ask my daughter what she wants." With those words, Crockett turned and walked away. He chuckled to himself. For a man about to lose his job, he had never felt better.

19

Mallie, we best be going," Crockett said as soon as he was in the door.

"Why Pa, it's only three o'clock?" Mallie protested. "I thought we might stay until dark."

"Something's come up," Crockett said without explaining. "Riley, will you be coming along with us?"

"If it's all the same to you, I just as soon stay awhile longer," he said. "Is it something I can help you with?"

Crockett shook is head. "Maude thanks again for the fine dinner."

Rose and Mallie exchanged looks. Mallie got up without another word and said good-bye. They walked away leaving Riley, Maude and Rose standing on the porch with worried looks on their faces.

Mallie did not speak but shot him worried glances until they were out of sight "What's wrong Pa?" she asked.

"I need to tell you something Mallie."

"Does it have anything to do with that man you went to see?"

"In a way it does and then in someway it goes back a long time. To when I sent you away."

Mallie searched his face. "You explained about that Pa and I've come to see where you had your reasons."

"You are a sweet child, Mallie. More than that, you have grown up to be a fine woman. That is why I need to tell you what I've done."

"Why thank you, Pa," she said, concern in her voice. "But what is it Pa that has you so worked up?"

"I didn't ask you what you wanted before I sent you away and that was wrong of me. You was old enough to know your mind. Now, I've gone and done something just as bad, I reckon."

"Please, Pa, tell me," Mallie begged.

He looked at his beautiful daughter knowing what he was about to tell her could turn her against him once more, perhaps forever. "I'm the one had you sent to Fish Camp to teach."

"What!" she yelled. "You went behind my back and had me sent without even asking me. Were you trying to make me hate you?" The color rose in her cheeks and she glared at him. Finally, she stomped away, her fist balled.

"I was trying to get closer to you," Crockett said weakly. "I thought if we spent some time together, you might come to know that your pa ain't such a bad man."

"Could you not have come to me and said those very words? Asked me how I felt about spending more time with you? Maybe I would have agreed to that. Did you have to take it upon yourself once again to know what was best for me?"

"There does seem to be some things I'm slow to catch on to Mallie," Crockett said, disgust in his voice. "Doing the right thing when it comes to you just seems to be one of them, but I have enjoyed having you so close by. The evenings we have spent together has been like having the best of my little girl and the best of her mama all rolled up together."

"You are right about one thing," she said softly, "I was just beginning to like you. I was just beginning to think I could trust you again." She shook her head and tears sprang from the corners of her eyes.

"I know I've hurt you, but I'm trying to make that right. That's why I'm telling you the truth about what I've done."

"Why now? Why tell me now? I might never have found out."

"'Cause I come to see how you might want to be in Elkmont. Life is rough up at Fish Camp and here you have folks you know."

"I have missed Rose and Maude, but I see them now and again." Then her eyes widened with shock. "You don't want me there. You have changed your mind and you don't like having me there," she said the pain in her voice.

"No, Mallie that's not it at all," he said stumbling backwards thrown off by the force of her words. He regained his balance and went to her. Appealing to her understanding, he reached out his hands. "I never want you to think that I don't want you around. These last weeks have been the happiest I've knowed since your mama died. It's you I was thinking about. I thought maybe...well, I come to see that there might be someone special you...somebody in Elkmont you might want to see."

His daughter, turning a deep shade of scarlet said, "You mean, Will?"

"Will?" he asked.

"Will Stenson."

Crockett did not know what to say. He stood puzzling over what to say next. He remembered the young fellow at the Combs' house that night and how Mallie had looked at him, but he had given no further thought and she had never mentioned him.

"You don't mean Will, do you?" she questioned. "Who do you mean?"

"Mr. Gerard," he said at last.

"Pierce Gerard!" Mallie exclaimed.

She looked at him first with shock and then puzzlement. After a few seconds, Crockett nodded.

"Has there been talk?" she asked.

Crockett shrugged. "Not that I've heard."

"Then how do you know Mr. Gerard?" she asked.

"Met him today. He's the man I went to see."

"You went to se Pierce Gerard? What did he want?"

"He wanted me to build a house for him."

"His cottage in Elkmont?" she asked. Not waiting for an answer she asked, "Why did he want you?"

Crockett hesitated rubbing his face with his hand. "Maybe he thought he was doing me a favor, logging being dangerous and all."

"I don't understand. Hundreds of men around here are logging for a living. Why would he be so concerned about you?"

Crockett winced.

Mallie's eyes widened. "Did he mention me?"

"He said he knowed you."

"Don't lie to me Pa. We are past that."

"He said the two of you was friends."

"That isn't all he said, is it?" she said glaring at him.

"He said the two of you had dinner at the hotel," Crockett said slowly, each word like pulling teeth. He could see Mallie puffing up with anger. "And he said he give you the loan of his horses."

Mallie marched up and down in front of him hands on her hips. "All that is true, but what call did he have to tell you that? I have done nothing to be ashamed of Pa."

"I never said you had," he said, "and I never asked him about none of that."

"There's more isn't there," she demanded.

Crockett scuffed his shoe in the mud like a young boy caught doing wrong. "Mallie honey, I never meant to tell you any of this, I just wanted you to know that it was all right if you wanted to come back to Elkmont."

"If I wanted to come back, I would have found a way."

"I know that now, Mallie," he said hesitating.

"Tell me," she demanded.

"He might of already arranged to have you sent back. The way he sees it, the two of you might be more than friends."

"Of all the effrontery," Mallie exploded. "What a prideful, vain peacock of a man. How dare he assume anything about me. If he thinks a meal and the loan of a horse is the price for Mallie Hamilton, he has a thing or two to learn. I am not the ignorant mountain girl he thinks I am. I am not someone to be played with like a chess piece."

"Mallie be careful. He's a rich man. He knows a lot of people."

"You think I've been a fool, don't you?"

"You're nobody's fool, Mallie, but you don't know how the world can be sometimes."

"Why do you think he asked you to work for him?"

"He knows a lot about us, about our family. Maybe he thought it would…" he hesitated, "make you happy."

"Or make me feel more obligated to him," Mallie said mostly to herself. "What did you tell him about the offer of a job?"

"I turned him down."

Mallie smiled, and then her smile faded. "It wasn't an offer was it?"

"I reckon, I better give up poker," he said grinning.

"What did you tell him about me moving back to Elkmont?"

"I told him a smart man would be asking you about that."

Mallie surprised him by throwing her arms around him. "I love you Pa," she whispered.

He hugged her gently, felt her heart racing in her chest, felt his own heart jump. "I love you too, Mallie. I always have."

"Do you have any cash money on you?" she asked abruptly.

Surprised, he pulled her arms loose and looked at her. She put her hands on her hips and waited. He felt in his pockets, pulled out five one-dollar bills, all the money he had and handed them to her.

"Thanks Pa," she said her face somber. "Wait here, I'll be right back."

He watched as she took off walking toward Elkmont. "Where are you going?" he shouted.

"To the Wonderland Hotel," she shouted back, without turning.

"Lord almighty," Crockett gasped and took off after her.

Mallie walked arms pumping, the dollars clasped in her fist. When they got to the station, she turned and said, "I'm the one doing this Pa."

He looked at his daughter and he knew that she was right. She was the one to do what needed doing.

"We could both lose our jobs?" she said searching his face.

"We got by before, we'll get by again."

Crockett watched as his daughter threw back her shoulders and walked up the long flight of steps. He leaned against the station railing arms crossed and waited.

Mallie stopped at the top of the steps to catch her breath, her pulse beating in her throat and roaring in her ears. She steeled herself and opened the door to the hotel. Pierce sat in a chair by the fire drinking coffee. A group of men stood around laughing and talking. "Pierce Gerard," she called out.

He looked up, surprise on his face. His face lighted up with a smile that quickly faded. Jumping up, he walked toward her. "Mallie, I am surprised to see you here. What a pleasure."

He seemed afraid to stop talking. The men by the fire watched out of curiosity, but looked away when she glared at them. Pierce came closer until she stopped him with a look. She clenched her jaw to stop her chattering teeth. "Thank you, but I don't wish to be any more indebted to you, Mr. Gerard."

"Mallie, what's wrong?" he asked quickly

"You once told me that one of the things you liked about me was that I speak my mind."

"That's true," he said, but his voice was questioning.

"Well, this is for the dinner at the hotel," she said throwing the dollars on the floor, "and for the use of your horses."

Pierce's eyes registered shock. "Mallie, what are you doing?"

She glanced over his shoulder. The men at the fire busied themselves with conversation. Pierce shifted on his feet, his jaw working. Mallie smiled to think she was making him uncomfortable. "I'm speaking my mind, Mr. Gerard. You told me that other folks in my life had tried to make me do things I did not want to do. Never knuckle under, you said. Now, I find you are just like the rest of them."

Pierce reached out and took her by the wrist. "You have been talking to your father. Did he tell you he was the one who had you sent to Fish Camp?"

"He told me everything," she hissed. She stared back at him, determined he would not stop her with cruel words.

He shook his head. "You have me wrong, Mallie. I only meant to help."

"Why is it when people mean to help me, they never ask me what I want? I'll tell you how you can help. Don't ever try to buy me or my pa again. You don't have enough money. Don't ever threaten us again. You don't have enough power to make us bend." Pulling loose from his grasp, she spun around slamming the door behind her. She stood gasping for air, her knees trying to fold under her like spindly saplings. When she felt the door open behind her, she whirled around to see Pierce. She backed up putting her hands out to keep him away.

"Mallie let me explain," he begged.

"No, don't explain. You'll just try to justify your actions."

"Mallie, you are behaving like a child. Do you know how much you humiliated me in there?"

She gave him a withering look. "And you are behaving like a father," she snapped. "Yes, I do know how much I humiliated you in there. Do you know how much you have humiliated me for believing you were a nice person who simply wanted to be kind only to discover I had been a fool?"

His shoulders slumped and he sat down in a rocking chair, head in hands. When he looked up at her he looked older, his gray eyes rimmed with dark circles. "Mallie, the truth is...," he said hoarsely.

"The truth," she agreed. "Do you know the truth?" She waited, but Pierce seemed unable to collect his thoughts. Was the truth so difficult for him, she thought. She turned to go just as Pierce spoke.

"After that day I saw you with Will. The day the two of you had been riding, I realized that well, Will is young and handsome and I thought perhaps." He waved his hand, but said nothing more.

Pierce looked at her his eyes pleading. He seemed so uncomfortable with what he was saying she almost asked him to stop. It occurred to her that he was about to tell her that he had cut off Will's funding. "What else have you done?" she demanded.

Instead of answering her, he said, "then you moved to Fish Camp and. . ."

"And...?"

"And I thought I was losing you," he said forlornly.

"You don't have me to lose," she said, incredulous at his words. Her mind raced back over everything she had said to Pierce that might have made him think that she had feelings for him, but her mind was a jumble of thoughts and anger seared through her. "Answer my question, what else have you done. Did you cut off Will's money?" she asked in a rush of words, already knowing the answer. His look told her everything. "How could you?"

"I have the right," he said, his old arrogance coming back.

"I thought you cared about his work."

"There are hundreds of people who could do what he is doing."

"You just don't want *him* to do it."

"It is after all, my money," he said.

"In your world, that justifies everything you do, doesn't it?"

"Yes, it does, Mallie," he said forcefully. "You may not understand this, but in my world it does."

"What did he say?" she asked.

"He didn't seem all that surprised," Pierce said with a shrug.

"He knows you better than I do," she said almost to herself.

"Mallie, he has nothing to offer you. He comes from a poor family. The life he has chosen will never provide you with the security you deserve. Do you really want to live from one handout to another?"

"Whatever life I live will be one of my own choosing. I thought I had made that clear to you."

"Mallie, I love you," he blurted out suddenly. "I am forty-two years old and I have fallen in love. I am not the kind of man who believed that would ever happen." He gave her a wry smile and his face showed puzzlement as though no one could be more surprised.

She almost said 'again you mean', thinking of Will's mother, wondering about Christina, whether he had ever loved her. For once, she held her tongue unwilling to betray what Will had told her. "Pierce, I never led you to believe that we were more than friends."

"I have a lot to offer you, Mallie. I am a wealthy man. You could live the life most women could only imagine."

A sharp breeze blew across the porch and she shuddered and brushed a loosed strand of hair from her face. "I have had opportunities to marry rich men. That is a life I can imagine Pierce, and I want none of that."

"Then imagine the life you do want Mallie and I'll buy it for you."

"I am not one of your business ventures," Mallie said, shocked that he still could not hear her words. "Besides, this time you miscalculated the risk."

"I told you once that I rarely take risk unless it is something I truly want."

"Unless it is truly something you think you can buy," she countered. Pierce looked deeply offended but said nothing.

"This is the life I want," Mallie said with a sweep of her hand toward the mountains. "I want to be free to live my life the way I choose here in the mountains. That is all I have ever wanted. Can you buy that?"

"Don't underestimate me Mallie."

"I won't Pierce. Never again," she said. "But you must never underestimate me. I am a part of these mountains. I am like the tallest peak, the stone core, with all the sandstone and shale washed away and I have survived while all else was worn away." Turning on her heels, her back rigid, she walked down the long flight of steps. With the heat of his stare burning her back, she held her head high, lifting her eyes to the mountains.

20

It was a day full of promise. One of those rare December days in the Smoky Mountains when the sun woke up, peeked through the clouds and smiled. Mallie stopped, turned her face to it, and relished the warmth knowing that by dark it could be snowing. She loved the way the mountains seemed to pluck the passing weather from the sky with such whimsy. The winter had been unusually warm and dry. Storm clouds had gathered off and on through the fall, with ominous chest pounding and flashing fury, only to be ignored by the mountains.

The dry leaves crunched beneath Mallie's feet as she strode up the mountain headed to the farm. The rhododendron leaves, once green and vibrant, were lying brown and curled at her feet as she walked the path. It had been three weeks since her run in with Pierce and she had heard no more from him. Oddly, she had no misgivings about what she had done. She had gone over it from every side and her spirit would not allow for anything else, even though she worried for her pa's sake what Pierce might take upon himself to do now.

Her pa acted as though nothing had happened. He had never mentioned it after that day, when on their trip back up to Fish Camp, she had told him what she had done. He had merely listened and nodded as she relived those few minutes that, at the time, had stretched out like hours. At one point, he had chuckled to himself and she had caught a glint in his eye as thought he might be proud of her. Now, at odd moments she would catch him humming as they sat by the potbellied stove in her house. At times, he seemed lost in thought, but then he would look up at her and smile.

Mallie walked faster, eager to get over the ridgeline past where the men were logging. It was Saturday and all around her, the din of machinery and men at work filled the air. Fallen logs, limbs and slash covered the logged over areas around her, as she walked the narrow path toward Miry Ridge.

As steep as the hillsides were, it was hard to believe the loggers would soon be moving farther up Fish Camp Prong. The men had already started to joke about tying themselves into their beds at night to keep from rolling out and down the mountain in their sleep. As difficult as Fish Camp was for the wives and children of the loggers, she could only imagine life for them perched on even steeper slopes up the mountain.

She would take the same path her pa had taken many times, she had learned, to Dripping Springs Mountain in search of Cole. She had not seen her brother since the ride up the mountain with Will. It worried her that winter was coming on, even if it had been mild so far. At Fish Camp, she had awakened in the morning with tiny flakes sparkling on her quilt where they had drifted in through the cracks during the night and higher up heavy snows had fallen twice.

As she reached the point where the trail took the ridgeline, the woods were open and the wind blew furiously driving the currents up the mountain like a chimney. The winter outline of the trees was gray and higher up the mountain covered in ice. How cold it must be for her brother sleeping alone in a cave or under the shelter of branches, she thought. Despite the bright sun or as though to mock it, the bitter cold clamped onto Mallie like a ghost and howled its sinister warning. She shuddered and her heart fluttered briefly with fear. It is only the wind, she thought, rushing on ahead.

Shaking off the chill, she dropped down off the ridgeline where the fissures in the cliff face sent out its chilly breath. She stopped and faced the cliffs as though demanding to know what message they had for her, but there was nothing, only a sudden stillness.

Heading into the woods, the familiar path soothed her. With the canopy of leaves gone, the woods were light and open. Light snow still lay in the shady spots. Before long, her long stride and pumping arms had warmed her. Under her work jacket, she wore a lighter jacket, a denim shirt and overalls with the legs rolled up. Covering her overalls, she wore a black cotton skirt. In her knapsack, she carried some soda crackers and hoop cheese she had bought at the commissary, along with an extra shirt for Cole. If she could not convince him to come home this time, she would leave him the extra shirt, the overalls and the jacket before heading back down the mountain.

Soon her feet found a rhythm and her mind rested in the peace of the woods. She had another reason for coming to the farm today. Will had sent word from Elkmont the day before that he had come in on the train and he would meet her there by noon.

He had not asked for an answer from her about her feelings, but Mallie had made up her mind as to what she was going to do. It had come to her with a sureness that left no room for doubt. For her whole life, she had known what she wanted but she had forged ahead alone against the wishes of others as they heaved their doubts upon her. When she stood up to Pierce Gerard, she had spoken the truth. She had known all along the direction her life was meant to take and now no one could tell her otherwise.

Mallie lost in thought stepped out into the clearing of the farm before she realized she had come so far. The farm seemed even more overgrown than before, but still the sight stirred memories that were rare and precious. This time she did not mourn the garden overgrown with brambles or the stones falling from the top of the chimney. Nature was simply taking back what they had shared for a while. Her pa had told her that it was not only the poor soil that had made the farm fail but also his own bitterness. After her mama had died, he had been so bitter; his very touch had poisoned the plants. If that were true, the poison had washed away with time and now the land had given birth to stubby evergreens, and blackberries bushes, the hearty survivors of the mountains.

Stopping to collect some sedge from an open field, she planned to use it to make a broom to sweep out the cobwebs in the cabin. As she stepped up on the back porch, the field mice and chipmunks that had found a home there scrambled to safety. "It's all right little ones, you will have your home back soon enough," she said with a smile.

Taking off her extra coat and skirt, she hung them over the back of one of the chairs. She put her knapsack on the floor and surveyed the room. She was not sure why she felt this compulsion to clean the cabin. It made no sense, but the work soothed her. For over an hour, she busied herself cleaning and dusting. She collected firewood and built a small fire to warm the room. Everything she did was overlaid with memories from her childhood, her mama humming songs as she cooked, her pa telling stories at night by the fire.

When she was satisfied the room was as neat as she could make it, she took off to the stream. Washing her face and hands in the freezing water sent a shiver through her that shook loose the last of her worries.

Wishing she had brought a line and some bait, she watched as the trout jumped and sparkled in the pool. There was no time for fishing, she thought, Will would be there soon.

The walk back warmed her. She slipped out of the overalls she wore and took off her work shirt. Underneath she wore her white blouse with the narrow collar edged in lace. Putting on her black skirt, she brushed out the dust with her hand. Not having a mirror, she rubbed her hands lightly over her blouse and skirt checking that everything was in place and hoping she looked nice.

Then she went out to sit on the porch to take down her long hair. She shook her head to loosen the last of the pins combing the cobwebs from her hair with her fingers. Before she could pin it back into place, she looked up to see Will coming toward her. His mouth split into a full-faced smile when he saw her and his arms waved wildly. She jumped up, laughing and waving. Quickly she pulled back her hair and stuck the pins in at random. As she took off running, the pins flew out and her hair tumbled back down her shoulders. Will took off his pack breaking into a run. Meeting him halfway, she threw herself at him in the last few steps. His strong arms folded around her and his fingers entwined in her hair. He kissed her on the mouth and then pulled her face away to look at her. Then before she could speak, he gently kissed her eyes, cheeks, and nose all the while whispering her name. When she could catch her breath she said, "Will, I've missed you so much."

He grinned down at her. "I was hoping that was what this meant."

She laughed, blushing warmly. Fussing with her hair but could find only two pins.

"Leave it down," Will said. "I've never seen your hair down before. It's beautiful."

"Will, what would folks think," she said.

Will looked around as though to say, there was no one there but the two of them. "I would say there isn't a creature here that doesn't envy those beautiful locks."

"Oh, Will," she said, "stop teasing me."

"Never Mallie, never," he said picking her up and twirling her around. "Not until I've teased the seriousness out of you."

She turned her head up to the sun, closed her eyes and let him spin her until Will stumbled and they both fell to the ground laughing. They lay in the grass catching their breaths. Mallie looked up at the dreamy blue sky, crisp and cloudless and felt the earth spin beneath her. Feeling like she was tumbling between the ground and the sky, she reached out and placed her hand on Will's arm. The quiet stillness of the moment surrounded her. She realized how much she wanted to spend an endless procession of days likc this with Will.

"Are you getting cold?" Will asked.

"Yes," she admitted, realizing how foolish they were to be lying on the cold ground. "We had better get up before we catch our death." She jumped up brushing off her skirt and offering her hand to Will. "Let's go to the cabin. I've got a fire going and some dinner for us."

"Dinner is an offer I never refuse," he said, scooping up his pack throwing it over one shoulder as he got up. They walked on and Will stuck out his hand to her. He looked up at the sky and sighed. "Isn't this a glorious day? This is our day, Mallie, our day to enjoy just the two of us."

Mallie took the hand he offered and looked up into his dark eyes. They sparkled with pure delight. There was no sign of what had gone on between him and Pierce or any sign that he was at all worried about the future. She would not be the one to bring it up and spoil the day for him. "Yes, Will, this is a perfect day," she said at last.

"Every day we spend together will be perfect Mallie," Will said confidently. "I promise you that."

"That's the least a girl could expect," she said taking up Will's teasing way.

"The least you say, then I must find more to give you," he said as though pondering the thought. "What if I promise to love you forever?"

"Forever?" she mused, as though she was considering the possibility.

"Beyond forever then," he said growing suddenly expansive. He held his arms to the sky and said, "Throughout eternity." Then he took her chin in his hand and kissed her.

"Will," she whispered overwhelmed by his wholehearted love for her.

"Am I scaring you?"

"A little," she confessed.

"Only a little, then you are coming around," he said with a grin. "Soon you will realize that we were meant to be together and that I will never leave you."

"Don't say that," she gasped. She felt her heart hit against her chest.

"You think that because your mother died and left you that I will too?"

She looked at him stricken by her fears.

"All right, I promise I will never leave you unless someone more interesting comes along," Will said.

Mallie punched Will on the shoulder and marched on ahead. She could hear him moaning in pain, but she refused to turn around. When he came up behind her and kissed her neck, she leaned back into his chest.

"It's going to be fine, Mallie."

"When I'm with you Will, I believe that."

When they reached the cabin, Will said, "It's such a beautiful day, let's take our dinner and walk up to the cave."

Mallie collected the knapsack and they walked up through the farm to the rocks where she and Cole had played as children. They scrambled to the top of the boulders and Will spread his coat out against the chill of the rock. Mallie laid out the soda crackers and hoop cheese. They ate heartily, Will grinning at her with full cheeks. When they had eaten most of the crackers and cheese, Mallie pulled out a surprise. "Maude sent some fried pies by Riley and I saved you one," she said, handing it to him like a prize.

"Maude's fried apple pie. My stomach has been calling out for these since I left Elkmont," he said, eating the pie in two bites. Then he looked at Mallie sheepishly.

"I had my fill of what she sent," she lied.

He nodded, his mouth full, still chewing. When he finished, he fell back on the rock and sighed. "Mallie, I have to be the happiest man who ever lived. I have a full stomach, the warm sun on my face, and the woman I love by my side."

"Well, I can see what is most important to you," she said pretending to be upset.

"Ah, it's not often a man gets a home cooked meal of soda crackers and cheese."

Mallie laughed. "You can look forward to a lifetime of such cooking." Realizing what she had said, Mallie's hand flew to her mouth in surprise.

Will reached for her pulling it away from her mouth and kissing her fingers gently. "That's an offer I don't think I can pass up," he said smiling.

"Are you not worried?" she blurted out before she could stop herself. Will rose up on his elbow and looked at her his brow furrowing.

"I know about Pierce. I know that he stopped giving you the stipend."

"Mallie we both knew that would happen."

"Did you tell him about your discovery?"

"He knows. That is one of the reasons he stopped funding me. He won't have me make a name for myself."

"That's so unfair. Doesn't that make you angry?"

"Why be angry? It is his money, Mallie. He can and will do with it what he pleases."

"What are you going to do now?"

"For now, I am going to enjoy this day," he said simply.

"What about your trillium?"

"Mallie, I have come so far and I have discovered things far greater than I ever imagined. I have to believe that a way exists for me to do what I have dreamed about all my life. I can't believe that a dream that has carried me through worse hardship than this could so easily die."

"Do you not get discouraged?"

He sat up letting go of her hand and putting his arms atop his knees. His eyes grew dark as though his thoughts had drifted far away. When he looked back at her, his face was sad for just a moment and then he was himself again. "I do worry about one thing, that there may not be enough time," he said at last. "Nature is both perfect and fragile. A plant finds its place on earth. A place with just the right soil, the perfect amount of rain and sunlight and there it will prosper. It will grow there in harmony with all the other plants because it has found everything it needs."

"Just like your trillium," she said.

"Yes," he agreed. "It has found its perfect place on earth. In all my searching I have found it only in that one small cove on the side of a mountain." He looked at her with wonder in his eyes.

Suddenly she realized what he was trying to tell her. "And if that place changes, it may not survive."

"Yes," he nodded. "If they log the trees, it will die."

"Will, what can we do?"

"You and I may not be able to do enough to save the plants that have found a home here," he said simply. "It's going to take powerful people to save the trees, people with money and influence."

People like Pierce Gerard she thought, but said nothing. She slumped down folding her hands into her laps, and then she popped back up excitedly. "Cole said that there were people interested in saving the trees. You told him about just such people."

"There has been talk about a national forest."

"What would that mean?"

"It would mean the trees would be more protected. If the trees were logged, there would be rules to be followed, like not taking all the trees and replanting."

"Would it save the plants?"

He shrugged. "You know there are places so beautiful in this country, they have been set aside to be preserved forever."

She sensed something more in his words. He had given a lot of thought to what he was saying. "These mountains are as beautiful," she pointed out.

"Very few people know anything about the Smoky Mountains, Mallie, and many of those who do, see them as a nuisance. I talk to the local businessmen in Knoxville and all they want is a road through the mountains to connect to North Carolina. They have commerce on their minds. If they could, they would level these mountains."

Mallie knew the shock of his words showed on her face, but she said nothing. He jumped up and walked around as though suddenly filled with more energy than he could contain. She watched as he walked to the edge of the boulder and looked out over the valley. The sun had burned through the blue haze leaving only the faded colors of a dying autumn.

"Two years ago the United States government made Glacier Montana a National Park," Will said. "There are eight other national parks. Now, that land can never be changed or destroyed."

"That's what you want, isn't it Will? You want the Smoky Mountains to be a National Park."

"That would be my dream, Mallie."

"Then that is my dream too, Will," she said solemnly. "We need all of this to never be changed or destroyed," she said looking out over the valley.

Laughing aloud, Will stood up and pulled her up by the hand. "How can we be denied then, two such wise and noble people?"

"We'll find a way," she said, hoping she sounded more lighthearted than she felt and wanting more than anything for her words to be true.

"Spend the night Mallie," Will said, his back to her as he put wood on the fire.

Mallie did not answer but busied herself setting out the coffee and other things she had brought for Cole. After dinner on the ridge, they had drifted down the trail to the cabin wrapped in contentment enjoying the cool, thin air of winter. They had stopped to admire the gray-green of lichens on the boulders, to listen to the scolding of a squirrel displeased by their presence and to catch the occasional scent of balsam in the air.

"You'll want to see Cole," he added when she did not speak. "Are you afraid your pa will worry?"

"He knows I came up to see Cole," she said, her cheeks turning warm. She had not mentioned meeting Will. "And he knows I can take care of myself." Since that day she had confronted Pierce, her pa treated her differently with a kind of prideful admiration most men reserved for their sons. There was another reason she hesitated to answer. Will had assumed that from the moment he saw her sitting on the porch waiting for him that she loved him. That she had come to tell him just that. If she stayed, it would mean he was right. When she turned, he was standing looking at her. He put out his arms and she walked into them.

"Mallie I want us to be together. I have loved you from the day I first heard your name. From the first time I saw you, I knew I loved you. Marry me Mallie," he whispered into her hair.

"Will how are we to live? You have your work. I can't leave the mountains again," she said fervently.

"I will be wherever you are. This is your place on earth Mallie. These mountains are a part of you. I could never take you away from here."

"Will I do love you," Mallie said. Thinking of her mama who had left her family to be with a man she hardly knew but loved beyond reason, she understood at last the love they shared. She relaxed into Will's chest. Her hand tingled, the skin burning as she reached to touch his face.

He kissed her softly on the lips. His fingers caressed the nape of her neck as he kissed her again. "Don't worry about anything, Mallie. We will live like the flowers. Every day when the sun comes up we will lift our heads in joy. We will give no thought to how we are to live, for together we will have all we need."

He lifted her in his arms and she clung to him. For once, she gave no thought to tomorrow, but let herself feel the warmth of him, the joy of love and the hope of thousands of such days ahead.

21

As soon as Crockett raised his hand to knock, the door flung open. Martha's radiant smile greeted him. He smiled back nervously.

"I've been expecting you," she said.

Crockett felt his fate turn on those simple words. The blood rushed around his head and then headed to the pit of his stomach. He had to plant his feet wide apart on the porch to steady himself. "I've come to tell you about Riley," he finally managed to stammer.

"Come on in, dinner is ready."

Crockett followed her toward the kitchen, but stopped short when he heard voices. She turned to look at him, once again smiling. "I reckon, you've got company, I might ort to come back later."

"It's just my brother and his wife come to Sunday dinner. Come on in, I have told them about you. They want to meet you."

He was both surprised and pleased to learn that she had told her family about him. He had been curious to know if she had given as much thought to him since they had last met as he had given her. It was a wonder that she could know anything about him to tell her family after their brief meeting, but then he felt that he knew her too.

"Mama, its Crockett come to see us again," Martha said as they entered the kitchen.

"Martha's been a looking for you," Lizzie said. "Your friend is better ain't he?"

He could see the color rise in Martha's cheeks. He had to clear his throat before he could speak. "Yes ma'am. Fit as a fiddle. He's right proud of all you done for him. Would of come hisself, but his son has a new baby and they took off to

Wears Cove to see it. He wanted me to thank you." That was not the whole truth. Crockett had told no one he was coming to Gatlinburg, for he wanted to see Martha on his own. He had never shared his feelings about Martha even with Riley for it was too close to the bone. Besides, he was a little embarrassed by such an unexpected turn of events in an old man's life.

"No need to thank me," Lizzie said with a small wave of her hand. "When you're old and blind, it's good to be of use to somebody."

Before Crockett could protest, Martha said, "Crockett, this is my brother, Cordell and his wife, Katie."

Cordell stood up to shake Crockett's hand. He was not a tall man, but broad shouldered and lean from hard work. He flashed a friendly smile and Crockett could see some of Martha's kindness in his face. "Good to meet you," Crockett said. His wife looked much younger than he did. She nodded shyly and he nodded back politely. He noticed for the first time that she had a small baby asleep in her arms.

Martha motioned for him to sit down next to Lizzie. He took his seat and she sat down next to him. The family bowed their heads without a word and Cordell said a prayer of thanks. Crockett could tell this was their custom and they had done this hundreds of times before. The sight made him long to have his family around him. He wanted to look up and see Mallie and Cole sitting across the table laughing and teasing each other as they had done as children. Moreover, for the first time, the other face he pictured at the table was not Rebecca's but Martha. It surprised him that he felt no shame in that. Somehow, he felt Rebecca would approve, that she had a hand in bringing him here.

The table was laden with bowls of food and Martha passed one after the other to Crockett until his plate was overflowing. He ate heartily as was his custom. When he looked up, he was relieved to see that the rest of the family enjoying their meal. Martha got up several times without a word and filled everyone's glasses with fresh milk. When Crockett felt himself growing full, he rested.

"Martha tells me you are a logger," Cordell said, holding his fork upright resting it for the moment, ready to resume eating any time.

"I've logged most of the East Fork of the Little River, Jakes Creek and now Fish Camp."

"Do you like logging?" Martha asked.

"It's a living," he replied truthfully.

"I know what you mean," Cordell said. "I used to work at the tannery in Walland some time back. That was a hard way to make a living, but I was younger then."

"They's some things a man don't want to do more than once in his life," Crockett said sympathetically.

"Still, it was a living. My first wife did not care for living in Walland. Her people had always lived in Maryville. She was accustomed to more than I could give her. When she died giving birth to our daughter and then the baby died a week later, I moved back up here."

He had said the words without any pity. It was just a fact of his life that he had lost a wife and child. Crockett felt ashamed of himself for the grief he had carried so long. By doing so, he had taught his younguns not to forget or forgive and never trust life.

"I farm a little," Cordell went on, "and do some scouting for folks coming up from Knoxville to hunt and fish."

"That sounds like a good life."

"It suits me. I like to be outside. I never was much for schooling. Martha here is the smart one of the family." He looked at his sister with the same teasing look brothers reserved for sisters. "Besides, it don't take much for us," Cordell said tilting his head toward his wife. "Katie's folks own a big farm over in Cades Cove. I help'em out when I can. They do right well with it."

He looked at his wife with such delight Crockett had to look away. "I miss farming now and again," Crockett surprised himself by saying.

Martha took his plate and replaced it with a large slice of apple pie. She poured him a cup of coffee before sitting back down. "You should go back to it," Martha said softly.

He did not know what to say. If you had asked him before today, he would have said he hated farming. Digging into his pie to cover his consternation, he said, "This is good pie."

"Martha made it," Cordell teased. "She's a good hand at most anything she puts her mind to. You know she teaches at the new school."

Crockett turned to Martha, his mouth full, and tried to swallow so he could ask her about her job. Seeing his distress, she put her hand on his arm and laughed a trilling laugh. It was the sound of a robin announcing spring. His arm burned where her hand had been. Glancing down, he looked, foolishly, to see if it had left a mark on his shirt.

"I don't teach the children. I teach weaving. The Pi Beta Phi sorority started a school here for the children, but they have cottages where the local craftsman can sell their work to tourists."

"I'd like to see it sometime," Crockett said. "I'd like to see your weaving."

"You men go on out to the porch and smoke," Lizzie said dismissing them. "Martha will clean up."

Crockett looked to Martha.

"Don't argue with Mama," she said sweetly. "I'll be out later. I want to show you around the place. And don't let Cordell get to you neither. He thinks he's my keeper."

He obediently joined Cordell on the porch where he was already rolling a cigarette. Crockett sat down in a rocking chair next to him.

"You like that chair?" he asked.

"It's right nice. Sets good."

"I made it."

"You done a good job."

"My mama and sister like to sit out here in the evenings. I like for them to have a good place to sit. They ain't neither one had an easy life. I like to think they are happy here."

He could tell that Cordell was protective of his sister even though he was the younger brother. "I don't mean your sister no harm. She done something good for me and I just come to tell her so."

"Martha has taken a liking to you. She likes most folks, but I can see where she thinks more of you than most."

"Martha is a fine woman," Crockett said. It was taking all his nerve to stay in his seat and not flee.

"Fine as they make," Cordell said drawing out his words. "Her first husband beat her," he said more quickly. "Worked her like a dog. She ain't had much interest in men since he died ten year ago. You can understand that, can't you?"

"I reckon I can." He found he was angry with a man he had never met dead ten years now.

"I kind of watch out for Martha. I wouldn't want to see her hurt."

"It won't come from me," Crockett said sincerely.

He could see Cordell relax and lean back in his chair to smoke. "No offense just had to be said, is all."

"None taken," Crockett said. He looked back over his life at all the times he had taken offense at someone's words. At times, he had jumped men for little more than a look. He wondered why what Cordell said or the way he looked him over did not bother him. Maybe it was because he did not want to spoil his chances with Martha who had asked so sweetly for his patience. He could hear the women in the kitchen talking and laughing amidst the clatter of crockery. Martha's words, uttered low from her throat, stood out among the women as it worked its way to him. He knew that he wanted to hear that voice again and it pleased him that he was not so weakened by disappointment that he could not hope for more.

Suddenly, Martha came out of the door, a brightly woven shawl around her shoulders. "Crockett," she said.

He jumped up to greet her. She walked off the porch and down the steps without a look back. He joined her without a look back at Cordell, whom he heard chuckling in the background.

"Don't put too much stock in Cordell," Martha said. "I used to have to wipe his snotty nose when he was too little to do it hisself."

Crockett laughed. "It don't hurt to have somebody looking out for you."

"I try to take care of myself mostly," she said searching his face.

"I've done the same."

"It gets lonesome," she said plainly.

He nodded, not meeting her eyes. He liked the simple way she had of stating her feelings and he told her so. Slowly they walked around the farm. She showed him the vegetable garden, and her chicken house and where she grew many of the herbs she had given him. She told him about how she spent her days weaving. The school, she told him, had allowed her to sell her blankets and shawls giving her cash money of her own. She laughed when she told him of how she had lived so long without money; she had put most of it in a jar and hidden it away unable to think of anything she wanted. She described a simple, peaceful life that Crockett envied. He wondered what he had to offer that she would be willing to trade such a life. Deciding he had nothing to give her but the longings of an old man, he decided to cut his visit short and head back over the mountain before he made a bigger fool of himself. Turning to tell her he would be going now, she surprised him by taking his hand and leading him to the barn.

Once inside she made him stand still. Out of the shadows came a gray and white cat. It rubbed against her skirt tail and she bent to pick it up. "She won't come to nobody but me," she whispered. "The others swear they've never seen her cause she hides out, but she comes to me." Martha sat the cat back down, pulled a hunk of cornbread from her pocket, and put it on the ground next to the cat. She gazed at the cat eating. "It's a good sign she'll come out when you're here."

"Do you believe in signs, Martha?"

"I do Crockett," she said earnestly.

"I don't know that I've been too good at reading signs in my life. If I'd been a little better at it, I might not have took so many wrong turns." Then without meaning to, he started to tell her about how he felt responsible for Rebecca's death and how his grief and bitterness had driven his younguns away. The guilt he felt over not doing right by them.

"Why Crockett," she said taking his hands in hers. "That's just life, there are good times and then there's hardship. You can't let one outweigh the other."

Could life be as simple as that, he thought. Being here with her, he could feel the rightness of her words. Martha walked out of the barn and strolled easily along a footpath that led to an orchard. Crockett followed her watching the sure way her feet met the path, the rise and fall of her hips beneath her skirt. When she reached a springhouse at the edge of the orchard, she stopped. He watched as she bent down, cupped her hand into the water and drank. When she looked up water dripped from her chin. Laughing she wiped her face with the back of her hand. He had never known anyone so at ease. "Cordell told me you ain't had an easy life."

"He prides hisself too much on looking out for me," she said with a crooked smile.

"How was it that all that didn't take you down?"

"I just always knew a change would come. I always feel like hard times is like the seasons. In the darkest times of winter, I always know spring is just around the corner."

"You're happy now, living here?" he asked.

"I have been," she replied and waited.

He stubbed his toe into the ground and searched the sky. "I don't reckon you'd be willing to risk all that on the likes of me," he blurted out.

She stood up and searched his face. "I've felt a change was coming," she said.

"I'm a pretty rough fellow. I have lived most of my life in the mountains and I've spent the last six years in one logging camp after another. That ain't much to offer a woman."

"Myles Clark, that was my first husband's name," she said.

He watched as she shivered and pulled the shawl tighter around her shoulders. "Can't say as I ever knowed of a Myles Clark," he said by way of conversation unsure of what was expected of him.

"He come from off somewhere else," she said with a wave of her hand. "I never loved him," she confessed. "I married him because I was older than most and I thought I could come to love him. He was not bad to look at and had money when we first married. I wanted to love him more than anything, but I just couldn't see my way clear to do it."

"Was he never good to you?"

"In the beginning, he could be kind. Trouble was, he wasn't cut out to be a farmer. It wasn't the life he pictured it to be. The more he failed at it, the more he took to drink and the meaner he got."

"Why didn't he just try his hand at something else?"

"He never said, but I got the feeling he'd tried most everything else."

"That can be hard on a man."

She looked at him, a sadness suddenly filling her dark eyes. "He wanted a family and as the years went by and I couldn't give him one, I think it made him hate me. I think when he looked at me; he saw everything that was wrong with his life in my eyes."

"What happened to him?"

"Drunk hisself to death."

"I'm sorry to hear it," he said honestly. "I'm sorry for him and I'm sorry for your suffering."

"I only told you that because I need you to understand something," she said matter-of-factly.

"What is it Martha?" he asked.

"You had a great love in Rebecca," she said.

"That I did. They's no denying that," he agreed.

"I've never had that Crockett, but I believe I could have that in you."

Crockett rubbed his hand over the stubble on his face and through his course red hair. "I admit I'm more than little surprised to hear them words come out of your mouth," he said.

"I'd rather hear you say it now, Crockett, if you're not interested in me," she said without pity.

"I couldn't be more pleased by such a pleasant turn of events, Martha," he said his face opening wide into a smile.

"Then I expect you'll be coming round pretty regular," she said taking his arm and leading him back toward the house.

He nodded.

"If you don't change your mind before then, I reckon we can marry in the spring."

"That would suit me just fine," he said. They strolled back toward the house, arm-in-arm talking like two people who had always known each other.

22

Feeling warm arms slip from around her, Mallie tried to come up from the depths of sleep. Briefly, she opened her eyes as her mind ran back through her memory trying to place where she might be. The room was oddly light, although she thought it must still be nighttime and the walls around her seemed strange but familiar. Then she remembered that she had spent the night with Will in her old family cabin. The realization brought her wide awake as she remembered how they had talked half the night about their future. She had agreed to marry Will Stenson in the spring. They would find a place here in the mountains to live where Mallie could teach and Will could continue his work. Life, she thought, had given her a gift of happiness she had not been expecting. Smiling to herself, Mallie stretched her limbs and sat up.

The smell of wood smoke still filled the room even though the fire had gone out some time in the night. The wind had howled up the mountain all night blowing down through the old chimney and the chinks in the cabin.

Will, she decided must have gone to collect more firewood. While she waited for him, she folded the blanket they had used for a bed. Smoothing the folds with her hand, she held the rough wool to her face and smelled his scent surprised again by the pleasure it gave her. Placing the blanket gently over the chair, she combed her hair with her fingers and straightened her clothes. When she had done all she could think to do and Will had not come back, she began to worry. Finally, she went to the front door and opened it. She was surprised to see Will leaning against the porch railing. He wore a serious look that was unlike him. She wondered if he had come to regret any of the night before, but then he turned to her and opened his arms.

She walked into them and relaxed into his strong embrace. Relief flooded through her. "I was worried. I woke up and you were gone."

"I'm right here," he said gently. "Did you sleep well?" he asked.

She nodded. "I thought I wouldn't sleep at all with the wind howling so, but I dropped off during the night."

"You were sleeping soundly when I got up," he teased.

"You'll soon discover I'm a girl who can fall asleep most anyplace."

"But most easily in the arms of the man you love, I hope," he said smiling down at her.

She should have blushed at the boldness of his words, but instead she felt the truth of what he said. "I can't deny it," she said and reached to caress his face. "You are the man I love and I will always."

"Mallie I am so happy," he said sighing contentedly. "Our life together will be a great adventure."

"I believe you Will," she said and thought dreamily of the days ahead. "Now, what is the man I love doing up so early? It's hardly daylight."

"It isn't daylight, Mallie," he said his brow furrowed.

"What do you mean?" she asked. "I can see the sun coming up."

"That's fire," he said pointing over the ridge toward Fish Camp.

"Fire," she said incredulously. "That's what's lighting up the sky. That's why I smelled smoke."

"It must have started yesterday and the wind whipped it up during the night."

"Pa," she gasped. Fire was something about which her pa always worried. With the trains coming and going each day sending out cinders along the way and skidders setup along side fallen trees, limbs and debris, he had a right to worry. He was always searching the skies for any sign of smoke and now, his fears had come true, Mallie thought.

"He'll be fine. I'm sure they've had time to get the families out."

"Do you think they'll stay and try to fight it?"

"I don't think there is much they can do at this point. It is so dry and there is so much slash on the ground. It's probably spreading way too fast."

"Could it reach us here?"

"It's still pretty far away and it appears to be going up the valley. The wind has died down for now so it should have slowed some."

Will spoke calmly, his words meant to be reassuring, but Mallie wondered if he could really know. "What should we do Will?"

"I think we will be fine but I had better take you back down over Jakes Gap. Pack only what you need and leave the rest. Put on those overalls, you can travel better. We'll go as soon as there's a little more light."

"What about Cole?"

"Cole is a smart man and he's worked as a logger. He wouldn't go anywhere near a forest fire," Will said firmly. "Stop worrying, now and get ready," he said more gently.

"I'm sure you're right," she said giving in to his urgings. She paused to give him a kiss. He put his hand on her head and stroked her hair. She turned to go inside, but not before she saw him looking out over the valley, his eyes dark and shadowed with worry.

They were making good time as they headed down toward Jakes Gap. Even though the sun had come up, the dark smoke blocked out the light and the air was becoming warm and thick making Mallie feel that the fire was uncomfortably near. Her eyes stung from the smoke and she wiped them with the back of her hand. She stopped when she saw Will looking back at her.

He smiled at her reassuringly. "Do you need to rest?"

Shaking her head, she said, "We need to keep going." In the time they had been walking, they had watched the fire come over the ridge spreading like a wall of flame as it spread from tree to tree.

"I think the fire is still moving mostly up. I think we are still safer going down as long as…."

"As long as what?" she asked.

"As long as there is no wind," he said simply.

"We've been lucky so far," she said encouragingly. "Do you think anybody is out looking for us?"

"I wouldn't want anybody out risking their lives to try to find us, but Rose was home when I left. She knows where I was going."

"Do you think she knows I'm here?"

He smiled. "She guessed. It was not too hard to pick up on how I feel about you. She seemed pleased."

"I hope she wasn't hurt that I hadn't shared it with her, but it just seemed like it was too close."

"Rose is a good friend Mallie. She'll be happy if you are happy."

"I know you are right about that. I can't wait to get back and tell her the news," she said cheerfully, as though they were just walking back from church. She realized they were talking about ordinary things to take their minds off trying to outrun a fire. Suddenly, Mallie had a terrible thought. "You don't think the fire could have spread to Elkmont, do you?"

"I don't think so, Mallie. I think it started higher up the mountain probably where they were logging. Even if it has spread, they'd have time to get out."

"Will I just thought of something. You left your pack at the cabin. What about your journals and sketches, you didn't leave them in your pack at the cabin did you?"

"No, I left them at the Combs' place. I'm sure someone there would think to take them if they have to get out."

"I hope so Will," she fretted. "It would be such a waste of all your hard work."

"Then we would have to start over again, together. I could teach you to sketch."

"That might be a lot like teaching a mule to dance," she said honestly, for she had never shown a talent for anything that required such patience.

Will laughed and then stopped abruptly as the wind started to swirl around them. They looked at each other and Mallie could see the look of fear in Will's eyes. Then it came up with a fury sweeping mercilessly up the valley driving the red-hot flames in searing blasts across the narrow gorge. It was their worst fear roaring to life. The wind had shifted in their direction. Like branding irons, the falling limbs carried sparks to new trees. As if by magic, the quiet around them was replaced by the terrible sound of hissing, roaring flames and the crashing of timber. Fire was rushing toward them from down below and incandescent flames licked at the sky. The heat became intolerable. "The wind," Will yelled as he grabbed her hand just as the valley below them ignited.

They ran back up the mountain the fire coming on fast casting shadows over their backs. Will was yelling at her but she could hardly hear him for the sound of the fire roaring down on them like an out of control train. Trees were crashing all around sending showers of sparks high into the sky. Mallie gagged on the smoke and fell to the ground. Will picked her up and pushed her on toward the top. Her heart was beating out of her chest and she thought she might faint when a hand reached out from above her. Blinded by the smoke, she took it without thinking and it pulled her along. She called out to Will but her voice was lost in a world on fire. The flames were scorching the back of her clothes as she was thrown full force into the stream. Someone jumped in on top of her in the freezing water as the flames passed over them. Mallie held her breath for as long as she could and then pushed up against the body on top of her to catch quick gulps of air. Each time she could feel the heat of the fire before she went back down. Finally, after what seemed like hours, the body lifted off her and she sat up choking and gasping for air. As the smoke cleared, she could see the stream was covered in ashes. She looked up to see the face of her brother, Cole standing above her. He reached out his hand and lifted her up. "Cole," she said hoarsely, "it was you."

"Mallie are you all right?"

"I think I am," she said hoarsely, her throat raw from the smoke. Her body shook uncontrollably from the fear that was just now gripping her. "But look at you. Your hands are burned and your hair is gone."

Mallie watched as Cole touched the top of his head. The flames had burned off his hair as he lay covering his sister in the water. "We could have been boiled alive," Cole said.

"Oh Cole," Mallie moaned. "I'm so sorry. You risked your life to save me." She went to him and put her arms around him feeling where the fire had burned through the back of his clothes and into his skin. "Where's Will?" she cried out suddenly as realization hit her that he was not there with her. "He was right behind me."

"He probably jumped in downstream from us. It is still plenty hot out there. Wherever he went in, he may have to wait it out a while. We'll wait here a while and then I'll go look for him."

"I'll go with you," she said firmly. Cole looked at her and said nothing. They both looked out over the devastation. The power of what they were seeing showed on their faces. The gray green forest of hours ago was gone. In its wake, the blinding heat and crackling flames had left a mass of charred wreckage. Fallen logs still smoldered all around them and the valley was devoid of anything green. The sight of so much horror brought back the clawing fear of the last hours. Mallie fought back her tears. Her concern now was for Will. She called out his name over and over her voice a harsh, raspy sound. Cole took up her cry when she could no longer make a sound. She bent down to the stream and brushed the ashes away with her hand. When she cupped her hand to drink, she felt Cole's hand on her arm.

"Mallie, don't drink that water," he said gently. "If it's run through a lot of ashes from upstream, it could have lye in it."

She opened her hand and let the water run out. "It'll kill the fish then won't it?"

"More than likely," Cole said.

She stood up, a sudden resolve filling her. "I can't wait any longer, Cole. I have to go look for Will. He could be hurt."

He did not try to stop her. "Stay close and watch yourself," he said. "You take to the creek and I'll walk out a ways and come back to you."

Their progress was painfully slow. All around them were burning stumps and hot ashes, and fallen trees blocking the path. They picked their way carefully back down the mountain. Mallie worked her way as close to the creek as she could get, climbing down banks and over boulders. At the bottom of the ravine, she spotted something. It looked like a body, still and broken on the rocks and her heart caught in her throat. As she struggled to get down the bank, she could see that it was a deer, legs broken, eyes still wide with fear. It had fallen down the bank running in terror from the fire. She wondered how many more animals had died in the flaming wall that had passed over them, but she wasted only a moment on the thought before scrambling back up the bank. Her hands were black and burned from the heat. Blisters were forming on her palms and she could feel the heat of the ground through the soles of her shoes. Still she pressed on desperate to find Will. She knew that he was somewhere hurt and waiting on her to find him. Just as he had pushed her on up the mountain to Cole's waiting hand, she would find him now and save him.

When she first saw Cole kneeling by a fallen log she did not recognize him with his blackened face and scorched hair. He looked up to see her staring at him. When she started toward him, he held up his hand to stop her. It was then she saw the tears in his eyes and her heart stopped. "Will!" she screamed as she took off running.

Cole met her halfway trapping her in his arms. "Mallie don't go over there."

"Is it Will?" she whispered.

"He was caught by a falling tree Mallie."

"I have to go to him. He needs me."

"There's nothing you can do Mallie."

"Let me go Cole." She walked slowly unable to make her limbs move any faster. When she reached him, Will lay crushed beneath a tree. The merciless fire had burned off his beautiful black hair and his ever-smiling face was still twisted from the pain he must have felt in those last moments. The sight of him seared her worse than any fire could have. All the joy and hope of their last day together burned away in a blaze. She sat down in the ashes and cried, her tears falling on Will's battered face. He had promised he would never leave her, and in the end, he had not been able to keep his promise. He had sacrificed himself to save her.

"Mallie come with me now. We need to go down and let folks know what's happened."

She shook her head fiercely. "I have to stay with Will."

"We will send some men up to get him Mallie. I'll come back up with them and we will bring him down."

"I can't leave him Cole. You go on now. I'll stay here until you get back."

"Mallie, you don't know what you are saying. You're not yourself right now."

"You are wrong Cole. I am myself. I am now entirely myself and I intend to stay here with Will. I will not leave him alone here."

"I'll be back as soon as I can round up some men," he said giving in reluctantly.

There was no need to hurry, she thought but merely looked at Cole. She was not even sure when he left, for her mind was already caught up in the stillness. A fleeting shadow floated in front of her. The fragrance of leaves, mosses and fresh stream water enveloped her. She and Will were walking in a rhododendron thicket and he was pointing out the plants that surrounded them. He turned to her, his smile radiant. In the solitude and stillness of that moment, she knew he would never leave her.

23

The sky was a gray slab that weighed heavily on the funeral procession as it made its way slowly to the Elkmont Cemetery. Mallie walked behind Will's mother and sister who had taken the train down the night before. The rumor was Pierce Gerard had paid for their fare on a private coach and put them up at the Wonderland Hotel at his expense.

Mary Anne wept quietly her shoulders slumped. Mrs. Stenson was dry eyed, her face tight and her back ramrod straight. She had been kind enough to Mallie, without showing any interest in getting to know her or anything about the last days her son had lived. Mallie could not blame her for she had lost two people she loved to the mountains. She was just grateful that Will's mother had allowed her to bury him at Elkmont near the mountains he loved.

People had come from all over to pay their respects. Death in the mountains was a time of unselfish concern for the family of the deceased. Folks gave of their time and themselves to come and show genuine sympathy and respect. They traveled by wagon, horseback and foot from great distanccs. Not all of them knew Will, but came simply because of Crockett Hamilton and the Combs family. The women cleaned and dressed the body and the men dug the grave. The setting up had been at the Combs' place because it had been the closest thing to Will's home in the Smoky Mountains.

Cole walked beside Mallie, looking stiff and uncomfortable in his black suit. He had shaved off his beard, exposing the pale skin beneath, and what remained of his scorched hair stuck out on the sides in patchy tufts. Mallie thought he looked like the awkward young brother she had known so long ago, but her heart told her that boy was gone, burned away by a fire that had changed them both.

After the fire, when Cole had come back with help, some of the men had tried to tell her it would be best if she left the body to them and went on down the mountain. Telling her she needed rest and food, they tried to pry her hands loose. Cole had backed them off, telling them to let her be. In the end, they had all come down together through the ashes and destruction. Will's body strapped to the horse, she had walked alongside, her hand always on him.

At the cemetery, Crockett, Riley and the other loggers who were carrying the casket set it down by the graveside and stood back solemnly. Their faces grim, they looked down at the ground afraid to look into the eyes of the mourners, for they had survived the fire and the relief they felt at being alive was a heavy burden.

The fire had started from a spark off a skidder. It had spread quickly fed by the slash that covered the ground and the high winds that whipped about the mountains. Nevertheless, it had been a small fire after all. The rains had come the morning after they had brought Will down. The sky had opened up as though seeded by the fire and quenched the scorched hillsides. No one else had been hurt, although some of the men had bemoaned the loss of board feet and a few days work. Still the men took it as a warning that next time they might not be the lucky ones. Mallie could hear the preacher praying, but his words were lost to her. What meaning could they have, what hope could they give her? She felt nothing. Even as they lowered the casket into the ground, Mary Anne's wails piercing the air, and Mrs. Stenson's body racked by shudders, she felt nothing. Her only desire was to be alone with her grief, to be done with all of this, the preaching, the kind words, the sad looks.

At last, it was over and everyone turned to go. Most of them would be coming by the Comb's place to eat and say their last condolences. Maude had been preparing food all morning and the neighbors had brought in covered dishes until there was no more room in the house for more.

Pierce Gerard stood off to the side his face pale and tired. Mallie had not spoken to him and he did not attempt to approach her. Mrs. Stenson walked quickly to him, Mary Anne coming to her side. He reached out his hand but she did not take it and slowly he lowered it to his side. Mrs. Stenson spoke to him, her voice rising and falling. Mallie thought she might be thanking him for all his help but her voice grew louder, her face red and twisted. She was accusing Pierce of being responsible for her son's death because he had given him the money, because he had encouraged his foolish dreams. Her daughter, worry showing on her face, took her mother's elbow urging her to come along. Mrs. Stenson pulled her arm away and slapped Pierce across the face. He neither flinched nor moved, accepting the blame, along with a mother's grief.

Mrs. Stenson turned and walked away. She and her daughter would be catching the train back in the morning. Mary Anne stopped to hug Mallie. "I'll write to you Mallie. Will loved you so much. He spoke of you in all his letters." She stopped speaking and tears welled up in her already swollen eyes. "He loved you so much and he was so happy."

She gave Mallie a helpless look and patted her arm before she walked away. Mallie nodded but her throat was too dry and tight to speak. As Cole led her away, she turned to see Pierce holding back, standing alone, the last to leave.

Mallie covered the food with clean dishtowels and helped Rose dry the last of the dishes. Friends and neighbors had stayed for hours filling up the house, milling about eating and drinking. Many of them had told stories of Will. She had wandered in and out of their talk wanting to know every detail of their stories of Will and at the same time, not wanting to hear a word of it as each story reminded her of something precious lost. She had thought of his roaming as a solitary act. It surprised her to hear that he knew many of the seasoned mountain guides and had stayed with families as far away as Cades Cove. "He stayed with us a while," a mousy little woman said to the crowd gathered round. "We live up Curry Mountain. Taught the boys to tie all manner of knots and hitches. They pestered him till I had to tell them to go to bed, but he'd just smile and say how it wasn't no trouble, he liked doing it." She backed away slowly, overcome by having spoken up.

"That boy liked most everything best I can figure," a wiry little man said.

"I know what you mean," Cole said to encourage him.

Unlike Mallie, Cole had joined in telling stories, reliving the times he had spent with Will. She did not resent it. That was what folks did at funerals to show respect. It was just not in her to join them.

"I come across him up on Siler's Bald one morning," the man went on. "I'd been out huntin' when I seen him standing out in the field looking up at the sky. He just stood there as I come up on him and then he turned and smiled. He knowed all along I was there," the man said with wonder, "but he wasn't a bit afraid. Then he said the oddest thing. He said, 'I was just listening to the wind in the trees and watching the hawks fly overhead and I thought about all that goes on up here when we are not here.' It come off strange to me. Then he begin to tell me about all the things he saw around him and the way he seen things, it was like it was a magic show. He just seen things different from most folks." Several folks nodded as though they had a similar experience when they had met Will. Others looked as though they wished they had met him. Mallie walked away unable to hear any more.

At some point, Crockett, Riley and Cole slipped out and Mallie watched out the window as they got their shovels and headed back to the cemetery. They were going to fill in the grave. It was a sacred act reserved for close family and friends. She should feel only kindness toward them for this act, but instead she felt a rage well up in her and she wanted to run and stop them, to scream at them that they had no right. She saw herself running ahead, spreading her arms, falling face first into the grave to stop them. Turning to see Maude and Rose staring at her, she could bear it no more. Their looks of sadness and pity filled her with the sense of a chance not taken. She wheeled on her heels, went to her room and slammed the door.

Rising at midnight, as had become her custom, she went out into the night. Sometimes, she sat on the front porch and rocked until dawn. Other times she wandered the woods. She spent her days sitting about the house; her hair uncombed turning her hand to nothing. Unable to go back to teaching, she cared for little else. She shunned all offers of comfort from Maude, Rose and even Cole. Kindness was unbearable to her and she preferred the solitude of her grief to the questioning worry in their eyes.

There came a time each night, usually just before dawn, when she could bear it no longer and she would take off running through the woods, screaming and tearing at her clothes, lost in madness. Crying out for Will until her throat was raw; wondering why she was still alive when he was gone.

Stepping off the porch into the light of a full moon, she watched as a cloud passed swiftly and then another. The night was chill and snow was coming. Rose had been talking about it at supper, as Mallie sat barely touching her food. All the old folks said the signs called for a big snow, biggest of the year they predicted. The thought had struck her then as to what she would do.

She did not wear a coat, or carry any food as her feet headed down the familiar path. Guided by a sureness she had not felt in months, she walked up the mountain toward home.

It was nearly dawn, when she stepped out into the clearing. She had not been back to the farm since the fire. Holding her breath until she saw the cabin silhouetted against the light, she was overwhelmed to scc it still there. If they had stayed at the cabin, they would have been all right, she thought and it was like a knife ripping through her. But it was too late for regret and soon there would be no need. Her pa was the one who had told her about freezing to death. At the time, he had meant it as a lesson to caution her when she was a child against staying out too long, or getting lost in the woods. "The cold can take your mind," he had warned her. "So you can't think straight. It will make you want to go to sleep, but that is the last thing you want because to go to sleep is to die." She thought of his words now as she lay down on the ground in the field where on that perfect day, Will had come to her, laughing, swinging her around, and promising to love her forever. Magically, the snow began to fall and she smiled as the thick wet flakes covered her. She took it as a sign that Will was still with her and they would soon be together. Closing her eyes, she waited for his embrace.

His laugh woke her. She opened her eyes to see him smiling down at her. Without a word, Will took her hand and pulled her up. She threw herself into his arms, surprised to see that the sun was shining and there was no snow. It was spring and the world was green. "Oh, Will, I have missed you."

His laugh filled her with joy, washing away all the sadness she had felt in the last months. "I loved you from the beginning Will. From the beginning, I knew we would be perfect together and I knew you knew it too, but I was afraid. I'm not afraid anymore." Will looked into her eyes and she knew that for him there were never any regrets. It was all just as it was meant to be, perfect and forever. They walked hand in hand through the fields and over the ridgeline, Will pointing out the flowers in bloom and speaking of the beauty, he saw all around him just as she had known he would.

"Look Mallie, it's a trillium in bloom, the first one of the season. You know it takes six years before a trillium will bloom from a seed," Will said looking at her. "I never see a trillium in bloom without feeling a sense of wonder," he said.

She laughed because it was so like Will. He could never see a flower or a tree without seeing more as though he could look inside it. Suddenly, she could see it too, just as Will was seeing it and she knew it had been there all along, this joy, and this delight. "It is beautiful Will," she said.

They sat down at last to rest. They had walked such a long way it seemed and she felt her eyes wanting to close. Leaning back against a tree, she said, "I'm so happy Will."

"That's why I came back, Mallie. I want you to be happy."

"I am Will," she whispered. She wanted to say more. She wanted to open her eyes, to look at Will and reassure him that she had never been happier but her lids felt heavy as though weighted down.

"Promise me," Will said.

"Always," she answered, but she could not be sure she had said it out loud for she was drifting now, sleep overtaking her. There would be time, she thought, to tell him once again when she awoke.

"Mama, she's awake," Rose called out.

Mallie watched as Rose bent over her looking deep into her eyes. Then Rose ran off and came back with Maude in tow. They both stood looking at her. She was in Maude's big bed, which struck her as odd. Why was she not in her own bed? The bed piled high with quilts, was so heavy she could hardly move and a roaring fire burned in the fireplace. She tried to sit up and throw the covers off her, but she was too weak. "I was so sleepy," she said at last. "I remember falling asleep. Did Will carry me in?"

Rose and Maude exchanged a worried glance. "Your pa brought you down from Fish Camp three days ago," Rose said.

"Fish Camp?" Mallie asked puzzled. "Will met me at the farm. We walked a while but I didn't know we'd walked that far."

"Your pa found you," Maude said nervously ringing her hands. "It was just past daylight. You were on the edge of the woods sitting up against a tree nearly froze to death. Nobody knows how you got there. He carried you and warmed you by the fire. He sat by your side for two days rubbing your arms and legs trying to bring you back. Then when the snows cleared and he thought it was safe, he brought you down by train."

"It snowed? But it was spring?"

"Near a blizzard," Rose remarked. "Over two feet up at Fish Camp. Can't nobody figure out how you come through it alive."

"Rose, is Will all right?" Mallie said suddenly worried.

Rose looked at Mallie her eyes widening. She said nothing as tears welled up and spilled over onto her cheeks. A noise at the back door made them all turn. Rose and Maude parted like a wave as Crockett came into the room carrying firewood. "He ain't left your side except to keep the fire going," Maude whispered.

Surprised showed on Crockett's face when he saw Mallie awake and sitting up. Throwing down the firewood, he came to her, sat down on the bed feeling her face and hands as though he could not believe she was alive. Tears collected in the corners of his eyes and he wiped them away with the back of his hand.

Mallie looked into his eyes and saw it all written there, the power of grief. She saw the years lost, the turning away from friends, and family, the endless wells of sorrow leading nowhere. Seeing too, her life reflected there. It was the reflection of a mad woman giving herself up to grief, and sorrow just as her pa had done. Thinking of all the things Will had taught her of love and life, of his joy and hopes for them both, she knew this was not what he would have wanted. She would not live her life as her pa had. Her grief would have meaning and purpose. And she knew then what had happened. Will had come back to show her the way. He meant for her to have a full and happy life as his would have been had he lived. It was his gift to her and she knew then what she would do. It would be her gift to Will.

She reached out, took her pa's hand, and smiled.

24

It was spring in the Smoky Mountains and the dogwood, redbud and the delicate new green leaves of a dozen other trees decorated the hillsides. Robins sang their morning song as Mallie sat on the porch of her cottage on Jakes Creek and took in the bright, warm air with its fragrance of phlox and the whiff of the blooms from the apple orchard in Elkmont. Pierce had given her the cottage in the spring of 1913 when they had married and she had never missed a spring or summer there in twenty-nine years.

Pierce had been a good husband to her and a good father to their four children. Although he could be ruthless in his business dealings, he had never again tried to use his power on her. In all ways, he had treated her as an equal. He had loved her with a depth and fervor she could never understand but she came in time to cherish. Because he loved her so much more than she could ever love him, he never asked anything of her. He saw in her the natural beauty and wildness she saw in the mountains around her. When he had died last winter, she grieved the loss of a man who had kept every promise he had ever made to her.

In the spring after Will died, she had come to Pierce with a simple proposal. With his promise to do whatever he could to get Will's trillium recognized as a new species and to do everything in his power to have the Smoky Mountains made into a National Park, she would become his wife. He had accepted her conditions without hesitation. They had a simple ceremony at her request and then moved back to Philadelphia where they spent much of every year.

Mallie did not know how much money Pierce had spent having Will's trillium researched and documented as a new species. He never mentioned the cost in dollars nor did he ever let on that he knew how much she loved Will Stenson and always would.

Joined by hundreds of forward thinking, influential people, Pierce had worked tirelessly, as had Mallie, to have the Smoky Mountains made into a National Park. He had returned with her on September 2, 1940 to Newfound Gap the day Franklin D. Roosevelt had stood with one foot in Tennessee and one foot in North Carolina and dedicated the Great Smoky Mountains National Park.

Mallie traveled back to the Smoky Mountains two or three times a year. She brought the children to Elkmont every summer where they took long hikes and swam in the cool water of the bubbling creeks. She taught them the names of nature. They learned to recognize hundreds of flowers and trees, and to distinguish a scarlet tanager from a gold finch or a chickadee. As the summers came and went, the mountains began to heal from the scars of logging, railroad beds and fires. Moreover, she taught them that lesson too. She taught them the lessons of courage, determination and hope that Will had seen so clearly in his beloved nature.

It was a source of great pride to her, that all of her children had made good lives for themselves. Thomas, the oldest, had gone into business with his father. He had his father's intense gray eyes and still demeanor even as a little boy.

Sara, the favorite of her Grandma Martha, had become a nurse. One summer, Sara had discovered her Grandma Martha bandaging up the broken wing of a baby bird that had fallen from its nest. Sara had begged to help and soon took over its care. Martha began to teach her all she knew about healing. When Sara finished nursing school, she had come back to the mountains to work at the clinic of the Pi Beta Phi School.

Martha had married her pa soon after Mallie had married Pierce. She had made a good home for Crockett, and Mallie was glad for the measure of peace he had found. He had given up logging having lost his taste for it after Will's death. In the summer of 1922, a fire had come once again, this time burning for over two months. It started on the northern flank of Blanket Mountain and burned over Dripping Springs Mountain taking the farm and cabin leaving no trace of what had been.

Maude and Riley had moved back to Wears Cove and gone back to farming. Rose had married a farmer and lived nearby. Mallie saw her every time she came to Elkmont. Rose had born six children, but four had died in infancy filling up the family cemetery with tiny head stones. Who could say, what the true measure of sorrow might be, Mallie thought and yet Rose seemed content with her life.

Cole was living with his wife, Beth Ann, in Gatlinburg. After the fire, Cole had gone to live there and met a young teacher. Beth Ann had supported him while he had gotten his schooling at the University of Tennessee. Now, they had both come back to the settlement school. Cole was teaching shop courses to the local boys, while trying to bring older folks to teach mountain skills. The young boy who had always wanted to flee the mountains had found himself at home there.

Mallie knew Sara was safe, but it was Alberta the youngest daughter, she worried most about. She was in New Mexico teaching at a mission school. Alberta, of the flaming red hair and matching temperament had vowed never to marry but to make her own way in the world. They had fought endless battles for all of Alberta's childhood, for she had found every rule and every normal constraint intolerable. Mallie worried about her, but knew that she would not be the one to rein her in from whatever vistas she sought.

It was Seth, the youngest son, who was closest to her heart. Because he was the baby, the other children had allowed their mother to indulge Seth. They too found his sweet smile and infectious laugh irresistible. It was to his credit that with the whole family doting on him, he never grew spoiled.

He had grown up with her love of nature. As a small child, he had poured over the sketches and journals Will had left behind. He was the one who, every summer, could not be coaxed to sleep inside but insisted upon camping out even if it was only in the woods near the cottage. When he was older, he would take off for two weeks at a time, hiking and camping in the woods coming home worn thin and exhausted but full of stories of all that he had seen. Seth was the one who was going to school to be a botanist. Seth's sunny disposition and joyous nature, made Mallie turn and look twice when he was speaking. Seth's dark eyes were always trying to convey some wonder he could not put in words.

It did not surprise her that the spirit of a man long dead could inhabit the body of her beautiful son, for Will had been with her all along. He had guided her steps along the way; pointing out the joy of life to her, she could have so easily passed by. It was in her nature to turn away, to blink, and to miss the magic that was life, but he would not leave her to her musings for he would come to her like a gentle breeze and whisper to her of life's enchantments.

With the signing of the law in 1926 to form the Great Smoky Mountains National Park, Mallie felt a sense of peace, but also one of sadness. Many of her friends had sold their farms and cottages and moved away. She had stayed finally accepting the government offer of a lease. She would return to her beloved cottage until her death. Then she and Will would be free to wander the mountains forever, each day a new adventure.

As for now, the full weight of the season was upon her and the mountains called to her. She walked down the cottage steps and up along the Little River. The day was brilliant and shining, awash with the yellow-green of a world coming alive. The clear, sparkling stream splashed over giant boulders passing on its journey hillsides bursting with wildflowers. Dainty dwarf irises, wild ginger and purple-fringed orchids filled in the spaces between the graceful fiddlehead ferns. Mallie smiled and turned her back reluctantly on such delicate grace and headed on up the mountain. The world meant something different to her here amidst such peace and beauty, but she had something she needed to do. She would make her way up the mountain as she had done every year since that day long ago. After all, it was April and the trilliums were in bloom.

Discover the novels of Loletta Clouse

Call 1-865-693-5678 to order by phone, or use this form to order by mail.

TITLE	PRICE EACH (includes shipping)	QUANTITY	TOTAL
Wilder	$15.95	______	______
The Homesteads	$15.95	______	______
Mallie	$15.95	______	______

Tennessee residents must add $1.20 per copy for state sales tax. ______

Total amount enclosed ______

Send check or money order to:
Chicory Books
PO Box 31131
Knoxville TN 37930

Please send book(s) to the following address:

Name ________________________________

Address ________________________________

City ________________________________

State ______________________ Zip Code ______

Discounted prices are available for the purchase of ten or more books. For details call Chicory Books at 1-865–693-5678.